FLAMES OF ATTRACTION

D0556495

NEW YORK TIMES BESTSELLING AUTHOR

BRENDA JACKSON

FLAMES OF ATTRACTION

A Westmoreland Novel

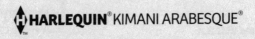

HARLEQUIN® KIMANI ARABESQUE®

FLAMES OF ATTRACTION

ISBN-13: 978-0-373-09130-0

Copyright © 2013 by Harlequin Books S.A.

This edition published April 2013

The publisher acknowledges the copyright holder of the individual works as follows:

QUADE'S BABIES
Copyright © 2008 by Brenda Streater Jackson

TALL, DARK...WESTMORELAND!
Copyright © 2009 by Brenda Streater Jackson

Recycling programs for this product may not exist in your area.

For questions and comments about the quality of this book, please contact us at CustomerService@Harlequin.com.

Printed in U.S.A.

HARLEQUIN®
www.Harlequin.com

CONTENTS

THE WESTMORELAND FAMILY

Scott and Delane Westmoreland

John (Evelyn)　　　　　　　　　James (Sarah)　　　　　　　　　Corey (Abbie)
　　　　　　　　　　　　　　　　　　　　　　　　　　　　　　　Madison

John (Evelyn)

② Dare (Shelly) — AJ, Allison
③ Thorn (Tara) — Trace
④ Stone (Madison) — Rock, Regan
⑤ Storm (Jayla) — Shanna, Johanna, Slate
⑥ Jared (Dana) — Jaren
⑧ Durango (Savannah) — Sarah
⑨ Ian (Brooke) — Pierce, Price
⑩ Casey (McKinnon) — Corey Martin
⑪ Spencer (Chardonnay) — Russell
⑫ Clint (Alyssa) — Cain
⑬ Cole (Patrina) — Emilie, Emery

James (Sarah)

① Delaney (Jamal) — Ari, Arielle
⑦ Chase (Jessica) — Carlton Scott
④ Quade (Cheyenne) — Venus, Athena, Troy
⑮ Reggie (Olivia) — Ryder

① *Delaney's Desert Sheikh*
② *A Little Dare*
③ *Thorn's Challenge*
④ *Stone Cold Surrender*
⑤ *Riding the Storm*
⑥ *Jared's Counterfeit Fiancée*
⑦ *The Chase is On*
⑧ *The Durango Affair*
⑨ *Ian's Ultimate Gamble*
⑩ *Seduction, Westmoreland Style*
⑪ *Spencer's Forbidden Passion*
⑫ *Taming Clint Westmoreland*
⑬ *Cole's Red-Hot Pursuit*
⑭ *Quade's Babies*
⑮ *Tall, Dark…Westmoreland!*
⑯ *Dreams of Forever*

THE DENVER WESTMORELAND FAMILY TREE

Raphel and Gemma Westmoreland

Stern Westmoreland (Paula Bailey)

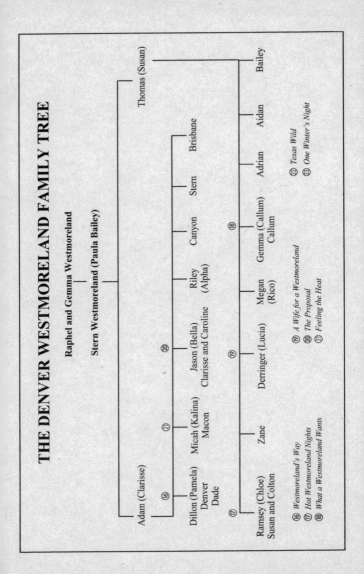

Thomas (Susan)

Adam (Clarisse) ⑯

Dillon (Pamela)
Denver
Dade ⑰

Micah (Kalina) ⑰
Macon

Jason (Bella) ⑳
Clarisse and Caroline

Riley
(Alpha)

Canyon — Stern — Brisbane

Aidan

Bailey

Zane

Derringer (Lucia) ⑲

Megan (Rico)

Gemma (Callum) ⑱
Callum

Adrian

Ramsey (Chloe) ⑰
Susan and Colton

⑯ *Westmoreland's Way*
⑰ *Hot Westmoreland Nights*
⑱ *What a Westmoreland Wants*

⑲ *A Wife for a Westmoreland*
⑳ *The Proposal*
㉑ *Feeling the Heat*

㉒ *Texas Wild*
㉓ *One Winter's Night*

Dear Reader,

When I first introduced the Westmoreland family, little did I know they would become hugely popular with readers. Originally, the Westmoreland family series was intended to be just six books, Delaney and her five brothers—Dare, Thorn, Stone, Storm and Chase. Later, I wanted my readers to meet their cousins—Jared, Spencer, Durango, Ian, Quade and Reggie. Finally, there were Uncle Corey's triplets—Clint, Cole and Casey.

What began as a six-book series blossomed into a thirty-book series when I included the Denver Westmorelands. I was very happy when Harlequin Kimani Arabesque responded to my readers' requests that the earlier books be reprinted. And I'm even happier that the reissues are in a great two-books-in-one format.

Flames of Attraction contains "Quade's Babies" and "Tall, Dark…Westmoreland!" These are two Westmoreland classics and are books #14 and #15 in the Westmoreland series. In "Quade's Babies" I united my two popular families—the Westmorelands and the Steeles—in a story you don't want to miss. And in "Tall, Dark…Westmoreland!" we find out how two people who shouldn't have even been friends become lovers.

I hope you enjoy reading these special stories as much as I enjoyed writing them.

Happy reading!

Brenda Jackson

A man that hath friends must show himself friendly:
and there is a friend that sticketh closer than a brother.

—*Proverbs* 18:24

To the love of my life, Gerald Jackson, Sr.
My one and only. Always.

To everyone who enjoys reading about those
Westmorelands, this one is especially for you.

QUADE'S BABIES

Chapter 1

"Sir, the plane is about ready to take off. Please shut down your laptop and fasten your seat belt."

Quade Westmoreland followed the flight attendant's instructions while thinking just how many times he'd heard such a request while flying aboard a commercial aircraft. Over the past eight years he had grown accustomed to the luxury of Air Force One where using a laptop during takeoff was not only welcomed but necessary.

He glanced around. At least he was in first class, which wasn't a bad deal, and no one was sitting in the seat beside him, which made things even better. He didn't like the feel of being crowded or cramped. He liked having his space. That was the reason he'd enjoyed his job with the PSF, Presidential Security Forces, dual branches of the Secret Service and CIA.

But if the truth be known—and there were only a few key individuals who actually knew the truth—his particular position entailed a lot more than protecting the president. After the terrorist attacks of 9/11, the PSF was created and he'd become a part of the elite team. His job was to keep tabs on the president's travels abroad and make sure everything associated with the trips, especially the security, was dealt with prior to the president's visit. It was his responsibility to protect the commander-in-chief from behind the scenes at all cost.

That was the reason he had been in Sharm al-Sheikh, Egypt, the night he had met Cheyenne Steele.

Cheyenne Steele.

Just thinking about her brought an automatic tightening in his chest, as well as a stirring in another part of his body. The woman had gotten that sort of response from him from the first time he had encountered her that night walking on the beach. He had actually felt her presence before seeing her. And when he had gazed into her face, a deep physical attraction had unleashed fierce desire in him, a degree to which he had never felt toward any other woman in all his thirty-six years. It had been hot. Unexplainable. And luckily for him, the attraction had been mutual.

It didn't take long to discover that she was just as physically attracted to him as he was to her, and after a few brief moments of small talk, she accepted his offer to share a drink…in his hotel room.

Although he had known she would be safe with him, he had initially questioned her decision until they'd gotten up to his room. Before going inside with him she had made a smart move by using her cell phone to contact the female friend she was traveling with to let her know where she would be; specifically which room and at which hotel on the beach.

Cheyenne was the only part of her name she had exchanged with him that night and, considering how they'd met and the activities that had followed afterward, he hadn't been sure if Cheyenne had even been her real name. She had been pretty secretive, but then so had he. And like her, he had only shared his first name.

He had constantly thought about her since that night and then a few days ago, while visiting his relatives in Montana, he had seen her face on the cover of a magazine. And it was pretty damn obvious that she was pregnant.

In fact, she looked ready to deliver at any moment. Since the magazine had been October's issue and it was now the first of December, a million questions had been going through his mind. The first of which was whether or not he was the man responsible for her condition.

They had used protection that night, but he would be the first to admit his passion for her, his desire to mate with her, had been uncontrollable. And somewhere in the back of his mind he seemed to recall at least one of the times in which there had not been a barrier. Whether it was true or just a figment of his imagination, he wasn't certain. Even if he had used a condom each time they had made love, condoms weren't without flaws, and when you made love as many times as they had, anything was possible. Even an unplanned pregnancy.

She was the only one who could put his mind to rest by telling him whether or not the child—which should have been born by now—was his. If it wasn't, she must have slept with someone else around the same time she had slept with him. That was something he didn't want to think about. And if the child was his, he would do the right thing—the only thing a Westmoreland could do if they were foolish enough to get caught in such a situation. He would ask her to marry him to give their child his name. After a reasonable amount of time they could file for a divorce and part ways.

He could tolerate a short-term wife if he had to. He had recently retired and was about to embark on another career. He had joined a partnership with a few of his cousins to open a chain of security offices around the country.

He refused to be reminded that a marriage of convenience was how things had started out between his brother Durango and his wife, Savannah, and that they were now a happily married couple. Quade was glad things worked out the way they had for them; however, the situation with him and Cheyenne was different.

Durango had fallen hard for Savannah from the first time he had seen her at their cousin Chase's wedding. But it had been lust and only lust that had driven his desire for Cheyenne that night. If it had been more than that, he would have taken the time to get to know her. He'd only had one goal in mind after meeting Cheyenne and that was finding a way to get her into his bed.

One of the downsides of his former job was the long periods he'd had to put his social life on hold. It had been during one of those times, when his testosterone had been totally out of whack, that he met Cheyenne. He'd gone a long time without a woman and Cheyenne had been a prime target for a one-night stand.

But he hadn't meant to get her pregnant if that's what he'd actually done. So here he was on his way to Charlotte, North Carolina, to find out if he was the father of her baby. He had contacted the ad agency and discovered not only that Cheyenne was her real name, but that she was also a model, which was the reason she had been on the cover of that magazine. He shouldn't have been surprised to learn of her profession since she had to have been the most beautiful woman he'd ever met. On the cover of that magazine with her pregnancy proudly displayed for the camera, she had still looked radiant and breathtakingly beautiful.

Quade felt the plane tilt upward as it took off. He leaned back in his seat and closed his eyes, deciding now was a perfect time to relive those long and passionate hours he had spent in bed with Cheyenne nearly ten months ago.

Quade felt hot, edgy and he couldn't sleep.
Muttering a curse, he eased out of bed and looked around the hotel room.

The president was to arrive in two days and Quade and his men had checked out everything, especially the route the motorcade would be taking. There had been rumblings of a planned protest, but a spokesman for the Egyptian government had contacted him earlier to say the matter had been taken care of.

He wondered if the bar downstairs was still open. He could definitely use a drink to take the edge off. For some reason this place and sleeping alone in this bed was reminding him just how long it had been since he'd had any sort of intimate physical contact with a woman. Too long.

Instead of getting a drink, Quade decided to take a walk on the beach. He eased into a pair of jeans and pulled a T-shirt over his head. After sliding his feet into a pair of sandals he checked the clock on the nightstand. It was almost one in the morning.

As he left his room, closing the door shut behind him, he thought about the phone conversation he'd had with his mother earlier. She had surprised the hell out of him by saying his cousin Clint had gotten married.

He had just seen his cousin a few months before at his brother Spencer's wedding. They had talked. Clint had been excited. He had just retired as a Texas Ranger to become a partner with Durango and a childhood friend, McKinnon Quinn, in their horse-breeding business. Not once had Clint mentioned anything about a woman. And now he was married? There had to be more to it than the romantic tale his mother had weaved.

Within no time at all Quade had caught the designated elevator, the one that would take him six levels down to a patio that led to the beach. Most of the hotel was empty. The majority of the rooms were already reserved for the president's visit. The first lady would be present on this trip, along with a number of other dignitaries. The visit would last three days and Quade would be working nonstop behind the scenes the entire time.

He inhaled deeply as the scent of the ocean filled his nostrils, and after taking a few steps his sandals hit the soft sand, making him feel as if he was walking on marshmallows. Sharm al-Sheikh was a beautiful place, a developed tourist resort on the Sinai Peninsula that catered to the rich and famous. Even in the moonlit night, he could make out the large five-star hotels that dotted the shoreline.

A number of his men had made plans to hang around after the president's visit to relax and unwind. Unfortunately, he wouldn't be one of them. He had promised his mother that he would be returning to the States in time to make an appearance at the christening of his cousin Thorn's son.

Quade had to admit that he always looked forward to returning home to Atlanta whenever he could. The Westmorelands were a large group and getting even larger with all the recent marriages and births. And then there was the possibility that

they might find even more Westmorelands if the ge-
nealogy search his father was conducting proved
out. It seemed that their great-grandfather had a
twin everyone assumed had died while in his early
twenties. It appeared the black sheep Raphel West-
moreland, who had run off with a still-married
preacher's wife at the age of 22, was still alive. Both
Quade's father and his father's twin brother, James,
were eager to find any descendants of their long,
lost wife-stealing, great-granduncle Raphel.

Quade had been walking near the shoreline for
a few moments when suddenly he felt an intense
yearning in the pit of his stomach, an incredible
ache that ran through his body.

He stopped walking as his gaze took in the
stretch of beach in his path. It was dark and he
could barely see, because a haze had covered the
earth in front of him, some sort of low-hanging
cloud. He took a cautious glance around him as
the ache got more profound. And then seconds later,
a woman appeared out of the mist.

She was absolutely the most beautiful woman
he had ever seen.

He blinked to make sure his mind and his eyes
weren't playing tricks on him. His gaze traveled
down the length of her body, taking in her white
linen pant set and the mass of dark, luxurious
hair that flowed recklessly around her shoulders
and cascaded around her face. He felt his body re-
spond to her presence. He tried to get his breathing

back to normal while at the same time wondering what was going on with him. Why was he reacting to her this way?

She had seen him at the same time he had seen her and he watched her reaction. By the look in her dark eyes, she was feeling whatever it was that he was feeling. It had her in the same intense sexual grip. He could sense it. Just like he could sense the pull he felt toward her, specifically her mouth. She had the kind of lips that made you want to do naughty things to them, lick them, taste them forever. They had a shape just for kissing and were the kind that any man's tongue would want to wet and tease.

"You're out rather late, aren't you?" he heard himself asking, feeling the need to say something before he was forced to do something he would later regret. He was known as a man with iron-clad control, but you wouldn't know it now. He was being reduced to melted steel.

"I could say the same for you," she said. Her accent told Quade she was an American. Before now, he hadn't been sure. The sound of her voice was soft and seductive. But he had a feeling it wasn't intentionally so. It probably couldn't be helped since it went with the rest of the alluring package she presented. Was she someone he should know, a movie star perhaps?

"I couldn't sleep," he said.

Then he saw the lift of her shoulders, and noted

*the way the soft material of her blouse draped
around them, showing a nice cleavage with up-
lifted and firm breasts pressing against her blouse.
He also saw her smile and his stomach clenched
and his throat tightened.*

*"Some nights aren't meant for sleeping. This
could be one of them," she said, her voice stirring
the unbridled lust that was flowing through his
veins.*

*Her response made him consider the possibility
that she could very well be coming on to him. If
she was, then she had done so at a time when he
was ripe for the picking. Normally, he didn't pick
up women, no matter how tempting they were. He
had a list of his usual partners back in D.C. who
knew the score. He didn't have time for serious
relationships and the women he bedded knew it
and accepted it. There wasn't a woman alive who
could make a claim for Quade Westmoreland, in
no shape, form or fashion.*

*He sighed ruefully, wondering how she would
handle the question he was about to ask her. "I'm
Quade. Would you like to go up to my room for a
drink?"*

*She took a step closer, stared at him as if study-
ing the outline of his face in the moonlight. And
then her gaze shifted and scanned the full length
of his body and the dark gaze that finally slid back
to his eyes nearly took his breath away for the second time that night.*

"And I'm Cheyenne," she finally said, offering him her hand. "And I would love joining you for a drink."

The moment their hands touched Quade felt it all the way to his toes. His eyebrows snapped together in confusion and he wondered why he was behaving like a man desperate to get laid. A man without any control or willpower. A man whose needs were being exposed. And frankly he didn't care too much for the thought of being that way. He needed to take a step back or knock some sense into his head.

Instead, still holding her hand, he leaned closer to her, inhaled her scent. "Let's go now," he said, hoping and praying she wouldn't change her mind. "I'm staying at the Bayleaf," he added as they moved in the direction of his hotel.

He held her hand as she walked beside him. At first they said nothing and then she said, "This isn't common behavior for me."

He glanced over at her. "What isn't?" he asked, deciding to pretend he had no idea what she was talking about.

"Following any man this way."

He slowed his pace. "Then why are you now?"

He studied her features. Saw the confusion in her eyes and knew she was just as baffled as to what was taking place between them as he was. "I don't know. I just feel this strange connection between us. It's like I know you when I really don't. For heaven's sake, I just met you barely five minutes ago."

"I understand," he said, and really, he did. He actually understood because he felt the same way, although he hadn't a clue as to why. And for the moment maybe it was just as well. All he knew was that he wanted her in a way he'd never wanted another woman. It seemed his level-headed nature was being placed on the back burner, falling victim to a need he couldn't describe. It was a need that was taking over his senses.

"And what brings you to Egypt?"

Her question, spoken in a soft voice, sent a quiver through him. There was no way he could tell her the real reason he was there. No one, not even his family, knew the full extent of what he did for a living.

He glanced over at her. "Mainly business. What about you?"

She met his gaze. Held it. "Business, as well."

He wasn't sure if she was telling the truth and a part of him figured she wasn't. However, he wouldn't lose any sleep over the fact that she wanted to keep secrets since he was keeping a few, too.

Suddenly it dawned on him that there was one question that he had to ask her. He stopped walking and she automatically stopped beside him and met his gaze with questions in her eyes.

"I see you aren't wearing a ring, but nowadays that doesn't mean anything, so I think I should ask anyway just to be sure. Are you married?"

There was something about the look that appeared on her face that let him know what her response would be even before she spoke. "No, I'm not married. Are you?"

"No."

She nodded, and he knew at that moment that she believed him. It was hard to accept that she could trust him so easily when he always found trusting others outside of his family and inner circle of friends nearly impossible.

He saw that the patio where the elevator was located was only a few feet away. He glanced out at the ocean and knew she followed his gaze. There was a soft breeze flowing, a seductive breeze, and there was something about how the waves were hitting against the shore that was blatantly sensual.

He looked back at her and felt a frisson of heat flowing through his veins. Her hands, the ones he was still holding, felt warm. He gave her features a good assessment, letting his gaze scan her face in detail. They were now standing in a lit area and he could see more of her. Everything. Her perfectly shaped eyebrows, high cheekbones and mussed hair made her look even sexier.

Then there were those dark eyes that returned his gaze, while acting as a magnetic force, pulling him in as he continued to look at her in silent consideration. She was younger that he originally thought. "How old are you?" *he heard himself ask.*

He could tell she hadn't liked his question and

watched as she squared her shoulders. "I'm twenty-eight. How old are you?"

He continued to hold her gaze and felt the smile that played around his mouth when he said, "Thirty-six."

She nodded. "That's a nice age."

He couldn't help but chuckle. "In terms of what?"

"In terms of being a man who knows what he wants."

She was so right. In fact, he wanted to make her aware of just how right she was. Deciding it was time to be serious, he tightened his hold on her hand and gently pulled her closer, pressing her soft body against the hardness of his. He wanted her to feel just what she did to him. Just how much he wanted her. How aroused he was. And he knew the exact moment she did know.

Quade saw the glint of full awareness in her gaze and watched her nervously lick her lips with the tip of her tongue. He was suddenly hit with an urge to kiss her, to taste her lips.

He lowered his head and like a magnet, her lips were pulled toward his. Then slowly their mouths connected and the moment they did so a deep throb of intense hunger and desire shot to every part of his body. That iron-clad will that he was known for slowly began dissolving as he took hold of her tongue and began mating with it, deepening the kiss, hungrily tasting every area of her mouth, leav-

ing no part untouched. He heard her moan and likewise, he moaned, too.

He couldn't break the kiss, couldn't stop his mouth from devouring her in a way he had never done any woman. It was as if the taste of her was something he needed, an element he had to have. And it didn't help matters that she was so responsive. Passionate. Desirable.

Although he could have stood there and kissed her forever, he knew more than anything that he wanted to escalate things to the next level. His mind was filled with the thought of pure pleasure. His body was attuned to the need for sex. But then he also felt something else, something he couldn't put a name to that made a warning to be cautious that clamored through his head more profound. But it wasn't any match for the feelings of need overtaking him.

Reluctantly, he pulled his mouth free and watched as she inhaled a deep, shaky breath. He watched further as she closed her eyes as if fighting for composure, some semblance of poise and control. He wanted none of that.

"Are you sure you want to go inside with me?" he asked, when she reopened her eyes. He released her hand, needing her to be certain. He knew what would happen once they got to his room.

He held her eyes and, in a way, almost dared her to break the contact. She didn't. Instead, she reached up and looped her arms around his neck and brought her mouth within a heated breath of his.

"Yes," she said after a moment while holding tight to his gaze. "Yes, I'm sure."

And then leaning up on tiptoe, she joined their mouths once again.

Chapter 2

"Cheyenne, will you please stop being so stubborn and difficult."

Cheyenne Steele rolled her eyes upward. Leave it to her two sisters, Vanessa and Taylor, to try to gang up on her, while trying to convince her to think their way. Any other time she would have conceded, just to be left alone. But not this time. Although she was still considered the baby in the family, now she had a baby of her own. No, she quickly corrected, she had babies of her own. Three of them.

It still amazed her that nearly eight weeks ago she had given birth to triplets. Her doctor had suspected the possibility of multiple births early, and the sonogram she'd taken by her third month had confirmed his suspicions. She had been shocked. The Steele family overjoyed. And she had let them convince her that she needed to come home to North Carolina to be around family when the time came for her to deliver.

The main reason she had agreed was because she had wanted her babies born in the United States instead of Jamaica where she had been living for the last three years. As a professional model she moved from place to place, and one day while on a photo shoot in Jamaica, she had stumbled across what she considered her dream home and hadn't wasted any time purchasing it.

The problem her sisters were having was her announcement at dinner today that once the doctors had given the okay for the triplets to travel, she would be returning home to Jamaica. She was hoping that would be the first of the year.

"Be realistic, Cheyenne," her sister Taylor was saying. "Handling one baby isn't easy and you have three. You're going to need help."

Cheyenne frowned. The problem she had with her family was the same one she'd always had. Being the youngest of the three daughters, no one wanted to acknowledge her capabilities. That was why she had left home after graduating from high school to attend Boston University and only returned for visits. On the advice of Taylor, who was the financial advisor in the family, she had purchased a home in Charlotte a few years ago as an investment. That purchase made it possible whenever she did come home for extended visits for her to have a private place to stay.

"And I will have help," she said as she opened the

refrigerator to pull out the salad she had made earlier. "My housekeeper will be there and I've hired a nanny for the babies to assist me."

"But it's not the same as having your family close by," Vanessa replied.

Cheyenne closed the refrigerator door and then leaned against it. She studied the two women who were putting up a fierce argument as to why she and her babies shouldn't return to Jamaica. Her sisters were beautiful, both inside and out, and although they were getting on her last nerve, they were the best sisters a girl could have.

Vanessa, the oldest at twenty-eight, was the one who after getting a graduate degree at Tennessee State had returned home to Charlotte to work at the family's multimillion-dollar manufacturing company alongside their four male cousins—Chance, Sebastian, Morgan and Donovan. In June, Vanessa had married a wonderful and handsome man by the name of Cameron Cody.

Taylor was the second oldest at twenty-six. Taylor had chosen not to return to Charlotte after college to work for the family's company. Instead, Taylor had set her sights on New York after accepting a position with a major bank as a wealth and asset manager. Taylor was also married to a wonderful and handsome man named Dominic Saxon and the two were expecting their first child in a few weeks. Taylor and Dominic made Washington, D.C., their primary home, although they traveled quite a bit.

"You guys know how I feel about the two of you

trying to mother me. I wish you wouldn't do it," she said, and immediately saw the guilt on their faces. Although she knew they only wanted what was the best for her, they were breaking a promise they had made on her twenty-first birthday, which was to let her live her life, regardless of the mistakes she would make along the way. They had pretty much kept that promise...until now.

"I know taking care of three babies won't be easy," she said. "But I'm determined to do it. Thanks to you, Taylor, I have enough money not to work for the next eight months or longer if I have to. The modeling agency knows my plans and is giving me the time I need. Besides, it's not like me and the kids won't come back for frequent visits. And I promised not to leave before your baby arrives, Taylor, so the two of you can relax. I don't plan to sneak off during the night."

She saw the reluctant smiles that touched their faces. Then Vanessa spoke and said, "I'm going to miss my nephew and nieces. I've gotten so attached to them."

"Then I expect that you'll come visit us often. Since Cameron purchased that house next door to mine, it sure makes things convenient."

Vanessa laughed and shook her head. "Yes, it does."

Cheyenne then stared at her other sister and figured something else was on Taylor's mind. Typically, Taylor was the one known to stay out of everyone else's business, mainly because she had this thing about anyone getting into hers. But lately, and seemingly with a lot of frequency, Taylor tended to ask questions that no one,

not even their mother or male cousins or Vanessa—
who sometimes acted as if it was her God-given right
to know everything—would dare ask. Cheyenne had a
feeling what was on Taylor's mind and it wouldn't be the
first time during the past ten months that she had asked.

"Okay, go ahead and ask me, Taylor."

Taylor frowned while absently rubbing her stomach. "Why? So you can tell me it's none of my business again?"

"Umm, go ahead and ask. I might surprise you this
time."

She saw the doubtful look on Taylor's face, but she
knew Taylor wouldn't be able to resist. "Okay, I want
to know who fathered my two beautiful nieces and my
very handsome nephew."

Cheyenne closed her eyes briefly and could see the
face of the man just as clearly as if he was standing
right there in front of her. His facial features were embedded deep into her memory and would always stay
there. And she had a feeling her son would be a constant reminder of him. Although her daughters had inherited a lot of Cheyenne's mother's Native American
ancestry—exotic features like high cheekbones and an
abundance of thick straight-looking black hair—her son
favored his father. She had thought that very thing the
moment he had been placed in her arms. He had his father's dark eyes with the slanted eyebrows and the full
nose and what already appeared to be a stubborn chin.
But what she noticed immediately was the shape of her
son's mouth. It definitely belonged to his father. She, of

all people, should know after the countless times during that one single night she had plastered hers to it. There had been no doubt in her mind on that particular night, just as there weren't any now, that Quade had to have been the most handsome man she'd ever met. And his maturity had set him apart. He hadn't played any games with her, but she had with him…at least at first.

She had lied to him about her age, stating she was twenty-eight instead of twenty-three. She'd feared that, had she been truthful, he would have walked away from her that night and there was no way she could let him do that. She had been attracted to him in a way she had never been to anyone else and she had wanted to explore what such a deep attraction meant.

"Cheyenne?"

Her eyes snapped open to find her two sisters staring at her. "Okay, his name is Quade and I met him on a beach in Egypt. It was a one-night fling." She saw the latter statement didn't seem to shock her sisters, possibly because they may have done the same thing at some time during their lifetime.

"And what's this Quade's last name," Vanessa asked, staring at her over her glass of cranberry juice.

Cheyenne hunched her shoulders. "Don't know. We were more interested in getting into each other's bodies than we were last names."

Neither of her sisters said anything at first and then Taylor asked, "And you're sure he wasn't married?"

Cheyenne inhaled deeply. "He said he wasn't, but I wasn't completely truthful about everything with him, so he might have fibbed a little about one or two things with me. However, I believe he was telling the truth about not being married."

Vanessa raised a brow. "And just what did *you* lie about?" she asked.

Cheyenne moved away from the refrigerator and crossed the kitchen to the cabinet over the sink to pull out her teapot. "My age," she said, turning back around to face her sisters, wanting to see their expressions when she answered. "I told him I was twenty-eight instead of twenty-three." She saw the tightening of both of their features.

"And you think he believed it?" Taylor asked.

"Yes, on that particular night I'd gone for a walk on the beach after a long day of doing a photo shoot. My makeup was still on, which probably made me look a little older."

Vanessa snorted and rolled her eyes. "Or he figured you were ripe for the picking and didn't even care."

Cheyenne laughed softly and said, "If he figured that, then he was absolutely right. I saw him and wanted him just as much as he wanted me."

She couldn't help but remember that night. Every single detail was burned into her memory. Never in her life had she desired a man as much as she had him, and on first sight. Her attraction had been immediate, her surrender had been ultimate and the ten hours that followed had been breathtaking, absolutely the best hours she had spent in any man's bed. And although her experience was limited compared to some women, with those she could compare the difference was beyond measure. Quade had made her beg, scream and become a captive to passion of the most intense kind. She had literally been at his mercy the entire night.

"Cheyenne?"

It was only then that she realized that one of her sisters had been trying to get her attention. "What?"

"I know I asked you this before; it was during the time you were in your seventh or eighth month, and I inquired whether or not you felt you should try and find this guy and you said no. Have you changed your mind about that?" Vanessa asked.

"No," Cheyenne said, shaking her head. "It was a one-night stand and he didn't expect anything out of it, except what he got…what we both got that night—extreme pleasure. I don't blame him for getting me pregnant. He used a condom each time. I saw it. I guess one must have malfunctioned."

Taylor chuckled. "I think that's an understatement, don't you? Must have been one hell of a night to produce triplets."

"It was." She crossed the room to stand in front of them. "I finally got Mom to go home after convincing her I could handle things on my own tonight, and now I want the two of you to do the same. Dinner was great and I appreciate the two of you joining me, but I want to get some rest before the babies wake up. They're still sleeping and if they stay on schedule, I'll only have the six o'clock feeding to deal with."

"But what if they want to eat at the same time?"

Vanessa asked, seemingly alarmed at the thought of her sister caring for the babies alone. Someone had been there with her on a rotating basis since she and the babies had come home from the hospital. Even the wives of Chance, Sebastian and Morgan, had taken turns. Both Sebastian's and Morgan's wives, Jocelyn and Lena, were expecting and used the same excuse Taylor had—they were getting some practice time in.

"If that happens, then two of them will have to wait their turn. They have to start accepting the routine sometime," Cheyenne said with a smile. The one thing she was blessed with was the fact that at least her daughters had begun sleeping through the night. Her son, however, was another story.

"Come on, Taylor, let's leave since she's determined to get rid of us," Vanessa said with a laugh. She helped a very pregnant Taylor out of the kitchen and through the living room.

"Only so I can get some sleep," Cheyenne said. "Besides, if I keep either of you here any longer, your hubbies will come looking for you."

All three of them knew that was true. Because Vanessa's husband traveled a lot, whenever he was home Cameron rarely let her out of his sight. And since Taylor's baby was due the first week in January, her husband, Dominic, also kept her on a tight rein.

After her sisters had left, Cheyenne went into the nursery to check on her babies. Each was in a crib and the room had been beautifully decorated with a Noah's ark theme, compliments of Sienna Bradford, an interior decorator who was also Vanessa's best friend since grade school. Sienna, who had given birth to a beautiful baby boy last year, had offered to decorate the nursery.

Cheyenne's announcement that she would be having triplets had sent excitement spreading through the Steele family, since there was no record of multiple births in the family. More than once Cheyenne had wondered about her babies' father. Did he have a history of multiple births in his family?

The doctor had asked her a number of questions about the man who had fathered her babies, and she hadn't been able to answer any of them. It probably hadn't taken her doctor long to determine she had gotten pregnant by a man she hadn't known for long.

Stealing a few quiet moments while the babies slept, she decided to stretch out on the sofa instead of on the bed. Cheyenne kicked off her shoes to lie down, feeling confident she could handle things just like she had told her mother and sisters. The baby monitor was sitting on the coffee table and would alert her when they awakened.

She had spoken with Roz Henry, her agent and good friend. Roz had fully understood Cheyenne's decision to put her modeling career on hold for a while until the babies got older. Right now the thought of leaving them with anyone while she traveled didn't sit well with her; and she just couldn't see having their nanny travel with her just to take care of the babies. She wanted to be a stay-at-home mom for at least two years, and with her wise investments she would have no problem doing so.

The house was quiet and Cheyenne felt her eyelids getting heavy. Today had been laundry day. She had washed the babies' laundry earlier and would fold it later. Her mother had encouraged her to get out and do something while volunteering to stay there and watch the babies. Taking her mother up on her offer, Cheyenne had gone to the hair salon and had planned to pay a visit to a nail salon, as well, but she had begun missing her babies and had rushed back home.

Cheyenne's eyes drifted closed and automatically she thought about her babies' father.

"Quade."

It was an unusual name and she couldn't help wondering if it was real. Whether it was real was not important now, but it could possibly be later when her children grew up and asked about their father. What on earth would she tell them?

The truth, her mind suddenly interjected. She would tell them the truth and would even assist them in finding him one day if that's what they wanted to do. With only a first name to go by it would be like looking for a needle in a haystack, but she was certain even with the limited information she had, the man could be found eventually. While pregnant she had even entertained the idea of hiring a private investigator to locate him, but she had to consider the possibility that given her circumstances, he might not want to be found. Not every man relished the thought of being a father, and he was one three times over.

Thinking of Quade made her want to relive that night

and her mind automatically went back in time, to a night
that had changed her life forever.

*He pulled her into his arms the moment they
entered his hotel room and closed the door behind
them, locking it. He took her mouth, thrusting his
tongue inside while tangling his hand in her hair
to kiss her deeply, even more so than those other
two kisses they had shared on the beach.*

*She eagerly returned the kiss, thinking he was
very proficient. He had a skill that almost brought
her to her knees. When she was convinced she
would melt in his arms, he broke off the kiss, took
a step back and, with his gaze holding steadfast to
hers, he eased down the zipper to his jeans.*

*She watched him remove his jeans, treating her
to a strip show, the likes of which she had never
seen before. He removed every piece of clothing except for a pair of black boxers. Sexy was too mild
a word to describe how he looked at that moment.
Tempting wouldn't even do justice. He had broad,
masculine shoulders and a taut, firm stomach.
What caught her attention was all the thick, curly
hair on his chest that extended down his stomach
and tapered in a lush line down past the waistband of his boxers. She wanted to reach out and
feel her way through the hairs on his chest before
following the path downward.*

And when he eased his boxers down his legs, that

*part of him that had been straining against them
sprang free, making her eyes widen to see its size.*

She swallowed as she stared at him. Entranced.
Never before had any man looked more beautiful, so stunning, so blood-thickeningly gorgeous.
He didn't seem to have a problem standing there
naked and fully aroused in front of her.

"Now for your clothes," he said, making her fully
aware of what he expected her to do. In fact, he
backed up a few more steps to sit on the edge of
the bed to watch. The way he stared at her made
her nervous, but not in an uncomfortable way. It
was the type of nervousness that intensified the
nerve endings in her body and made her even
more aware of him as a man. Because of her profession she was used to getting in and out of her
clothes rather quickly, but never had she done so
for an audience or more specifically, for one man.
The thought of doing so for him sent an unexplainable thrill of excitement through her.

Feeling bold, brazen and downright hot, she held
his gaze while taking off her blouse and heard
his sharp intake of breath and watched his eyes
darken when he saw she was not wearing a bra.
She had been complimented on the shape and size
of her breasts many times, especially by other mod-
els. They were the kind of breasts that women tried
to imitate with enhancements. She was proud hers
were natural.

She kicked off her sandals and then slithered out

of her pants, working them down her thighs, knowing that he was watching her every move. She was left with one remaining piece—her underwear— a barely there thong that didn't leave anything to his imagination. Everything was basically there, exposed, right before his eyes, and for some reason she didn't feel uncomfortable when his gaze shifted to latch on to her feminine core with an intensity that heated her skin all over.

"Come here, Cheyenne."

He said her name with a huskiness that she felt all the way to the bones and the look in his eyes made her realize even more so just how much he wanted her and how much she wanted him. Her feminine side longed for a connection with him in the most intimate way.

A sexy smile touched his lips as he held his hand out to her. On bare feet she slowly crossed the room and he widened his legs so that she could stand between them. He then pulled her close to bury his face in her chest, right in the center of her breasts, and inhaled her scent. And then she felt it, the wet flick of the tip of his tongue against her nipple. She felt the heat of desire when he closed his mouth over it, latching on to it and sucking it like a newborn baby. A ripple of sensations tore into her, hot and intense, and she automatically reached out and caught hold of his shoulders to keep from falling.

The greedy way his mouth was devouring her

*breasts made her throw her head back and release
the breath she'd been holding. He continued to suck
on her nipples with an intensity that made all kind
of pleasure points gather in the area between her
legs. She felt herself getting wet in the center and
just when she thought she couldn't handle any
more, she felt his hand lower to that area. And when
he touched her there, heat radiated from deep inside as he stroked her.*

*Her legs parted wider for him, giving him ac-
cess to anything and everything he wanted, and
his fingers entered her and began to explore her
sensitive flesh. He first stroked with mild, featherlike
caresses to get her comfortable with the invasion,
and then with heated strokes that elicited groans
of pleasure from her.*

*Nothing or no man had ever made her feel this
way before. Her entire body felt achy with need. And
if anyone had told her she would be in the hotel
room with a man she had just met on the beach,
she would never have believed them.*

*She knew, given her profession, most people
would find it hard to believe that when it came
to sex she barely had any experience. There was
that one guy in college and another she had fan-
cied herself in love with while working in Philly
as a television reporter. But when it came to the
bedroom, neither had known a thing about sharing. It had been all about them fulfilling their own
selfish needs.*

Quade was the first man she had been intimate with in four years. It hadn't been a conscious effort on her part to abstain. Things had just worked out that way.

But this was different. She had been intensely attracted to him from the first, so intensely attracted that she could see herself making love with him right there on the beach if he had wanted it that way.

Suddenly he pulled back, removed his hand from inside her and she felt an immediate sense of loss. She met his gaze, stared as deeply into his eyes as he was staring into hers and watched as he inserted the finger that had been inside of her into his mouth, licking it like it was a lollipop of his favorite flavor, and letting her know how much he was savoring her taste. Seeing what he was doing made the muscles between her legs clench, stoked her desires into a feverish heat.

He stood and she felt herself being lifted into his arms and placed on the bed. He leaned over and caught his hand in the waistband of her thong and then slowly eased it down her legs. Instead of tossing it aside he brought the thong to his nose and inhaled deeply, as if he needed to know her intimate scent. She was at a loss to do anything, but stare at him.

And while she lay there naked, her entire body exposed before his eyes, for his pleasure, he moved his hand upward from the bottom of her feet, then

*pausing at her center, zeroing in on her feminine
mound as if the sight of it fascinated him. Her
breath caught when he began stroking between her
legs before sliding another finger inside her again,
testing her wetness, making her moan out loud.*

*"Quade." She said his name, a deep moan from
her mouth. "I need you." And at that point she did.
Every cell in her body was vibrating with that need.*

*"I'm going to take care of you, I promise," he said
while he continued to stroke her, building tension
inside her. "But if I don't taste you now I'm going
to go mad."*

*She caught her breath, almost held it when he
slid down on the bed and placed a warm kiss on
her stomach before arranging her legs over his
shoulder, bringing him face-to-face with her feminine mound. He was so close she could feel his
heated breath on the swollen lips of her feminin-
ity. She closed her eyes and let out a deep groan the
moment she felt his heated tongue on her flesh, and
then he pushed that tongue deeper inside her and
began moving it around in firm, hard strokes, then
pushing in deeper, withdrawing then inserting it
back in deeper and deeper again, over and over.*

*She soon discovered he was methodical and in-
tense with his kisses no matter where he placed
them. Holding tight to her hips with his mouth
locked on her, he was using his tongue in ways
she didn't know it could be used, taking it places
she hadn't known it could go and giving her the*

most intimate French kiss possible while greedily feasting on her.

She screamed when a climax hit with the intensity of a train derailment. She felt her body break into tiny pieces filling her with a degree of pleasure she had never felt in her life.

She felt him leave her momentarily, watched through a heated gaze as he reached into the pocket of his jeans to pull out a condom. She watched him sheath himself before rejoining her on the bed and settling between her trembling thighs where the aftershock of a gigantic orgasm still lingered.

He leaned down and kissed her and she could taste the essence of herself on his lips, and then she felt him, the head of his hard and thick manhood pressing at her wet center. She craved the contact, was almost desperate for the connection, and was consumed with an abundance of heat that was generated by his desire for her and hers for him. He was building a need within her, one that made her feminine core throb. And as if he felt her need, he pulled back from the kiss, met her gaze to see her expression and reaction when he slowly began entering her.

Their gazes continued to hold, stayed connected as he began penetrating her deep, stretching her wide, filling her with the very essence of him. She was extremely tight and for a moment she read the question in his eyes and decided to respond before he could ask.

"No. It's just been a long time for me," she explained. She hoped her words had sufficiently removed any inkling that she was a virgin.

"Then tonight we'll make up for lost time," he said huskily, slowly pressing deeper inside her, filling her to capacity.

"We're perfect together," he said, and it was then that she realized just how deeply embedded inside her he was. All the way to the hilt. Their bodies were joined as tightly as any two bodies could be. They just lay there, him on top of her, inside her, while they stared at each other, taking in just what that moment meant and contemplating what would be the next move.

"I'm going slow to make it last," he whispered just seconds before he began moving. Flexing his hips, he ground his hard masculine thighs against hers for deeper penetration with each stroke into her, lifting her hips up with the palm of his hands and locking her to him to fill her even deeper.

He started off with slow, even strokes, just like he said he would do. Then the tempo changed, the rhythm was switched and he began riding her faster and with more intensity, with an even deeper penetration. He threw his head back and a guttural groan escaped from deep within his throat. Her body was in tune with his, with every stroke, and she felt sensations filling her, taking over her, setting off another explosion inside of her.

She sank her nails into his shoulder, screamed

his name when everything was ripped out of her, igniting every nerve ending, every single cell. She could feel every strand of hair on her head, every intimate muscle clench him, pulling everything out of him as he kept going, thrusting into her with an intensity that brought on another climax. She screamed his name again at the same time he screamed hers. And she felt him shudder inside of her, actually felt the condom expand under the weight of his release.

It took awhile for the sensations to begin to fade. He leaned forward and kissed her, thrusting his tongue back and forth into her mouth the same way he had done to her feminine core earlier and making her come again just that easy. Never in her life had she enjoyed such pure pleasure—such deep, piercing satisfaction.

Moments later after he released her mouth she pulled in another breath as she felt limp, lifeless, completely satiated. And then Quade lifted up slightly, raised his head to meet her gaze. At that moment something touched her deep. Then he slowly lowered his head as his fingers caressed her cheek and seconds later he was kissing her again, a lot gentler this time, while whispering that he hadn't gotten enough and wanted more.

She couldn't help but inwardly admit that she hadn't gotten enough and wanted him again, as well. She could tell from the feel of him getting hard inside her all over again that what they shared was only the beginning....

The ringing of the doorbell interrupted Cheyenne's dream. She opened her eyes, a little annoyed at the intrusion. Standing, she stretched her body trying to fight off the lingering sensual sensations of her dream. When the doorbell sounded again she quickly moved to the door. The last thing she wanted was for her babies to wake from their nap. More than likely her visitor was one of her male cousins who periodically dropped by to make sure she was okay. She had to admit they were thoughtful and always had been, even while thinking they'd been somewhat overprotective of her while growing up.

She took a quick look through the peephole and blinked. Her eyes then shot open wide as she looked out the peephole again. Because she had just dreamed about the father of her babies her mind had to be playing tricks on her. There was no way he could be outside on her doorstep. The sun had set and the person was standing in a shadowed area of the porch so she couldn't completely make out the man's face. But from the build of his body—especially the broad, masculine shoulders—reminded her so much of *Quade*. Her one-time lover. The man who was constantly a part of her dreams.

She found her voice, yet it was shaky when she asked. "Who is it?"

"Quade."

She sagged against the door as a gush of shocked breath rushed from her lungs. *Why was he here? Had he somehow found out about her babies?*

"Cheyenne, I need to talk to you."

His voice was just as she remembered; ultra husky and as sexy as any man's voice had a right to be. Knowing she couldn't keep him standing outside forever, she garnered as much strength as she could and slowly began twisting the doorknob while asking herself how she would handle seeing him again when the mere thought of the man sent lust ripping through her body.

The door opened and she immediately met his gaze, finding it hard to believe that this wasn't a dream and he was actually here, standing on her doorstep—in the flesh. The air surrounding them suddenly became charged—just as it had that night. And she couldn't help noticing that also just like that night, his body was molded into a pair of faded jeans and a pullover shirt. Both oozed a degree of sexuality that warmed her skin and created an intense yearning within her. The man was as darkly handsome as she remembered. Even more so.

To make matters worse, he was staring at her the same way he had that night on the beach and it didn't take a rocket scientist to recognize that look of blatant desire in his eyes. Like before, he was getting to her without very much effort and she fought back the urge to reach out and touch him, while convincing herself that her hormones were out of whack and making her crave something she really didn't want and definitely something she didn't need.

Inhaling deeply she tried to relax, fight off the shock of seeing him. She was determined to find out why he was there while refusing to consider that somehow he had found out about the triplets.

"Quade? I don't understand why you're here," she heard herself say. "I didn't expect to ever see you again."

He continued to look at her. "I didn't expect to ever see you again, either," he said softly, yet in a masculine tone. "But I saw you on the cover of a magazine. And you were pregnant."

She nervously licked her lips, having an idea where this conversation was headed. A part of her regretted that she had allowed Roz to talk her into doing that magazine cover. And what on earth was he doing looking at an issue of *Pregnancy* magazine?

"I want to know one thing."

Cheyenne sensed what he wanted to know but asked the question anyway, preferring not to make assumptions. "What do you want to know?"

"Did you have my baby?"

Chapter 3

Quade felt his insides tighten, not knowing what Cheyenne's response would be, not even sure from the way she was looking at him if she would even give him one. The trouble was, he didn't plan on leaving until she did.

Until now he'd never given any thought to being a father. In fact, a wife and kids weren't on his list of goals he'd wanted to achieve in life. There seemed to be enough of his brothers and cousins doing a pretty damn good job of being productive and replenishing the earth with more Westmorelands, for him to be needed in that role. However, if he was the father of her child, then he would take full responsibility, and the sooner she knew it the better.

"Westmorelands take full responsibility for their actions," he said, as if that explained everything. He tried to downplay the stirrings in his groin that had started the moment she had opened the door. And when she lifted perfectly arched eyebrows the stirrings increased.

"Westmoreland? Is that your last name?" she asked.

He studied her to see what about her was different from that night. She looked a lot younger than twenty-eight and the color of her eyes seemed darker than he recalled. But her lips, full and enticing, were just as luscious as he remembered. She was wearing a pair of jeans and a T-shirt that stretched across firm breasts. Her waistline looked small, not indicative of a woman who'd given birth to a child, but her hips had curves that hadn't been there before. He, of all people, should know. He had touched and tasted every inch of her body.

"Quade?"

When she said his name, he realized he hadn't responded to her question. "Yes. Westmoreland is my last name." It also made him realize just how little they knew about each other. The only thing they did know was how much they could satisfy each other in bed. "And I take it that Steele is yours," he decided to add.

She nodded slowly. "Yes, Steele is mine."

Now that they'd gotten that out of the way, she still hadn't answered his question—the most important one and the reason he was there. "Are you going to answer my question about the baby?"

Cheyenne wasn't sure if she should answer him. Although there was no doubt in her mind that he had a right to know, she just wasn't certain he would be ready for her response. He was inquiring about a baby. How would he handle the fact that there were three?

She let out a sigh as she studied the handsome face staring back at her. It was a face that still had the power to make her pulse race, her heart beat faster and cause goose bumps to form on her arms. And worse still, it had the power to make her vividly recall every single detail of the night they had spent together.

Fully aware of the lengthening silence between them and the fact she could tell by the tightening of his jaw that he was getting annoyed she hadn't responded to his question, she said, "I think you should come in so we can talk about it."

"Do you?" he asked in what she picked up as a rather cool voice.

"Yes." She took a step back and opened the door a little wider in invitation.

He continued to stare at her for a moment before crossing the threshold into her home and closing the door behind him. It wasn't until he was inside that she became fully aware of just how tall he was. Her cousins and two brothers-in-law were tall men and Quade would fit right in with them. His presence seemed to dominate the room and there was an air about him that said he was confident in his masculinity. Confident, even arrogant.

"You're stalling."

He had come to stand directly in front of her and she was all too aware of his presence. "Am I?" she asked, fighting the tightness in her throat.

"Yes, and I'd like to know why? I would think my question was simple enough," he said in a tone that let her know he was getting even more agitated. "You were pregnant. The baby you gave birth to was fathered by me or by someone else. All I want to know is, was it me?"

Anger simmered in her belly at the thought that he could assume she had slept with someone else, but then she had to be reasonable—he didn't know her. The only thing he knew was how quickly he had been able to get her in his bed and without very much effort. He had been a total stranger yet she had gone to his hotel room, stripped naked and had made love to him almost nonstop all night long.

She inhaled deeply and then asked. "And if I were to say that it wasn't you?"

He gave her a smile that didn't quite reach his eyes. "Then I apologize for seeking you out and wasting your time."

"And if it was you?" she asked softly. "Not saying that it was," she hurriedly added.

She saw a hardening in his gaze. "To be quite honest, you really aren't saying anything," he said, crossing his arms over his chest. "Why can't you just give me a definitive answer?"

Cheyenne placed her arms over her chest, as well. "It's a bit complicated."

He lifted a brow and gave her a probing look. "Complicated in what way? Either I'm the one who got you pregnant, or I'm not. Now which one is it?"

His gaze burned into hers with a warning that said he was impatient, and tired of her not giving him a straight answer. She swallowed the lump in her throat and then said. "Yes, you're the one. But…"

"But what?"

From his expression it was hard to tell if he was disappointed or elated about being a father. Probably the former, since she figured most men preferred not becoming a daddy from a one-night stand. "There wasn't *a* baby," she said.

She actually saw the glint of concern that flashed in his eyes. "Did you lose it?" he asked softly.

"No," she said quickly. "That's not what I meant."

He stared at her. His expression then became rather chilling. "Then how about telling me just what the hell you did mean."

She glared at him. He was getting angry and so was she. She placed her hand on her hip and took a step closer to him with fire in her eyes. "What I mean, Quade, is that I didn't give birth to one baby. I gave birth to three."

Quade's mouth dropped open in shock. He had seen the size of her stomach and, although his cousin Cole had joked at the possibility she was carrying more than one baby, Quade had dismissed it, assuming the baby was just a big one. She'd given birth to triplets—Westmoreland triplets. The first in his generation of Westmorelands. He couldn't help but smile at the thought. Damn.

"Is there something that you find rather amusing?" Cheyenne asked in a somewhat annoyed tone. He glanced over at her. She looked as if she was ready to throw something at him. He could just imagine how hard it would be to give birth to one baby. But three…

He shrugged broad shoulders. "No," he said, quickly wiping the smile off his face. "Are they okay?"

The anger eased from her eyes somewhat with his question of concern. "Yes. They were born eight weeks premature and had to remain in the hospital for almost three weeks, but now they're fine."

"I want to see them," he said, wanting to make sure for himself.

From the look that suddenly appeared in her eyes he could tell his brisk and authoritarian tone hadn't helped matters, but at the moment he didn't care. If he had fathered babies, he wanted to see them. She said they were okay, but he wanted to see them for himself.

"No."

Now it was his eyes that were narrowing. "No?"

"That's what I said."

He stared at her. She was trying to be difficult. The look on her face was proof of that. He was used to his orders being followed. Okay, he would concede that he wasn't still with the PSF and she wasn't one of his men. But still, had he requested something of her that was so complex?

"Is there a reason why I can't see them?"

"Yes. They're asleep."

He studied her. "Is there a reason you can't wake them up?"

For a single minute she looked like she wanted to hit him over the head with something again. "Yes. It will interfere with their sleep pattern. If I disturb their sleep now, they will stay up later tonight and I would like to get a good night's sleep."

"Fine, I won't wake them, but I want to see them."

"No."

"Yes."

Tension sizzled between them and finally through gritted teeth Cheyenne said, "Fine, but you better not wake them."

"I said I wouldn't," Quade said in a furious growl. People used anger to mask a lot of things, even hard-cast lust like he was feeling now. Just the thought that she had given birth to his babies made him want to reach out and pull her into his arms and kiss the pout right off her lips. That would only be the start....

"You better not wake them. Now follow me."

She turned and he couldn't help but smile as he followed her down a long hallway. Damn, she was feisty. She hadn't been that night in his hotel room. Then she'd been passionate, seductive and *very* accommodating. He shook his head in disbelief. *He was a father.* Not that he planned on being one, but now that was beside the point. *So what was the point?*

He dismissed the question and glanced ahead at Cheyenne, more specifically her shapely backside. He was partial to that part of a woman's anatomy and even with her clothes on he could vividly recall her naked behind. He had liked it, especially the way it was curved and how it had felt beneath the heat of his body. It had been a lovemaking position he had introduced her to, and a position she had enjoyed just as much as he had.

She stopped at a door and whirled around and glared at him, making him wonder if she'd read his thoughts. "You didn't ask, but I'll tell you anyway," she all but snapped. "I have a son and two daughters."

The sex of the babies didn't matter to him. All that mattered was that they were his. "*We* have a son and two daughters," he corrected her by saying.

She stared at him—actually glared at him—some more. "You don't seem surprised that I gave birth to triplets."

He shrugged. "Not really," he said softly, trying to follow her lead and keep his voice down. "Multiple births run in my family. I'm a twin."

The look of surprise on her face was priceless and reminded him of just how little they knew of each other. "You didn't mention it that night," she all but accused.

"I had no reason to do so. If I recall, we didn't do much talking."

At that instant, by the look in her eyes, he knew his words were forcing her to remember. Then just as quickly he watched as she schooled her features to reflect casual indifference. "I don't remember," she said with deliberate coolness.

He smiled. She was lying and they both knew it.

However, if she wanted to pretend she didn't remember anything about that night then he would let her.

"And although you haven't even asked me what their names are, I'm going to tell you anyway," she said in a tone that implied she was still annoyed with him. "My daughters are Venus and Athena, and my son's name is Troy."

He nodded. They were nice names.

"There's something that you should know about Troy."

He lifted a brow. Concerned. "What?"

"He sometimes develops a bad disposition, especially when he's hungry. He always wants to be fed before his sisters, and he always wants to be the center of attention."

"Typical Westmoreland."

"They were born Steeles."

He let out an aggravated sigh. "Only because I wasn't here to make things otherwise. I'm here now."

He could feel the tension once again sizzling through them. "Meaning?" she asked.

He crossed his arms over his chest. "Meaning, since you have confirmed the babies are mine, that will entail a number of things."

"Like what?"

He saw a flicker of defiance in her eyes and knew whatever "a number of things" were she would put up a fight. "I'd rather not discuss them now. I just want to see the babies."

He had a feeling she was a woman who was used to

calling the shots and didn't appreciate his entrance into her life. Well, that was too bad. Babies had been the product of their one night of sexual lust, and although becoming a father had been the last thing on his mind, that very thing had happened. And just like he'd told her and would again tell her just in case she hadn't gotten it, a Westmoreland took responsibility for his actions, no matter what they were. That code of ethics had been drilled into every Westmoreland from day one and it would be his responsibility to teach that same code to his son and daughters.

A son and two daughters.

He inhaled deeply at the thought. What on earth was he supposed to do with babies? He liked kids well enough, but had never intended to have any of his own. He had enough nieces and nephews—either already born or presently on the way, and then all his cousins had begun having children, which meant he was constantly having a slew of young cousins being born. But now, of all things, it looked like he had three of his own to add to the number. He could just imagine his family's reaction when he told them. His mother would go crazy. Sarah Westmoreland was determined to get all the grandkids that she could out of her six sons.

"Remember, you aren't to wake them."

Her words intruded in on his thoughts. "I don't need to be reminded, Cheyenne."

She rolled her eyes and opened the bedroom door. He followed her in and glanced around. There were several painted animals on the walls and he immedi-

ately recognized the theme. Noah's ark. Must be a popular one since his cousin Storm's twin two-year-old
daughters had their room decorated in the same way.
He sniffed the air. The room even smelled like a nursery. The comforting scent of baby powder, oil and lo-
tion lingered in the air.

Quade's attention then came to rest to the three white
baby cribs and he suddenly swallowed when he fully
realized what this moment meant. Something akin to
panic surged through his veins. He was used to just
looking after himself, and for the past few years, he
had done a pretty damn good job doing so considering all the sticky situations he'd been in while working
for the PSF. Now he would be responsible for others,
namely three babies that were his. In a way, that was
scarier than protecting the president. He had a feeling
being a father was going to be one hell of a challenge.

He glanced over at Cheyenne. She was going to be a
challenge, too. There was a lot about her that he didn't
know. But the one thing he did know was that she had
chosen to bring his babies into the world instead of not
doing so. Women these days had other options and considering everything, he was glad of the decision she had
made. He let out a long sigh and slowly followed Cheyenne over to the first crib.

"This is Venus," Cheyenne said as a way of introduction. "She's the youngest and weighed the least when
she was born. Because she weighed less than three
pounds at birth, she had to stay in the hospital's special care baby unit two weeks longer than the others."

Quade glanced down at the baby covered by a pink blanket and his breath caught in his chest. He held his hands tight by his sides, tempted to reach out and touch her, just to see if she was real. Her little head was covered by black hair and she seemed to be sleeping so peacefully. She was such a fragile little thing. He silently vowed that one day under his love and protection she would grow to have incredible strength and would never have to worry about anything.

"And this is Athena," Cheyenne whispered.

He glanced up to see that Cheyenne had moved to the second crib. He took a couple of steps to stand beside her to glance down at the baby sleeping in the crib. She was also covered in a pink blanket and like her sister, she had a head full of dark hair. She was bigger than her sister, but still she looked rather small. "How much did she weigh?" he asked in a very low voice, meeting Cheyenne's eyes.

"Barely three. She was born second."

He glanced back down and knew, like the other baby, this one would never have to worry about anything. He would make sure of it. Following Cheyenne, he moved to the third crib and blinked. His son definitely wasn't a small baby. He could probably make two of his sisters.

"Like I said. He likes to eat," Cheyenne said, and he could hear the amusement in her voice. "He was born weighing almost four pounds and now he's almost eight pounds."

"What do you feed them?"

"Breast milk."

Quade's gaze immediately went to her chest and saw the outline of her breasts pressed against the blouse she was wearing. His heart thudded at the memory that was so fresh in his mind of when his mouth had captured a hardened nipple between his lips and how he had indulged in a little breast time himself by sucking on her breasts the same way a baby would. He also remembered just how much she had enjoyed the little byplay.

"I take it that he was born first," he decided to say, placing his gaze back on his son and away from Cheyenne.

"Yes, and when he gets older, I'm going to depend on him to look after his sisters. Look after them, but not boss them around," Cheyenne said softly.

He lifted a brow and smiled. "Do I hear a little resentment in your voice? Did your brothers boss you around?"

She smiled back and moved away from the crib toward the door. When they were outside in the hall she said. "I don't have any brothers. My parents had three girls and I'm the youngest and yes, my sisters tried bossing me around. And then there are my male cousins. Four of them. And they were bossy, as well, although they were convinced being that way was for my own good."

For some reason the thought pleased him that she had people looking out for her. He bet she had been a beautiful child. She'd certainly grown up to be a beautiful woman. He could imagine all the men who'd come calling.

"So what do you think?"

He glanced over at her as they walked back toward the living room. "About what?"

She stopped walking. "Not about what, but about who," she said, more than a little annoyed. "What do you think of Venus, Athena and Troy?"

He shrugged, not sure he could fully explain to her or anyone just how he was feeling at that moment. He decided to try. "I never planned to get married or have children. My chosen career took me all over the country and would have been hell on a family."

"But do you like children?" she asked him.

"What's there not to like? To be totally honest, I've never been around a child for a long period of time. If you're trying to find out how I feel about them rather than what I think of them, then I would have to say that as strange as it may seem, I feel attached to them already. Seeing them in there, knowing they are a part of me, something the two of us created… I can't help but be overcome by it all. And just to think they are dependent on us makes me—"

"They aren't dependent on you, Quade. I'm not asking you for anything."

He stared at her for a long moment before he spoke. "You don't have to ask. They are mine, Cheyenne, and I claim them as mine. For a Westmoreland, that means everything."

He could tell that his words bothered her for some reason and she proved him right when she said in a frosty tone. "I think we need to talk."

"Evidently we do. Lead the way."

She did and he followed, getting the chance to ogle her backside once again.

Chapter 4

"Are we going to talk or are you going to wear out your carpet?"

Cheyenne finally stopped pacing and glanced over at Quade. Then she wished that she hadn't. He had taken the wingback chair in the room with his long legs stretched out in front of him. His T-shirt fit his body like a glove and showed off his broad shoulders. Then there were the handsome contours of his face that could still turn her on, basically tilt her world to the side of the irrational. It had been so easy for him to get to her that night. On several occasions since then her body had longed for his, distinctively craving for all the things she had experienced in his arms and in his bed. To say he had left a mark on her in more ways than one would be an understatement.

She knew they needed to talk, but she wanted to school her words carefully. He was the father of her babies and they both knew it, however, she wanted him to understand that Venus, Athena and Troy were just that—*her* babies. What he'd said earlier about claiming them as his bothered her because the last thing she wanted was for him to consider exercising any type of legal rights. Any thoughts of claiming them might give him even more ideas. What if he tried to dictate where she and the babies lived, what they did and what part he felt he should play in their lives? she wondered. She had grown up all her life under someone's thumb and she refused to let it happen again.

"I'm waiting."

She glared at Quade. If he was trying to get on her last nerve, then he was succeeding. Pursing her lips, she fought the urge to give him a smart-ass comeback. She needed to feel him out and couldn't waste her energy on anything other than that. "Why did you say that a Westmoreland's responsibility meant everything? It's like your family lives by a certain code of ethics or something. Please explain."

Cheyenne's pulse jumped a few notches and she drew in a deep breath when Quade shifted in his seat to another position. The air surrounding them seemed to stir, and she became besieged by a blanket of desire just from his body movement. Her senses went on alert and she thought that it wasn't good to react this way toward him. But she couldn't help it. She was honing in on him, remembering how he looked in a pair of black boxers and at the same time recalling just how he looked when he had taken them off.

"I'll gladly explain it," he said, interrupting her thoughts and making Cheyenne so very grateful he wasn't aware of her attraction to him. More than anything, she had to stay in control.

"You mentioned I didn't appear surprised about the multiple births and I told you I wasn't because I'm a twin. What I didn't add was that my father is also a twin. And his twin brother John and my aunt Evelyn also have a set of twins—Storm and Chase. My twin's name is Ian. On top of that, my father's youngest brother, Corey Westmoreland, fathered triplets."

"That many multiple births in one family?" she said, amazed.

"Possibly more according to my father. He's convinced a Westmoreland who appeared in the national newspaper earlier this year when his wife gave birth to quadruplets is related to us. Dad's now into this genealogy thing, trying to find a connection."

After a brief pause, he said, "Now to get back to your question, there are thirteen male Westmorelands from my generation and we're all close. Very early, when we began sniffing after girls, our fathers instilled in us one rule that would always govern a Westmoreland. We were raised to take responsibility for our actions, no matter what they were."

Cheyenne sighed deeply. "But that's just it. I don't need you taking responsibility."

"Doesn't matter."

She could see he would be difficult. He reminded her of her male cousins who were also hell-bent on living by some code of honor, some invisible creed. At least Chance, Sebastian and Morgan were. Donovan, the youngest of her Steele male cousins—the only one not married—was still trying to find himself. At the moment, Donovan was happy to find himself right smack in the middle of any woman's bed. But still, she was fairly certain if he ever got caught by being careless, he would do the right thing by the woman regardless of whether he wanted to or not. Whether he loved the woman would not be a factor. In his eyes—the eyes of a Steele—a union would be a justified restitution for exhibiting a lack of judgment.

Evidently Quade and his other Westmoreland male kin had the same thought processes. Well, she didn't need him or any man sacrificing themselves for her and her babies. Getting pregnant hadn't been intentional on her part, just like she knew getting her pregnant hadn't been his intention. It was an accident. It happened and she could live with it mainly because the results—Venus, Athena and Troy—had captured her heart the moment she had been told she was pregnant.

"Does that explain things to you, Cheyenne?"

Yes, it did, but she still was unsure how to deal with him. He was looking at her with dark, piercing eyes. He was waiting for a response.

She had a feeling that he was a man who did whatever he wanted to do, someone who was used to being in control. In the few relationships she had been involved in, she had tried avoiding men like him—men with the ability to overrule her heart, as well as her head. Keeping her senses intact wouldn't be easy with him, but she was determined to do so.

"Yes," she finally responded. "Although I think you're getting a little carried away."

He lifted a brow. "Carried away how?"

"While I can understand and appreciate you wanting to take responsibility for your part in my pregnancy, as well as acknowledging you fathered my babies, all I'm saying is that you don't have to take it any further than that."

Quade stared at her and a part of Cheyenne actually felt the heat of his gaze on certain parts of her. "That's very generous of you," he said with a smile that didn't quite reach his eyes. "But you have no idea just how far I plan to take things."

No, she didn't and that's what bothered her the most. She knew she could not deny him the legal right he had to be a part of the triplets' life. It would be a total waste of her time to try to fight him on the matter. She'd heard more than one account of where the courts sided with a father. But still, she would do anything and everything to make sure being a father wasn't just a passing fancy for him, a novelty he was enjoying at the moment but one that would wear off later.

Deciding it was time for her to probe further, she said, "So tell me. How far do you plan to take things?"

"All the way to the altar."

She blinked. "Excuse me?"

"You heard me right, Cheyenne. And given the nature of our situation I recommend that we proceed immediately."

Panic ripped through her. "And do what?" she all but stammered.

His response was quick, without a moment's hesitation. "Get married. What else?"

Evidently there *was* a "what else," Quade thought as he looked at Cheyenne's face. It looked as if shock had knocked her speechless. But that look would not hinder his plans. He had arrived in Charlotte earlier that day not knowing what to expect. He had figured he had possibly fathered a child, but he certainly hadn't expected to discover he had fathered three. Now, knowing that he had, there was no way he could walk away. Nor was there any way he could not do what was expected of him—expected of a Westmoreland.

"Is there a problem?" he decided to ask when Cheyenne continued to stare at him as if he had just provided concrete proof to her that there was life on another planet.

He could actually hear her clench her teeth before she said. "No, there isn't a problem. At least not on my end because I have no intention of marrying you."

"I wouldn't say that if I were you," he cautioned. "You might want to think this through carefully."

She tightened her mouth in a firm line and glared over at him. "There is nothing to think about. I have no plans to get married, especially to you. I don't even know you."

Returning her glare, he crossed the room to stand in front of where she stood. "Then I suggest that you get to know me. Like it or not, I don't intend for you or our children not to carry my name."

She tilted her head and glared up at him. "My babies and I have a name—Steele. Thank you much for your offer, but we don't need another one. I happen to like the one we have."

He stepped closer. "And I happen to like the name Westmoreland for you and our babies better."

"Too bad," she snapped.

"No, too good," was his response.

And too late, Cheyenne thought, when she noticed his gaze had zeroed in on her mouth and that he had taken a step even closer while continuing to hold her gaze. She returned his stare and for the moment she was unable to move. She was transfixed in place. Breathing was even difficult as she remembered that night almost eleven months ago causing heated desire to run up her spine.

Deciding she needed her space she took a step back, but he recovered the distance in record time. "Going somewhere?" he asked, reaching out to place his hands around her waist.

Her entire body reacted to his touch. How in the world could he get such a reaction from her when she was mad at him? Her body was treacherous when it came to his touch…just like before.

"Don't think you're going to seduce me into any-thing," she said, and then wished she hadn't said it when she saw the flash of challenge that lit his eyes. "I'm used to men like you," she decided to say. "I was raised around four male cousins."

"And?"

"And I know how to handle *you*."

A smile touched his lips. "Yes, I'd be the first to say that you do. If memory serves me correctly, you have the ability to handle me very well," he said, his voice was low and guttural.

She tried to ease back again, but his hand at her waist made it difficult. Instead she continued to stare at him, and literally stopped breathing when he began lower-ing his head toward her.

She wanted to resist. To move. To stop the kiss she saw coming. Instead, she braced herself for it, and heaven help her, she felt fire surge in the area between her thighs in anticipation of it. All the while she tried convincing herself that this was not what she wanted, but another part of her was declaring loud and clear that this was exactly what she needed.

His lips hovered close to her, so close the warmth of his breath moistened her lips. It seemed he was refusing to bring it any further and she couldn't help wondering why he was stalling.

He must have read the confusion in her eyes because then he said, "Go ahead and take it."

She stared at him, thinking that he had a lot of nerve. But then a lot could be said for nerves, she thought when she found herself inching her mouth closer to his. Then she quickly made a decision and decided to act on it.

She leaned in closer, latched on to his mouth, clung to it and the moment their lips connected and hers parted, he was there, his tongue invading her mouth and rattling her senses, reminding her of that night. And just like that night, passion, more potent than she remembered, ripped into her and she ensnarled his tongue with hers. He was kissing her with a hunger and a desire she only knew with him. It was intoxicating. Stimulating. Mind-boggling. She hadn't expected anything less.

And when he tightened his hold around her waist, he brought her body closer to the fit of his. It was then that she felt everything. The feel of her hardened nipples beneath her blouse that was plastered to his chest, the size of his erection that seemed to fit perfectly in the apex of her thighs.

Just like before.

And then those memories filled her mind. It was a night that had been like no other. It was a night that had introduced her to lovemaking of the most intense kind. Each of his kisses had left her mouth burning for more, his touches had sent scorching heat through her wherever he stroked…and he had made contact with every inch of her skin. There wasn't an area of her body that Quade hadn't touched or tasted.

Thoughts of the latter made her body quiver and the quiver seemed to pass from her to him. She could feel his erection swell even more against her.

She whimpered with pleasure when he deepened

the kiss, leaning in closer to make her arch her back.
It seemed that millions and millions of tiny needles of
desire were pricking her skin, spreading heat and she
knew he was trying to prove a point. Just like that night,
he was claiming her. Stamping his possession. Leaving
his imprint. Proving beyond a shadow of a doubt that
she might say one thing, but she meant another.

Cheyenne didn't like the thought of that and wanted
to pull her mouth free, but she found the only thing she
could do with her mouth was continue to devour him
the same way he was devouring her.

Suddenly, he tore his mouth away from hers and
placed his forehead against hers, in an attempt to catch
his breath. She did the same. Sucking in deep breaths
of air and feeling tender places in her mouth that his
tongue had been. He had been greedy, but so had she.
He hadn't just consumed her. They had consumed each
other.

He pulled back slightly and stared down at her with
eyes that were filled with desire. She recognized that
look in them. "As you can see, Cheyenne, nothing has
changed between us. We're as hot for each other as we
were before. Do you know how many times over the
past eleven months I've awakened during the night, as
hard as a rock, wanting to give us both pleasure? And
how many times I wished you were there in bed with
me so I could touch you all over, kiss you all over, just
like before? Then there were my dreams that served as
a recollection of all those positions we tried, all those
I taught you. Although I didn't intend to get you preg-

nant, it really doesn't surprise me that I did, considering everything."

Her mind became fragmented at all the memories he was bringing forth. He was right, considering everything, especially how much they had been into each other that night, although they had tried being careful, it wouldn't surprise her if they had begun getting careless and concentrating on pleasure more than on birth control.

That thought prompted her to say, "We might not have planned for them, but I don't regret them, Quade," she said, wanting him to know just how much a part of her they were. "They are my life."

"As well as mine."

She reared back, refusing to believe what he was saying. "No," she said sharply, lifting her chin up. "There's no way you can feel anything toward them this soon. You found out about them today. You just saw them."

He reached out and took her stubborn chin between his fingers, caressing the outline of it with his fingertips. "And is that supposed to mean they can't mean something to me? Do you think just because you carried them in your body that I don't also have a connection? Granted, a part of me wished I could have been here to see how your belly swelled each month, but I wasn't. But that doesn't mean their existence means any less to me."

Cheyenne looked at him, tried to weigh the sincerity in his words. It took more than potent seeds hitting a fertile egg to make a man a father. Maybe she was far too aware of what made a good father because she'd had one. Her dad had been a hard-working man who had cherished his wife and adored his daughters. The only thing she wished was that he'd laid off the cigarettes, which had resulted in him getting lung cancer and dying way too soon.

"Okay," she said. "You want to be a part of their life, but that doesn't mean you have to be a part of mine."

He smiled and the way the corners of his lips curved made a wave of desire run through her stomach. She fought hard to downplay the effect. "I think it would be hard separating the four of you," he said. "It's a package deal. I want them and I want you. I claim them and I claim you, as well."

Her gaze narrowed. "No. I won't let you. We are Steeles."

"Not for long."

She frowned. "Are you threatening me?"

He chuckled and gave her that look she had found endearing the first time she'd seen it. "No, I thought I was asking you to marry me."

"You didn't ask. You all but demanded."

"Then I apologize and will start over. Will you marry me?"

She shook her head. "No."

"Can I ask why?"

"I've told you why. I don't know you." And when he opened his mouth to speak, she quickly added, "Out of bed."

He didn't say anything for a minute and then. "All right, then I have a proposition for you."

Something warned her to be cautious. "What kind of proposition?"

"I want to give you the time to get to know me, just like I want to get to know you."

She stared at him. "Why?"

"Because according to you, that's the reason why you won't marry me. My job will be to try to impress you, sweep you off your feet and make you feel comfortable enough to consider the fact that you, me and the babies together as a family is the only way things can be."

Cheyenne didn't like the sound of that. She was an international model who traveled all over the country. What if he had a problem with her chosen career? And then there was that part of her job that no one, not even her family knew about. Her agent wasn't even privy to information about it, although on occasion Cheyenne used her professional model status to get in and out of places where she needed to be.

"And if I don't see things your way and agree to your proposition?" she asked, needing to know her options.

"Then I will seek legal counsel to see what rights I have as a father. If the five of us being together as a family is not an option, I need to make sure I have a legal right to be a part of my children's life. I'd rather not involve an attorney, of course, and prefer that for the sake of the babies we can reach some kind of a reasonable and acceptable resolution. But if not, I won't hesitate to take you to court for shared custody rights."

Shared custody rights. Her heart jumped at the very thought of her babies being separated from her at any time, especially while they were so young. She just couldn't imagine it happening. But then all she had to do was to stare into Quade's face to know that he couldn't imagine it being any other way…other than the option he had given her. The one where the five of them would live together, married, as a family.

She needed to think. She needed to be alone. Basically, what she really needed was him gone. Around him she couldn't completely think straight. "I need time to think about this, Quade."

"That's fine," he said. "I'm not proposing that we marry right away. All I'm asking for is time for you to get to know me. However, I want my children to have my name as soon as it can be arranged. I want them entitled to everything I own if something were to ever happen to me."

Cheyenne lifted a brow. *If something were to ever happen to him.* She didn't even know what he did for a living for crying out loud. "What do you do for a living?" she asked.

"I recently retired from working for the Federal Government."

"In what capacity?"

"Secret Service."

Her frown deepened. She wondered if the reason he had been in Egypt that night had anything to do with his job. Most men who worked in the Secret Service were in place to protect the president, but that had not been the case with Quade. The president had been expected to arrive in Egypt, but hadn't yet done so. That made her wonder...

It hadn't been a coincidence for her to be in Egypt that night. The first lady was to arrive with the president and Cheyenne needed to be in place, behind the scenes. She shook her head, finding the possibility that the two of them could be associated with the same agency under the umbrella of the Secret Service mind-boggling. "So, you're one of those men who stand guard over the president wherever he goes, possibly taking a bullet if things got that far."

"Yes, something like that," he said, his gaze never leaving hers.

She nodded. He was being evasive just like she had been a number of times when her sisters had questioned the reason why they couldn't always reach her whenever she traveled abroad.

"It's late and like I said, I need to think things through."

He nodded. "When are the babies' next feeding times? I'd like to visit when they are awake."

She looked off toward the babies' nursery. "They'll sleep for another couple of hours or so, but I prefer you wait until tomorrow to see them."

"Any reason you're putting me off?"

Cheyenne looked back at him. "Like I said, I need to think about things. And I think you need to think about things, as well."

He shook his head. "There's nothing to think about. I want to do the right thing."

She regarded him steadily. "And you think wanting to marry a woman you slept with once and who got pregnant by you is the right thing when there is no love involved?"

From his expression she could tell her question was running through his mind. "First of all," he said quietly, "I slept with you more than once in that single night. And the answer is yes. Marrying you and giving you and my kids my name is the right thing to do."

"Even when there is no love?"

Quade nodded. "Yes, even when there is no love."

At least he was being honest with her, she thought. There would be no love in their marriage. He hadn't come seeking her out because he'd fallen in love with her. He had just admitted that love had nothing to do with it. He was being driven by what he perceived as doing the right thing. "Would you like to come to breakfast?" she decided to ask him.

"Breakfast?"

"Yes, breakfast. The babies will definitely be wide-awake then," she said, deciding to give him at least that time with them.

A smile tugged at his lips. "Then breakfast it is."

She hadn't for one minute doubted that he would take her up on her offer for breakfast. She could tell he was eager to see the babies he had produced. "I'll walk you to the door."

She had gotten halfway there when she noticed he

wasn't following her. She glanced back at him. "Is something wrong?"

"I thought I heard something."

She perked up her ears while glancing at the baby monitor that was sitting on the table. The sound of a whimper followed seconds later by a loud wail.

"Troy is awake," she said, glancing at the clock on the wall.

He raised a brow. "How do you know it's him and not the girls?"

She couldn't help but smile. "I've gotten used to their various cries. Besides, he's louder than the girls." She chuckled. "Probably a male thing. If I don't go in and get him, he'll wake up his sisters if he hasn't done so already."

Without saying anything else, she quickly moved toward the nursery. And Quade was right on her heels.

Chapter 5

Once they entered the nursery, Quade hung back and watched as Cheyenne went directly to the bed where their son was lying. He swallowed as a scary sensation ripped through him. Hard-core-to-the-bone Quade Westmoreland, who could be as tough as nails, suddenly felt as soft as a marshmallow and totally out of his element. He stiffened, not liking the feeling one damn bit.

But that feeling of resentment quickly eased away the moment Cheyenne lifted his son into her arms. Emotions he had never dealt with before rammed through him, nearly taking his breath away and making him weak in the knees all at the same time. Now he knew exactly how his cousin Thorn had felt when his child had been born. Thorn had always been the surly one in the family, but Quade had seen another side of Thorn when he had held his son in his arms.

Quade inhaled deeply, quickly deciding that if Thorn, of all people, could handle fatherhood, then so could he. There were three newborn Westmorelands who were depending on him and he would not let them down. Whether Cheyenne liked it or not, he intended to be an essential part of his kids' lives. He decided right then and there that he would be an essential part of Cheyenne's life, as well.

As if she read his mind, Cheyenne turned and he saw her frown. The frown slowly eased away from her brow, but not before she had scanned the entire length of him with a heated gaze. His body automatically responded and the silence in the room seemed to thicken, lengthen. She may want to deny it, but it was there—that same sexual chemistry, the physical attraction that had held them within its clutches almost a year ago. As far as he was concerned, it was as potent as ever.

Deciding it was time to meet his son, Quade slowly began walking toward her, crossing the room with purposeful steps.

Lifting Troy up toward her shoulders, Cheyenne tried concentrating on the baby and not on Quade. But she couldn't stop her gaze from devouring him with every step he took toward her.

The man was fine. Every inch—from his muscled shoulders, to his firm stomach, to his tapered hips. And it didn't take much to make her recall having his oh-so-fine male body on her and inside of her.

And then there were the kisses. Case in point, like the one they had shared earlier. The one she had started, but that she had eventually become victim to. The man had a way with his tongue and could use it to nip, stroke and tease her into submission. It was an instrument of pleasure that delivered every time it entered her mouth.

She released a trembling breath thinking, if she didn't develop a backbone, she could become putty in his arms. She was almost already there. She hadn't been firm enough when he had suggested marriage and had even agreed to think about it. *What kind of nonsense was that?*

When he came to a stop in front of her, he reached out his hands. "May I?" he asked, surprising her by his request. When it came to babies, most men preferred taking the hands-off approach.

"Sure," she said, and slowly, gently eased her son off her shoulders and into his father's outstretched hands. She saw Quade's hands tremble slightly before holding their child in a firm yet gentle grasp. It was at that moment that she saw things clearly. Although he was putting up a brave front she could tell that he was really at a loss as to what to do now that he had the baby in his arms.

Quade nervously glanced up at her. "He's tiny."

She couldn't help but smile. "Yes, and just think he's the biggest of the three. Just wait until you get a chance to hold his sisters."

She could actually see the blood almost drain from his face and somehow managed to keep from laughing out loud. But not before he met her gaze and saw the amusement lighting her eyes.

"Enjoying yourself at my expense, aren't you?" he said, before looking down into his son's face.

Her smile widened. "You *did* ask to hold him." And it was then she noticed that Quade seemed to be frozen in place as he stared down at Troy. Following his gaze she saw why. For some reason, Troy was staring back at Quade. Holding his father's gaze with an intensity that seemed strange even to her.

"Does he stare at everybody like this?" he asked her.

Cheyenne glanced back at Quade. "No," she said honestly. "And it's not because you're the first man he's seen. My four cousins visit often." She shrugged. "I guess there's something about you that fascinates him."

"You think so?"

"Probably." Cheyenne decided not to add that something about him had definitely fascinated her when she'd first set eyes on him. "I need to check to make sure he's dry," she heard herself say. "Not unless you want to take a stab at it."

"No, that's okay. You have more experience with that sort of thing," Quade said, and then quickly, yet gently shifted the baby from his arms back to hers.

He moved aside when she headed toward the baby's changing table and watched as she went about changing Troy's diaper. She glanced over at Quade. "Just so you know, when it comes to changing a baby boy, you have to use defensive diapering."

He lifted a brow. "Defensive diapering?"

"Yes, or you may get caught. Changing the diaper of a little boy can be like getting shot in the face with a loaded water gun."

When Quade caught on to what she was saying she heard him laugh. The sound was rich, as well as sensual, and did something to her insides. "Okay, laugh if you want, but don't ever say I didn't give you fair warning."

"Okay, I won't," he said between chuckles. "When is your nanny returning?"

She looked over at him. "Nanny?" At his nod she smiled and said. "I don't have a nanny, Quade."

He looked taken aback. "You've been handling the babies by yourself?"

"Not completely. My mom has helped a lot, as well as other family members. But I told them that starting today I wanted to handle things on my own."

"But there are three babies," he said as if the very thought of doing such a thing was ridiculous.

She rolled her eyes. He sounded like her cousins and sisters. "Trust me, I know how many there are. Just like I know I can manage things."

"I see." A few minutes passed and then he asked. "Is that why you don't want me to take responsibility? Because you're trying to prove a point?"

She narrowed her eyes. "No. The reason I don't want you to take responsibility is because for some reason you think taking responsibility means getting married.

Shotgun weddings played out years ago. Women get pregnant all the time without getting forced into marriage."

"Yes, but none of those women got pregnant from a Westmoreland."

She picked up the baby and placed him back into her arms, hoisting him to her shoulder and began gently massaging his back. "Are you saying you're the first guy in your family who had a child born out of wedlock?"

"No."

"And all those others ended in marriage?" she asked incredulously.

A smile softened his lips. "Eventually, yes. Westmorelands can be a very persuasive group."

She clamped down on her teeth to keep from saying that they sounded like a very arrogant group to her. Instead she crossed the room back to him and said, "Troy's all done. Here, hold him for a second while I check on the girls."

Again he seemed at a loss as to what he was supposed to do when she placed the baby in his arms. "The girls are awake?" he asked, glancing over at the other two cribs.

"Yes, they've been awake. I told you earlier chances were Troy had awaken them."

"But they haven't said anything," Quade said as if amazed.

"Usually they don't, unless they're hungry or wet. They are good babies. Only Troy tries to be difficult. But then, he's a typical male."

* * *

Half an hour later Quade sat in a chair with a baby resting in each of his arms—his daughters—while Troy was being breast-fed by his mother. Quade tried concentrating on the babies instead of what was going on across the room, but he found it difficult to do so.

Cheyenne had referred to his son as a typical male and, true to form, once presented with a breast Troy had latched on to it with the same greediness that his father had months ago.

Quade shifted in his chair, actually envying his son and thinking his daughters would be next. He smiled, wondering if there was a way he could sign up for some breast time.

Trying to get such thoughts out of his mind, he glanced down at his daughters and studied their features. Beautiful, the both of them. Less than two months old and they looked like their mother. Pretty, smooth brown skin and gorgeous dark eyes were staring at him, but not with the same intensity his son had earlier. The girls both had coal-black, almost straight hair. Not for the first time, Quade wondered if perhaps Cheyenne was of mixed heritage.

He looked across the room. "You're mixed with what?" he asked, getting her attention. She had been staring down at their son, who was cradled to her bosom.

She looked up. "Cheyenne Indian. My mother is full-blooded Cheyenne. She and my father met at college. Of their three daughters, I'm the one who inherited her features, which is why she named me Cheyenne when I was born."

"And how many years ago was that?" he asked, holding her gaze. She had told him when they first met that she was twenty-eight, but today she looked a lot younger than that.

She smiled. "How old do you think I am?"

His gaze moved across her features and then said, "Younger. I thought so that night but wasn't sure, but now I'm almost positive you aren't twenty-eight."

She glanced down at her son before looking back at him and responded. "I'm twenty-four, but when we met I was twenty-three."

His gaze sharpened. "Why did you lie about your age?"

He watched as she chewed her bottom lip for a second before saying, "I figured had I told you the truth, you would have left me alone and I had wanted you too much that night to allow that to happen."

He blinked, surprised that her response was so honest. Knowing it was probably best not to make a comment, he tried to ignore the intense stirrings in his body that were the result of her words. Even now he was still amazed as to how they had met and the intensity of their attraction to each other.

"Tell me about your sisters and cousins," he said, deciding they needed a change of subject. From the smile that touched her lips, he could tell evidently she was close to her family just like he was close to his.

"My oldest sister is Vanessa. She's twenty-eight and

Taylor's next at twenty-six. Vanessa works in PR for our family business and Taylor is a financial advisor. The best there is."

He latched on to something she'd said. "Your family owns some sort of business?"

"Yes, it's a huge manufacturing company that was started by my father and his brother years ago. The Steele Corporation. Ever heard of it?"

He let out a low whistle. "Who hasn't? They have been in the news a lot as one of the few companies who don't outsource."

"Yes, and we're proud of that fact. Although Taylor and I don't work for the company, we're members of the board. After my father died, my uncle, along with his four sons, began running the company. Now my uncle has retired and Chance, Sebastian, Morgan and Donovan are doing a good job of handling things."

She paused a second as if thinking of her family. Then she began talking again. "Chance at thirty-nine is the oldest and is CEO. Sebastian is thirty-seven and is considered the troubleshooter and problem solver in the company. Then there is Morgan, who at thirty-five heads up the research and development department. And last is Donovan, who at thirty-three is in charge of the product development division. Chance, Sebastian and Morgan are married. Donovan is single and according to him, has no intention of marrying. He likes being a ladies' man."

Quade nodded. Donovan sounded a lot like his

brother Reggie. "What about your sisters? Are they married?"

"Yes, and Taylor is expecting. She's due to have her baby the first of the year and we're very excited about it." Cheyenne paused for a minute, then smiled and said, "Now tell me about these Westmorelands."

Quade shifted the babies in his arms to make sure they were comfortable before he began talking. "Like I mentioned earlier, my father has two brothers—his fraternal twin brother John and his younger brother Corey. John has one daughter, Delaney, and five sons—Dare, Thorn, Stone and the twins, Chase and Storm. My parents had six boys. Besides me there is Jared, Spencer, Durango, my twin brother Ian and my youngest brother Reggie." He paused a moment then smiled. "Uncle Corey is the one with the triplets—a girl named Casey and two sons, Clint and Cole."

"Wow! That's a large group."

"Yes, and we're all close. There's not anything one wouldn't do for the other. That's the way families ought to be."

The room got quiet for a second, and Quade decided he would call his cousin Chase in the morning. Chase was worried about him, he could feel it. It had always been strange how although Ian was his fraternal twin and Chase was Storm's, when it came to that special bond that twins shared, the bond had always been he and Chase, and Ian and Storm.

"That's enough for you, big guy," Cheyenne said to the baby, and interrupted Quade's thoughts when she shifted Troy from her breast to her shoulder for him to burp. The action gave Quade a quick glimpse of her uncovered breast, the whole thing, before she covered it up again. He was blindsided by a rush of sensations that nearly shook his body.

"It's Venus's turn."

Her words reclaimed his attention and he saw she had placed Troy back in his bed. "All right, we're coming to you." He stood with both babies in his arms and walked over toward her.

When she took Venus from his arms, their hands brushed and he felt a spark of desire. Their gazes met and he knew she'd felt it, as well. He cleared his throat. "Umm, what happens if you run out of milk?" Curiosity had gotten the best of him and he wished he could bite off his tongue after he'd asked the question.

He expected her to come back with some smart response, but instead she smiled and said. "I won't run out. I think my body has adjusted to their demands and has given me an unlimited supply."

"Oh."

She then slipped by him to sit in the rocking chair to nurse Venus. That left one baby to go, and Athena seemed to be willing to wait. She had yet to put up a fuss like her brother. "How long does it take you to finish feeding them?"

"I can usually wrap things up in about ninety minutes," Cheyenne said, looking at him. "Once fed they're off to sleep again. And usually they'll sleep through the night. Overall, they are good babies."

Quade returned to the chair, holding Athena, and the room got silent again. He'd noted that Cheyenne hadn't brought up the suggestion that he leave her and the babies. Although she hadn't said otherwise, he had to believe that she appreciated the fact that he was there. She might have been able to handle the three of them, but he was glad to be here to help out. After all, these were *his* babies.

"It's getting late."

"Yes, it is."

Their gazes met and he figured she was about to ask him to leave. Instead she said, "I have a guest room if you want to crash there for the night. There's no reason for me to send you off to a hotel this late."

Surprised by her offer he said, "Thanks. I appreciate it."

"And I appreciate you for being here. You helped out a lot."

He knew it probably took a lot for her to say that, considering she had wanted to flex her independence and not depend on anyone's help with the babies. "Are you sure I helped or did I get in the way?"

She smiled. "You helped, and I would never admit it to my family or I'd never get them to leave me and the babies alone, but I needed you here, especially when Troy woke them all at once."

Quade chuckled. "Yes, I'm beginning to think he's a little troublemaker."

A short while later he was handing Athena over to Cheyenne after she had finished feeding Venus and placed her back in her crib. Cheyenne had explained that Venus was always the one who lacked interest during feeding time and was the one who could benefit the most because of her weight.

"When do they go to the doctor again?" Quade heard himself asking.

"Next week."

He nodded. "I'd like to go with you."

She lifted a brow. "You plan on hanging around that long?"

"Yes, I do."

Cheyenne opened her mouth as if she wanted to say something, and then closed it back. Quade was grateful because he wasn't ready to hear anything she had to say right now, especially if it had anything to do with him not being a permanent fixture in her and their babies' lives.

He intended to change her mind about that and would start working on it. Tonight.

Chapter 6

"You make a good mom, Cheyenne."

Quade's strong, husky and sensual voice seemed to float across her skin like a soft caress reminding her of that night he had touched it all over. She inhaled, not wanting to go there. Instead she tossed a thank-you over her shoulder and kept walking toward the living room, knowing he was following close behind.

The babies had been fed and put back to sleep, but not before she had given Quade a quick lesson in diaper changing. He had even helped while she had given them a bath and dressed them in new sleeping attire.

And then Quade seemed determined to sit and hold Venus for a while, actually rocking her to sleep. From the questions he'd asked, Cheyenne knew he was concerned with Venus's weight. Although Cheyenne had tried to sound encouraging, she had to admit she, too, was worried about Venus. During their last routine doctor's visit, Dr. Poston had said if Venus's weight wasn't up to what he considered a satisfactory level, he would be putting her in the hospital's special-care baby unit for a week. There she would be fed by nasogastric tube.

Cheyenne hadn't told anyone of what the doctor had said, and had even led her family to believe the babies would be okay to travel home to Jamaica within a month's time. She hadn't actually lied because she wanted to believe that would be the case. But her youngest child seemed less inclined to take her breast milk, and no matter what Cheyenne did, Venus seemed unresponsive to any feeding stimulation.

"Are you okay?"

Quade's question cut into her thoughts and she glanced over at him before she took a seat on the sofa. "Yes, I'm fine, just a little tired. My family was right. Taking care of all three of them isn't as easy as I thought it would be. I had a schedule prepared and thought it would be a piece of cake. I guess I've been proven wrong."

Quade came to sit in the chair across from her. "Did you really think you were a superwoman?"

She chuckled. "I wanted to believe I was. I guess starting tomorrow, I'll begin my search for a nanny while I'm here."

"Are you planning to go someplace?"

Cheyenne felt the weight of his gaze on her and glanced up and met his eyes. They locked on hers. "Yes.

Charlotte isn't really my home. I've been living in Jamaica for the past couple of years. I have a home there. I wanted the babies born in America, so I came back here for their birth. It was never my intent to stay."

"Oh, I see."

She shrugged, thinking no, he really didn't see. Neither did her family. Her mother meant well and so did her sisters, but while they were here to help her, they had preferred doing practically everything for the babies and leaving her with nothing to do other than breastfeed them. Tonight, she had gotten her first real taste of motherhood by handling the babies on her own. Quade had offered his help, but hadn't forced it on her and she appreciated that. Tonight she had felt in charge, sure of herself and her abilities. She closed her eyes, thinking that if she could only get Venus to be more responsive to her feedings and gain weight, everything would be perfect.

"You're sleepy. Why don't you go on to bed."

She snatched her eyes back open and looked over at Quade, embarrassed that she'd almost fallen asleep while sitting. "No, I'm fine."

"No, you're not. You've done a lot today. Motherhood is no joke. I have an all-new respect for my cousins' and brothers' wives who are new mothers."

She smiled. "You make it sound like there are a lot of them."

He chuckled. "There are. Seems like an epidemic hit and pregnancy swept through the Westmoreland family like wildfire. But it has made both my mother and my aunt Evelyn happy since they'd always wanted a bunch of grandkids."

She nodded. "Do you plan on telling your family about the babies?"

A smile touched his lips. "Yes, but not yet. You think *your* family is bad. If I were to tell my mother she had more grandchildren somewhere, she would be on the first plane out of Atlanta."

"Atlanta? Is that your home?"

"It's where I was born and raised. I haven't actually lived there since I left for college."

"And what college did you attend?"

"Harvard."

She blinked in surprise. He was a Harvard man? For some reason that didn't surprise her. "That night that we met, you said you weren't married. Have you ever been married?"

"No."

"Any other children?"

He shook his head. "No. The triplets are my first and I feel blessed to have them. Thank you."

She knew why he was thanking her. "There's no reason to thank me. When I found out I was pregnant, I knew I wanted them and never considered any other option." She didn't add that she'd known they would be a constant reminder of him and their one night together.

"Okay, that does it. You're falling asleep on me again," Quade said.

Before Cheyenne could catch her next breath, Quade

had stood up, crossed the room and swept her into his arms. "Hey, put me down!"

"No. Not until I get you into bed."

Her heart jumped in her chest with his words. If only he knew the picture his words suddenly painted in her mind. "I can't go to bed yet, Quade. I have a lot of things to do."

He looked down at her. "Like what?"

She rolled her eyes. "I had my sisters over for dinner so there're still dishes in the sink that I need to load in the dishwasher. Then the babies' clothes that I washed earlier need to be folded and I need to take out the trash for tomorrow morning's pickup."

"Consider them all done. I'll handle it."

She glared up at him. "No, I can do it myself."

He glared back. "The only thing you have to do is take care of yourself, so you can in turn take care of my babies."

She frowned. "*Your* babies?"

A softening flickered in the depths of his dark eyes when he said, "Yes, *my* babies."

She held his gaze and swallowed deeply, knowing there was no way she could deny what he'd said. They were his babies. *Quade's babies.*

"Now are you going to be easy or will you be a troublemaker like our son?" he said, smiling.

She wished he wouldn't smile like that. Whenever he did, it stirred things up within her that she preferred to keep still. "Steeles aren't known to be troublemakers, so he must get it from your side of the family, the baby-making Westmorelands."

He chuckled. "We can do more than make babies. We can also be great husbands once we put our minds to it."

She rolled her eyes upward. "Spare me."

"Wish I could, but I can't," he said with a wry smile. "In fact, I plan to do just the opposite. Starting tonight I'm going to lay it on thick." After a brief pause, he asked, "Do you know what that means?"

She looked away from him and then said. "No."

He knew she was lying. She knew. "Well, then I feel obliged to tell you. By the time I'm through with you, Cheyenne Steele, you will be falling into my arms and agreeing to do anything I want."

She snatched her gaze back to him, curled her lips and said, "Why are you so arrogant?"

"Am I?" he asked as he began walking toward her bedroom with her nestled in his arms.

"Yes."

"Never noticed."

Cheyenne released a sigh, refusing to say anything else. She doubted it would do any good anyway. When he stopped walking, she glanced around and saw she was in her bedroom.

"Here you are," he said, angling her body to slide down his. Her sharp intake of breath was a dead give-away that she had felt his arousal as her feet slid to the floor. Some things she figured just couldn't be hidden. And, she thought further, the heat simmering between them was another thing neither of them could hide. It was just like that first night. She had wanted him then and she hated admitting that she wanted him now.

When her feet touched the carpeted floor, she still held on to his shoulders and it seemed her body automatically swayed closer to his as if it needed the contact. She studied his features. "Troy favors you."

He smiled as he tightened his hands around her waist. "Yes, he resembles a Westmoreland. And the girls look like you."

She nodded. "We did good, didn't we? We make beautiful babies."

"Yes," he said huskily. "The result of perfect love-making."

She gave a little pleased smile. "You think so?"

"I know so. Close your eyes for a moment and remember it."

Cheyenne could feel the heat of his gaze on her the moment she closed her eyes. And then she remembered. It was the same dream she'd had earlier, before he had arrived. She recalled everything. The wanting. The desire. But most of all, the sensations she felt the moment he entered her and how he had mated with her with an intensity that even now could change the level of her breathing.

"Remembered enough?"

She slowly opened her eyes. It seemed his face had inched closer to hers. His lips were just a breath away. "No memories are as good as the real thing," she said.

"You think not?"

"I do," she responded.

"And what do you want me to do about it?"

Oh, she knew exactly what she wanted him to do about it, although she knew better. It was an insane thought, but no more insane than the night they had met on the beach. And although he had appeared on her doorstep that afternoon, the first time she had seen him in nearly a year, her body knew him. Her body wanted him. And her body was making her realize that she had never gotten over him.

Knowing he was waiting for her to say something, she leaned up on tiptoe, shifted her hands from his shoulders and wrapped her arms around his neck. "What I want is to relive our perfect lovemaking all over again."

She felt his erection—large, hard and throbbing—pressed against her. "You sure that's what you want?" he asked, leaning in closer and using the tip of his tongue to taste the sides of her mouth.

"Yes," she whispered, now almost too weak to stand.

"Then go ahead and lie on the bed while I run out to the rental car to get my gear. My condoms are packed in there."

She eased even closer to him, cradling his hardness between her thighs. "They didn't work so well the last time," she decided to remind him.

He chuckled softly. "Yeah, I noticed."

"I'm on the pill now."

Quade had been surprised to learn that she hadn't been before. But then on that night he'd also discovered she hadn't made love to a man in a long time. "I need to bring my stuff in anyway and now is a good time to do it. I might not have the strength for it later," he said, seconds before lowering his head to kiss her.

He felt his arousal thicken the moment he entered her mouth. He had intended for this to be a gentle kiss, but the moment his tongue took hold of hers, he began sucking hard, needing to do to her tongue what he couldn't do to her breasts. He heard her moan and the more she did so, his body became filled with ardent need. His kiss went deeper and became far more demanding. Every cell within his body began to tingle and he knew if he didn't take control of the situation, he would be making love to her right here and now.

Quade slowly pulled his lips back from Cheyenne's, thinking he could keep right on kissing her, but was too eager to get inside her. "Lie on the bed. I'll be right back." And then he was gone.

He was only gone long enough to get his gear out of the car and quickly headed back inside toward Cheyenne's bedroom, only to stop suddenly in the doorway. She had gotten in the bed like he'd said, but was curled up in a fetal position, fully clothed and fast asleep.

He inwardly pushed away the disappointment to replace it with compassion. More than anything, she deserved her rest. There would be other opportunities for them to make love. He would see to it. Dropping his gear pack on the floor he crossed the room and grabbed a blanket off the chair to cover her.

She made a sound when she snuggled into the covers, but didn't wake up. He gazed down at her, she was sleeping peacefully. He then remembered another night she had slept peacefully, as well…in his arms after he had made love to her.

Deciding if he didn't leave her alone now, he would be tempted to remove his clothes and join her in bed, he left the room, taking his gear with him and headed toward the guest room. She'd said the babies would probably sleep through the night and if they did, that was fine. If they didn't, that was fine, too, since he was there and he could take care of them.

A half hour later, he had checked on the babies and Cheyenne for the third time, loaded the dishes in the dishwasher and folded the babies' clothes. He glanced around, wondering what was there to do next and then decided to give his cousin Chase a call.

Quade pulled his cell phone out of his pocket and punched in Chase's phone number. Chase was the cook in the Westmoreland family and owned several soul-food restaurants in Atlanta, as well as in other parts of the country.

"Hello."

"Chase, this is Quade."

"Hey, what's going on with you, man? You said you would call if you found her."

Quade rubbed the back of his neck. Yes, that's what he'd said to Chase, his brothers and the rest of his cousins before leaving Montana. All of them had known that he was on a woman hunt. "I found her, but things are kind of complicated."

"In what way? I felt you worrying about something."

Quade paused a moment and said, "Cheyenne was pregnant."

"Cheyenne?"

"Yes."

"That's her name?"

"Yes. It's Cheyenne Steele."

"Oh, okay. And has Cheyenne delivered yet?"

"Yes."

Chase waited as if he'd expected Quade to say something else and when Quade didn't, he said, "Hey, don't keep me in suspense. Is the baby yours?"

A smile touched Quade's lip. It was a very proud smile. "No, the baby isn't mine, but the *babies* are mine."

There was a slight pause and then Chase said, *"Babies?"*

"Yes."

"More than one?"

Quade couldn't help but laugh. "Yes, more than one."

"Twins?"

"No, triplets."

Chase whistled. Moments later he said in an astonished voice, "The woman had triplets?"

"Yes. Two daughters and a son."

"Congratulations!"

"Thanks," Quade said with pride nearly bursting his chest.

"How is everyone doing?"

"Mother and babies are doing fine. But…"

"But what?"

Quade struggled to keep his emotions in check. They were emotions he wasn't used to having. "The youngest of the three is the smallest. She's such a tiny thing and I worry about her."

Chase paused once again. "You sound like your entrance into fatherhood is going to be a challenging one. You're worrying already and she hasn't started first grade," he said.

"I know, man. But you'll see how things are one day when you get there."

Chase chuckled. "I'm already there. Jessica informed me this morning that she's pregnant."

A huge smile spread across Quade's features. "Congratulations."

"Thanks. When will you tell the family about your babies?"

"I'm working on the mother to marry me and don't need any interference until then."

"Okay. As far as keeping silent, you know you can trust me."

"Yes, I always have."

Moments later, as soon as Quade ended the call with his cousin he heard the sound of the doorbell. He moved quickly toward the door, not wanting the sound to wake up Cheyenne or the babies. He snatched the door open to find four men standing there. They were as surprised to see him as he was to see them. But he figured out quickly who they were—Cheyenne's four cousins— the Steeles.

The one who appeared to be the oldest of the four lifted a brow and asked, "Where's Cheyenne?"

"She's asleep."

"Asleep?" the one he figured to be the second oldest asked.

"Yes." Quade leaned in the doorway. He could tell the four had gone from surprised to cautious to curious. "I take it you're her cousins—Chance, Sebastian, Morgan and Donovan," he said, appreciating the fact that he had a very good memory.

"Yes, that's who we are," the oldest one said. "Who are you?"

Quade smiled. "We haven't met, but you'll be seeing a lot of me," he replied. He extended his hand to the men. "I'm Quade Westmoreland, the father of Cheyenne's babies. Would you like to come in?"

Chapter 7

"So, Quade Westmoreland, where have you been for the past nine months?"

Quade saw anger flicker in the eyes of Sebastian Steele.

The four men had come inside and stood in the living room, all in a single file, with arms folded across their chests staring at him, evidently waiting for his response to Sebastian's question. The room was filled with thick tension and a part of Quade understood. He, his brothers and cousins would be doing the same thing if his cousin Delaney, who had grown up overprotected by her five brothers and six cousins, had gotten pregnant and it had taken the man responsible almost ten months to show up.

The stubborn part of Quade felt he didn't owe these

men any explanation, especially if Cheyenne hadn't given them one. But then another part—the one that understood the role of a protector—could accept how they felt and didn't mind stating his case. Who knew? They might eventually become allies instead of enemies and help in his cause.

Mimicking their stance, Quade placed his arms over his chest, as well, sending out a strong message that he was not easily intimidated. "Trust me, I would have come sooner had I known."

Chance Steele lifted a dark brow and dropped his hands to his sides in surprise for the second time that night. "You didn't know?"

"Didn't have a clue." Quade decided not to go into any details.

"And when did you find out?" the one Quade knew to be Morgan Steele asked.

"A few days ago. I saw her, pregnant, on the cover of a magazine."

The four nodded as if they were familiar with that particular magazine. "And after finding out, you came directly here?" Sebastian Steele asked.

"Yes." Quade then felt it was his turn to ask a question. "At any time did Cheyenne mention who had fathered her babies to you?"

All four men shook their heads but it was Donovan Steele who spoke. "No, she's been withholding your identity. We figured she must have found out that you were married or something." He then frowned. "Are you married?"

It was Quade's turn to shake his head. "Not yet, but I hope to marry pretty soon."

Chance Steele lifted a brow. "Cheyenne?"

"Yes," Quade said, dropping his hands to his sides, loosening up somewhat.

It was Sebastian who chuckled. "Good luck. Cheyenne's stubborn as hell. She likes her freedom and detests anyone telling her what to do."

Quade rubbed a hand back and forth across his chin in frustration. "I gathered as much."

"But you did ask her?" Morgan wanted to know.

"Yes, several times, but she turned me down each time."

"But you won't give up," Donovan said. It was more a statement than a question.

"No, I won't give up," Quade stated, determined. "I'm a Westmoreland and one thing a Westmoreland does is take responsibility for his actions, no matter what they are. Had I known about Cheyenne's pregnancy, we wouldn't be standing here having this conversation now, trust me."

For some reason, he felt they did trust him, or at the very least they were beginning to. "So, do you have any ideas that might help change her mind?" he asked.

It was Sebastian who chuckled and then said, "Prayer might work."

Cheyenne shifted positions in bed and seconds later her eyes flew open.

She glanced at the digital clock on the nightstand and

when she saw it was almost ten at night, she kicked the covers off her and quickly swung her legs off the bed, wondering how she could have dozed off.

The moment she stood, she remembered. Quade. The kiss. Him leaving to go outside for his gear and condoms. She inhaled deeply thinking he never got the chance to put the condoms to any use. She had passed out on him. She hadn't known how tired she was until she had lain on the bed.

Wondering just where Quade was and knowing that she needed to check on her babies, she straightened her clothes and raked several fingers through her disheveled hair in an attempt to make herself presentable. Leaving her bedroom, she began walking down the hall toward the nursery. As she walked, Cheyenne swore she could hear male voices speaking in a hushed tone.

Raising a confused brow, she turned and continued walking and, when she entered the living room, she came up short. Quade and her cousins were sitting at her dining-room table, and of all things, they were playing cards. *What on earth!* When did her cousins arrive? Quade had to have been the one to let them in. Did they know who he was? And just what had Quade told them about their relationship?

She passed through her living room and stood at the entrance to her dining room, not yet noticed by the five men. When a few seconds passed and they still hadn't noticed her she cleared her throat.

"Just what's going on here?"

Five pairs of eyes turned toward her, and unsurprisingly it was her cousin Sebastian who spoke. "This guy claims he's your babies' daddy. So we figured before he could be allowed in the family, he had to prove his worth by playing a game of cards with us."

Cheyenne frowned. It was on the tip of her tongue to say that there was no way Quade would be a part of the family regardless of his card-playing skills. Instead she asked, strictly out of curiosity, "And how did he do?"

It was Morgan who leaned back in his chair, smiled and said, "Not bad. In fact, he won all of our money, which means he's definitely in."

"Besides," Donovan said, grinning, "we'll let him in anyway since motorcycle-racer extraordinaire Thorn Westmoreland is his cousin."

"I really like your cousins," Quade said as he and Cheyenne stood together at the door after seeing the Steele brothers out.

Closing the door, Cheyenne glanced over at Quade. "And it was obvious that they liked you, as well. Which has me curious as to what you told them."

"About what?"

"About us."

Quade smiled. So she was thinking of the two of them in terms of an "us." "I didn't tell any of our secrets, especially the details of how we met on the beach that night. I figured that part really wasn't their business. Besides, they were mainly interested in knowing where I'd been the last nine months."

Cheyenne headed toward the kitchen area. "Although my family asked, I never gave them your name."

"You didn't know my name. At least not all of it."

She glanced around the kitchen, seeing how clean it looked, appreciating his thoughtfulness in taking care of things while she slept. "I could have asked the hotel to check their records for the information."

"They wouldn't have told you anything."

She looked over at him. "Why not?" She wondered if he would admit that he had been there on government business that night…just as she had been. No information about him would have been given out, because it would have been considered classified.

"They just wouldn't have." He then quickly changed the subject by asking, "Does the kitchen meet with your approval?"

She smiled over at him. "Yes. Thanks. You really didn't have to do it. And I see you even folded the baby clothes."

"You don't have to thank me, Cheyenne. I enjoyed doing it. And I checked on the babies periodically and they seemed to be doing okay."

"Usually they sleep through the night. Every once in a while Troy might take a notion to cause problems, but otherwise, it's smooth sailing for the rest of the evening."

"And what time do they wake up?" Quade asked putting litter from the table into the garbage.

"Too early. Try around five in the morning."

"Whoa. That's early," Quade said as amusement lit his eyes before he turned to her refrigerator.

"I've gotten used to it," she said, and not for the first time noticed how Quade seemed to dominate the entire room. His back was to her as he put a couple of sodas away, and she realized he looked just as sexy from the back as he did from the front. Her heart jolted when she remembered earlier in her bedroom how the front of that body had pressed against hers.

Thinking it was time to shift her thoughts elsewhere she said, "Is Thorn Westmoreland really your cousin?"

Quade glanced over his shoulder at her and chuckled. "Yes, Thorn's my cousin. Have you read any Rock Mason novels?"

"Of course. I read as many as I could get my hands on while I was pregnant. Why?"

A smile touched Quade's lips. "Because Rock Mason's real name is Stone Westmoreland. He's Thorn's brother and my cousin, as well."

She blinked. "You're kidding, right?"

He shook his head, grinning. "No, I'm not kidding. I'm dead serious." Quade wasn't exactly sure why he was enjoying seeing the look of shock on her face so much. She looked totally beautiful whenever a bombshell hit her.

"Wow, that's great, and I really mean it. He's a fantastic author."

"I'll mention you said that the next time I talk to him," Quade said, before turning back around to the refrigerator. "Aren't you hungry?" he tossed over his shoulder.

"No. I usually don't eat a lot. In fact, I eat more now because of the babies. I have to do whatever it takes to keep my milk supply up."

He turned and his gaze automatically went to her chest and was ridiculously pleased when the nipples of her breasts seemed to press tight against her blouse, under the onslaught on his intense stare. Childbirth seemed to have made them fuller, and undeniably tempting.

A swarm of sensations seemed to engulf him and he knew the cause. That night in Egypt, her breasts, like all the rest of her, had been for his pleasure and he in turn had made sure she had gotten hers. And she had, plenty of times over.

Don't even try it, he thought to himself. *What you're thinking about doing is worse than taking candy from a baby.*

His gaze shifted from her chest to her face and he saw in her eyes the same need that he felt. He knew this was crazy, but the attraction between them was back. It was making his body throb.

He hadn't slept with another woman since the night he had shared with her. He hadn't wanted another woman, and now he knew why. He also knew things would always be this way with them—instant attraction, quick response, unhurried fulfillment. He had just walked back into her life today, shown up on her doorstep just this evening. But they didn't have to go through any long, drawn out preliminaries. Neither did they have to take time to get reacquainted, at least not this way. This was one area where they knew each other inside out. He knew exactly what he had to do to make her moan, calling out his name in a raspy tone while begging for more.

And he had become privy to all that information in one night.

Their time together in Egypt would always hold special memories for him and he hoped the same held true for her. And in the end they had produced three beautiful human beings who would be a constant reminder of that night.

"I thought you were taking something out of the refrigerator to eat," he heard her say.

Quade felt his mouth stretch into a smile as he crossed the room, closing the distance separating them. "It just occurred to me that I have a taste for something altogether different, and what I want isn't in the refrigerator," he said smoothly.

"Where is it then?"

He heard the nervous hitch in her voice and was able, without very much effort, to inhale her heated scent. His gaze raked over her and he took in everything about her. There was her beautiful brown skin—a complexion that was smooth and creamy, absolutely flawless. She had shoulder-length, dark hair that hung straight with a little curl at the ends, and black eyes and high cheekbones that gave her an exotic look. Then there was her body, as perfect as it had been before. It was still model-thin, but now there was a lushness, a ripeness, to her perfect curves that were the result of motherhood.

He came to a stop in front of her and reached out and took her hand and pulled her closer to him, plastering her body to his. She may have seen how aroused he was when he crossed the room, but now he wanted her to *feel* just how aroused he was.

Quade pressed his body even closer to her, exhilarated in the contact. He leaned forward and whispered deep in her ear while taking his free hand and lowering it to the apex of her thighs and touching her through the denim material of her jeans. "Here, Cheyenne. What I want to taste is right here."

Cheyenne knew this was madness, heated lust of the worst kind. But as she felt his hard erection pressed against her, all she could think about was him sliding it inside of her hot body. And she *was* hot. It seemed she had buttons only he knew how to push. She hadn't slept with another man since that night she had spent with him, and tonight, now, this very moment, her body was letting her know it. It was craving a time it had been fulfilled to an infinite degree.

"Do you remember how things were between us the last time?" she heard him ask. His voice was hot and husky against her ear, while his jeans-clad thigh brushed against hers over and over again.

"Yes, I remember," she said, barely getting the words

out. Sharp, sensuous tingles flowing through her made her want an intense sexual encounter with him even more.

"And do you recall how I had developed a taste for a certain part of you?"

She remembered. There was no way she could ever forget. The memory had returned to her numerous times. He had been intense in his hunger, extremely greedy, almost devouring her whole.

"And if I recall," he said, taking the tip of his tongue and caressing the underside of her ear, sending more sensuous shivers through her body, "you enjoyed it immensely. I would even go so far as to say you loved what I was doing to you."

Yes, she had. Under the onslaught of his mouth, his very skillful tongue, she had come apart, numerous times. Each had resulted in an orgasm that had shook her to the core, splintered her in a million pieces, only for him to put her back together again to start all over.

"Yes, I loved what you did," she said. There was no way she could lie and deny such a thing as not being true. She felt no shame in admitting what was fact. Especially now when she felt weak just thinking about it.

"I'm glad. And how would you like to experience that moment all over again? With my mouth worshipping you that way? Do you want it?"

She met his gaze. Felt the heat of his desire as his eyes burned into hers. What they had felt before was a crazy attraction that could only end one way, the way that it had. Now what she felt was intense sexual long-ing, propelled by an almost unbearable need. So she said the only words that she could. "Yes. I want it."

Chapter 8

Quade wanted it, as well. With a vengeance. With every part of his being. And tonight, just like the other time, he would give them both extreme pleasure. A part of him didn't want to rush anything. He had wanted to wait and not make love to her until she agreed to be his wife—until the time when she saw that he, she and their babies needed to be a family. And although their marriage wouldn't be based on love per se, it would be based on mutual respect, admiration and desire.

But then another part, the part that was oozing with a degree of desire he could only reach with her, didn't want to wait. This part wanted a repeat of that night in Egypt. Being around her had unleashed a host of memories he could not ignore. The fiery heat of them had burned a place into the core of his very existence.

He drew her closer to him, leaned his mouth within inches of hers and said, "Do you know how many days and nights I carried the memory of what we shared with me no matter where I went?"

"No," she said, breathing her answer across his lips.

"Too many," he replied in a low and deep voice, while his gaze still held hers. He reached down and took her hand in his. "And whenever I thought about how you would touch me with these hands, stroke me with the most erotic care, I could barely stand it."

Cheyenne recalled how his body had been so responsive to her touch. Her stomach trembled at the thought that she could do that to him, make him ache with a need for her that was as intense as the one she had for him.

She felt her senses begin to overload, her desire for him kick up another notch at the same time she felt him lift her off the floor to sit her on top of the countertop.

"Have you ever done it in a kitchen before?" he asked, while leaning down to remove her shoes.

"No."

He then straightened his tall frame and lifted a disbelieving brow. "Never?"

She lifted a disbelieving brow of her own, wondering if making love in a kitchen was some kind of fetish for him. "Why would you think I have?"

Quade smiled. "Because I can imagine you stretched out on a table as a very succulent treat."

He reached out and tugged her top over her head, exposing a very sexy black-laced nursing bra, which he quickly dispensed of. Breasts that appeared fuller sprang forth before his eyes. He couldn't wait any longer and gently cupped them in his hands and began lowering his head toward one firm nipple. When she offered no protest, he asked, whispering against the moist tip, "You have enough to share?"

Cheyenne knew she had to respond before she lost the power to think. "Yes. I have enough to share."

And then it was there, his mouth on her breasts, gently at first, using his tongue to caress her breasts and making her feel the way her nipples hardened in his mouth. Each stroke of his tongue aroused her, sent passion points escalating through her. His expertise astounded her, nearly made her weak in the knees while bathing her in sensual satisfaction that she knew was within her reach.

"Quade."

The erotic pressure of his mouth on her breasts was devastating to her senses, making her tremble. She cried out when an orgasm struck. It would have knocked her off her feet had she not been sitting on the countertop. She felt her inner muscles tighten, then loosen up. And she felt her control slipping as shock waves of pleasure rushed through her.

"Shh, you'll wake up the babies," he whispered, after pulling his mouth away from her breast. "There's a lot that can be said about getting breast-fed," he said, licking his lips and lifting her to her feet. "Now, to remove your jeans. You should be more than ready for me about now."

Her breath shuddered as she fought to remain standing when he crouched down in front of her, and after placing a wet kiss on her stomach, he proceeded to unzip her jeans and slowly ease them down her legs, leaving her clad in a pair of sexy panties.

"Cute," he said of the daisy print.

She grinned. "Glad you like them."

"Um, I like what they are hiding even more," he said, before easing the pair down. And then she was there, bare, exposed and he leaned back on his haunches to take it all in. And she knew, just like he had predicted, she was wet, hot and ready.

Quade's tongue suddenly felt swollen in his mouth, actually thickening in anticipation of the treat he knew he was about to have. He couldn't wait to taste the pulsing heat of her again. He wanted to kiss and cherish her secret place the only way he knew how. He stood back on his feet and then lifted her to place her back on the counter, easing her body close to the edge, lifting her hips with the palm of his hands.

Quade then took her legs and placed them over his shoulders and instinctively, she widened her legs just moments before he lowered his head and brought her womanly core to him, slipping his tongue into the warm heat of her.

He moaned out in pleasure the same time she did, holding firm to her thighs and hips, lifting her up to lock his mouth on her. And then it was on as pleasure raced through him with every stroke of his tongue inside of her. He held on tight to her as she cried out her pleasure at the same time she squirmed under his mouth, trying to get away one minute while trying to get closer the next. He felt her grab hold to those same shoulders her legs were wrapped around and he was too far gone to care if he was getting bruised or squeezed to death. If he was going to die, this way certainly had its merits.

And then he felt her body contract beneath his mouth as another orgasm hit her, making her bite back her scream. He took her in a deep, hungry kiss while grabbing hold of her hips, making sure she stayed in place, right where he wanted her.

He felt something he could only feel with her, a myriad of emotions and sensations that pulsed through him just from her taste, overwhelmed by the potency of her and what this was doing to him. He fought back the notion that the emotions he was feeling were anything other than unrequited lust and appreciation for the mother of his children.

Moments later, licking his lips, he released her. Scooping her up into his arms he carried her over to the cleared breakfast table and placed her flat on it. At her surprised look, he said, "I was serious about doing it in the kitchen with you," he said. Taking a step back he unsnapped his jeans and eased down his zipper. He quickly dispensed with his jeans and boxers.

"You look bigger than before."

He grinned and looked down at her. She was an eyeful, lying flat on her back with her legs apart. The thought of easing between her thighs, pressing into her almost had him blowing a sexual fuse.

He knew she was watching when he sheathed himself with a condom before coming back to her. He glanced around the room, took note of her stainless-steel appliances, her shiny tile floor and her granite countertops. What was there about being in a kitchen that made him want to stir up heat, and to make his own brand of sensuous delight?

Naked, he walked back over to her, leaned and took her mouth with the voraciousness that he felt. At the same time his hand automatically went to her center, and tested her. She had gotten wet all over again. Suddenly every muscle in his body tensed with a need so profound he pulled his mouth from hers to release a guttural groan. As he continued to stroke her, feel her heat, he wondered for the umpteenth time what there was about her that pushed him to devour her in such a primal way.

The table was just the right height and width and looked sturdy enough to withstand what he intended to do. It wasn't a workout table by a long shot but there would be a lot of action on it today. He looked at her and saw the heated glaze in her eyes. He stood between her legs and noted she had spread them even wider. He pressed his hips forward, guiding his hardness into her moist heat. The moment contact was made he threw his head back and the veins in his neck seemed to almost pop from pleasure. He sucked in a deep breath and pushed farther, going all the way inside of her, almost to the area that had carried his children for nearly nine months.

When he was lodged inside of her deep, to the hilt, he leaned down and captured her lips, needing to kiss her, the way a man would kiss a woman he cherished. She felt good—perfect. A beautiful memory transformed into reality once again.

The kiss worked them both up into a feverish pitch and he began moving inside her, holding her thighs to receive his entry and his withdrawal, over and over again. He breathed in her scent. He heard the sound of his name whispered from her lips, and felt her body adjust to his as if it was made just for him.

He began moaning deep in his throat when he changed the rhythm, thrusting deeper, going faster. She clung to his mouth. He to hers. Their tongues mated with an intensity that he felt all the way to the bones. When he eased his mouth away from hers, she said in a frantic tone "No. Don't go. Don't stop."

He had no plans to do either. And to prove that point he bent his head and reclaimed her mouth, kissing her with a hunger that was more voracious than before. The lower part of him continued driving into her, surging deep. She matched his rhythm, lifting her body off the table on each and every downward thrust.

Her inner muscles clamped him hard and he felt his engorged member actually break through the latex. Instead of pulling out, he released a deep shuddering groan just seconds before spilling himself inside her, spinning her into an orgasm right along with him.

"Quade!"

He came again, and so did she. It was crazy. It was passion at its deepest. Satisfaction at its greatest. With an urgency that shook him to the core he filled her womb once again, not sure if her birth control pill would be able to withstand the potency of such a release.

He pulled his mouth away and leaned up slightly. Their gazes locked. He sent her a silent message that if he had impregnated her again, they would deal with it. His way.

Seeing the frown on her face, he leaned down and kissed her, building sexual tension all over again. Moments later he lifted his mouth from hers only to trace kisses down her neck to her chest. She arched her back and groaned out his name and he knew, this was just the beginning. They had the entire night and he planned on using every second of it.

Cheyenne wasn't sure if she would ever be able to move again. So she lay still, with her eyes closed while releasing deep breaths of fulfillment and gratification. Quade had removed himself from inside her moments ago and she knew he had walked away, probably to get rid of the condom, although it hadn't served much purpose.

Her mind shifted to dwell on that, when she suddenly felt something warm and wet between her legs. She opened her eyes to find Quade standing there, wiping her with a warm cloth. Instinctively, she closed her legs.

"No, don't close yourself from me. Let me do this, Cheyenne. I want to do this. Open up again for me."

The kind gentleness of his tone made her do just what he asked and he continued to wash her with the most tender of care. "You don't have to do this, Quade." He had done the same thing before. Their first time together in Egypt.

He glanced up and met her gaze. "I know, but I want to."

So she lay there, willing, complacent, at ease in placing herself in his hands. And they were big hands, tender hands, gifted hands. And when she thought about all those hands had done, how they had made her feel, she knew they were skillful hands.

"Feel better?"

Actually she did. Given the intensity of their lovemaking, she knew she would feel some soreness, but it had been worth it. "Yes."

He nodded. "I'll be back in a moment."

She figured he was going into the bathroom to wash himself and she wished she had the strength to do that for him, return the kindness. But she doubted she had the strength to move. So she lay there and closed her eyes again.

Moments later, she felt herself being lifted from the table and cradled into strong arms. "We're going to bed now." She heard his deep, masculine voice whisper close to her ear. "And I will let you sleep for a while."

She knew he was letting her know they would be making love again and she had no problem with it.

When they reached the bedroom, he placed her in the middle of the bed and she glanced up at him. He had put his jeans back on, but had not snapped them back up. Nothing about him had changed. Stripped naked he looked good; with clothes on he looked good. He was awesome and she knew as strange as it would seem to some people, she had fallen in love with him.

If the truth was known, she had probably fallen in love with him on sight that first night, but had put the thought out of her mind as ludicrous, especially when she'd believed she would never see him again. But the moment the doctor had told her she was pregnant, some kind of torch had lit inside her, and she'd known she wanted a baby. His baby, which would always be a way to connect with him. A baby where their combined blood would flow through his or her veins.

She hadn't counted on triplets, but when she'd given birth to their babies, she had felt connected to Quade threefold. The only thing that kept her from accepting his proposal of marriage was the fact that she knew he didn't love her. He had an obligation, a sense of responsibility, but he did not love her. She couldn't have that kind of marriage with a man. Especially this man.

"Is there anything I can get you?" he asked in a soft voice, standing next to the bed.

"Um, yes, there is this one thing."

She scooted closer to the edge and stared at his erection that was pressing hard against his jeans before reaching out to slide her hand down his stomach, liking the feel of his hair there, past his navel to insert her hand inside his jeans to grab hold of his throbbing member. He hadn't put on his boxers. She smiled when she heard his sharp intake of breath while she used her other hand to pull his jeans past down his knees.

"Careful." Quade eased the word from between tight lips when Cheyenne's fingers curled around him. He doubted that she heard what he'd said since she looked so preoccupied at the moment. Her main focus was him and she seemed content to stroke him in a way that was driving him mad with desire.

"You like torturing me, don't you?" he asked when she continued her stroking, hoping and praying that she didn't stop. She certainly had a way with her fingers.

He heard her soft sigh and then she said, "No more than you like torturing me. I love touching you this way, and thinking this, in all its engorged glory, is responsible for my babies." She glanced up at him. "Our babies."

He didn't want to bring up the fact that pill or no pill, with a burst condom she could very well be pregnant again. The thought didn't bother him.

His attention snapped back to her when he felt something hot and wet touch him. Her mouth. He sucked in deeply as need flared in his belly. He grabbed hold of her head and tried pushing her away, but she was holding on to him, her mouth was locked around him. What she was doing to him made him weak in the knees.

"Cheyenne, why did you have to go there?" Instead of answering him, she gripped him tighter. And he threw his head back when she began devouring him, covering all of him, caressing every inch of him with her hot, wet tongue. And then when he thought he couldn't stand it a minute longer, she opened her mouth and pulled him in deeper.

"Oh, yes!" There was nothing else for him to say and when she dug her fingers into his thighs to hold her mouth in place on him, he nearly hollered. Not from pain but from pleasure so intense he could feel a tingling sensation all the way to his toes. And when he felt his groin about to explode, he grabbed hold of her shoulders and tried pushing her back. When he saw that she was refusing to move, he sucked in a deep breath as a ripple of sensations crashed through his nerve endings causing him to flex his hips.

And she still wouldn't let go, holding on to him with the strength of a woman who knew what she wanted. Moments later she jerked her mouth free to pull air into her lungs. He used that time to remove his jeans the rest of the way before joining her on the bed and pushing her on her back and entering her in one smooth thrust.

And then he was riding her, stretching her, returning the same sensuous torture she'd just given. He wanted to make love to her forever—wished he could—and knew he would carry the memory of glancing down and watching her mouth at work on him for the rest of his days.

And when he felt her coming, he pulled in a deep breath as waves of pleasure splintered down his spine. He knew at that very moment that Cheyenne was the only woman he would ever want.

* * *

"And you have to do this every morning around this time?"

Cheyenne glanced over at Quade and smiled. It was barely five in the morning and she was busy at work breast-feeding the triplets. As expected, Troy had awakened first, sending a cry through the monitor that he was ready to be fed.

And as the night before, Quade was sitting across the room with Venus and Athena in his arms. He was proving to be an attentive father, she thought. He had heard the monitor go off before she had and was already easing out of bed to check on the babies by the time she had awakened.

She was still overwhelmed at the thought of their night together. They had made love until they hadn't had any energy left to do anything but sleep, and he had held her in his arms while doing so. More than once she had awoken cradled close to him, and then had gone back to sleep content and at peace.

An hour or so later and the babies were fed and placed back in their cribs. "They'll sleep until around ten," Cheyenne was saying as they turned off the light to leave the room.

"When can they begin eating solid foods?" Quade asked as they walked together down the hall to her bedroom. His arm was slung over her shoulder and he had pulled her close to his side.

"Not until they are at least six months old according to their doctors. But at the rate Troy is going, it might be sooner for him. I can't wait until their next doctor's visit to see how much weight he's gained. The same holds true for Athena." She paused a moment and then said, "But Venus doesn't seem to be gaining weight as fast as the others."

"Yeah, I noticed. Are you worried about it?"

"Yes."

"Then come over here and let me relieve your worry for just a little while."

When they entered her bedroom, he took her hand in his and when he sat down in the rocking chair, he pulled her down into his lap. "I enjoy holding my babies and now I want to hold the mother of my babies."

Cheyenne rested her head on his chest, liking the feel of being in his arms, being held this way, inhaling his mesmerizing male scent. She could get used to his attentiveness, his protection and how he catered to her every need. His tender attention had nothing to do with sex. He was merely giving her what he thought she needed: a peaceful moment in his arms.

"I want to change the babies' names from Steele to Westmoreland as soon as it can be done."

Cheyenne lifted her head and glanced up at him. She knew it bothered him that his son and daughters didn't have his last name. At least she could grant him that one request. "All right. I'll contact my attorney later today."

She could tell by his expression that he was surprised and appreciative. "Thanks," he said, with deep emotion in his voice.

"You haven't said anything about a paternity test," she said, placing her head on his chest once again.

He looked down at her. "I don't need one. I know the babies are mine." That statement made Cheyenne feel good inside. Yes, they were his.

"Now what about yours?" he asked.

She arched a brow. "My what?"

"Name. I want to change your name, as well, Cheyenne."

She sighed, seeing they were back to that again. "I don't need to change my name."

"I think that you do" was his comeback. "I want to marry you."

But not for the right reasons, she thought. "I'm not ready to get married," she said, hoping she sounded convincing.

"Then I guess it's up to me to persuade you to think differently."

He leaned down and captured her lips with his and then she decided she didn't want to think at all.

Cheyenne eased deeper between the covers when suddenly she was jarred from sleep by the sound of the doorbell. When it rang again, she opened her eyes and remembered. She and Quade had awoken when the babies had stirred for their five o'clock feeding. Just as he'd done the night before, Quade had assisted by holding the other two babies as she fed one. After making sure they were dry and comfortable, she and Quade had returned to her room where he had held her in his arms for an hour or so. After that, they had made love several times before finally drifting off to sleep. That was the reason she was naked. He had awakened a few moments ago, dressed and left to buy them breakfast from a deli not far away.

Wondering if he had returned, she slid out of bed and slipped into her short terry-cloth robe and made her way to the front of the house. The last thing she wanted was for the doorbell to wake the babies.

She crossed the room to the door and peeped out. It was her sisters. After their conversation yesterday, why had they returned when they knew she wanted to handle the babies alone? She then figured it out. One of her cousins had probably told her sisters about Quade.

Inhaling a breath of annoyance, she opened the door and plastered a smile on her face. "Vanessa. Taylor. What brings the two of you visiting so early?" she asked, pretending she didn't have a clue.

She took a step back when they walked in. At least Vanessa walked in—Taylor wobbled in. She wasn't due for another month or so but her belly had gotten so big it wouldn't surprise Cheyenne if she didn't deliver before Christmas. But then, Cheyenne thought, as far as she was concerned nobody's belly had been as big as hers. She hadn't gained a lot of weight, just a lot of size.

"Donovan called this morning," Taylor told her, taking a seat on the sofa. "He told us about the card game last night. Chey, you know we don't like to pry, but we're worried."

"About what?"

"We heard the babies' daddy showed up yesterday after we left," Taylor said.

Cheyenne lifted an arched brow. "And?"

"And it looks to me like he works fast," Vanessa said, eyeing Cheyenne up and down. "I hate to tell you this, but you have passion marks all over you. Even on your legs. What is that all about?"

Cheyenne thought the entire thing too comical to get mad. "If you have to ask, Van, then…"

"This isn't funny, Cheyenne," Vanessa said frowning. "This guy shows up one day and already he's back in your bed. Do you deny it?"

Now that ticked her off. She stiffened her spine and said, "No, I don't deny it, nor do I consider it any of either of your business."

"You're our baby sister," Taylor said softly. "We care about you and don't want to see you get hurt."

"And I can appreciate your concern. But I told you yesterday that what Quade and I shared ten months ago was no more than a one-night affair. The only reason he's here is that he found out about the babies."

"Okay, if the babies are the only reason he's here, then why did you two sleep together?" Vanessa asked, moving to take a seat on the sofa next to Taylor.

Cheyenne couldn't help but smile. Evidently she needed to paint a picture, a very explicit picture, for her sisters. "It seems nothing has changed," she said. "Quade and I can't keep our hands off each other. It's this thing, this spontaneous combustion that happens the moment we are within a few feet of each other."

Now, that much she thought was true. "When we get like that, all we want to do is have a sex-a-thon. Anywhere. And at any time."

Her sisters stared at her, not knowing if she was really serious. "Do you really want us to believe that?" Vanessa asked, glaring at her.

"Why not?" Cheyenne said, moving to sit in a chair opposite them. "The two of you have had more extensive love lives than I have. Is it possible for such a thing to exist? At least the part about the spontaneous combustion?"

Her sisters continued to stare at her, not sure if she really wanted an answer. She couldn't understand why the two of them were hesitating in giving her one. Vanessa had shared a torrid affair with Cameron right before they married, although it had taken Cameron years to get her to finally admit she was interested in him. And Taylor was now as pregnant as pregnant could be because she and Dominic had gone on a procreation vacation together. Now they were as happily married as Vanessa and Cameron.

"Yes, there's a lot to be said about spontaneous combustion," Taylor finally said, smiling. "But I'm sure Vanessa would agree with me that being in love with the person is important, too."

Cheyenne nodded. "That's good to know, because I do love him."

Shocked expressions appeared on both of her sisters' faces. "But the two of you have only been together twice during a ten-month period. And both times, need

I remind you, centered on sex. Are you sure you're not confusing lust with love?" Taylor asked.

No one had to remind her of anything, Cheyenne thought. She and Quade had a great sex life. It was a start, wasn't it? But deep down she knew her sisters were right. Quade wanted to marry her for all the wrong reasons. He wanted to give his babies a name— his name. He wanted to give her his name, as well, but only because she was his babies' mother. Love had nothing to do with it. At least not for him. But for her, regardless of how many times they had been together and the reason for them, she truly knew she loved him. Maybe for her it had been love at first sight and she had only realized that fact when she had seen him again yesterday. She refused to believe that two people needed to have a long, drawn out relationship before they could fall in love. She was living proof that they didn't. It wasn't the quantity of time but the quality of time, and she and Quade had definitely spent good quality time together.

Besides that, there was something about Quade that was totally different from any of the men she had ever dated. Maybe it was his maturity—he was twelve years older than she was. There was a goodness about him that she felt whenever she was around him that had nothing to do with lust. How many men would go searching for a woman to find out if she had their baby just because they'd seen her pregnant on the cover of a magazine? He not only had come searching for her, he had come willing and ready to do what he considered as the right thing by her and their children.

She was about to open her mouth and say something when the front door opened. Quade walked in and his gaze went from her to her sisters before he closed the door. The smile that lit his face almost took her breath away and made her love him much more. Without waiting for introductions, he placed the grocery bag he was carrying on a table and he went directly over to her sisters and offered his hand. "Vanessa and Taylor, I presume?"

At their nods, his smile widened, and then he said, "It's a pleasure to meet the two of you. I'm Quade Westmoreland."

At least her sisters now understood how the sight of Quade had practically knocked her off her feet the first time she'd seen him. She could tell they had been just as overwhelmed by him as she had. There was no way they would not agree that Quade Westmoreland was a very good-looking man. Quade was handsome beyond measure and debonair to a fault. He practically oozed sexuality from every pore.

Instead of going to a deli like she'd thought, he had gone grocery shopping with the intention of surprising her with a home-cooked breakfast. He ended up fixing a feast and inviting Vanessa and Taylor to join them.

It didn't take long to see how captivated her sisters were with him. Not only was he a wonderful cook, he was a great conversationalist. Vanessa and Taylor hung on to his every word. Then it was their turn to ask him questions and they started off by asking him about his family.

They were astonished to discover all the famous people in his family. There was motorcycle great Thorn Westmoreland and author Stone Westmoreland, aka Rock Mason. He also told them about his cousin Delaney, who was married to a Middle Eastern sheikh. They had remembered reading about Delaney's storybook romance and wedding in *People* a few years ago. Then there were his cousins who owned a multimillion-dollar horse-breeding business.

When Taylor—whose business was growing a person's wealth and who was always on the lookout for potential clients—had inquired as to who was managing the Westmorelands' wealth, Quade responded that his brother Spencer was the financial whiz in the family.

Then they had asked him about his occupation. He told them he had gone on early retirement from a position in government to join his cousins in opening several security firms around the country, as well as a number of other business ventures.

It didn't take long to accept that Quade was not someone after the Steele fortune. He and his family were already wealthy. And it was also easy to see that he cared for his babies and would be a wonderful father to them.

Moments later, Cheyenne excused herself when she heard the sound of soft noises on the baby monitor. "Excuse me, everyone. Troy is awake," she said, pushing her chair back from the table, standing and making her way to the nursery. Quade smiled at her, and she could feel his gaze following her until she was no longer within his sight.

Cheyenne sensed something was wrong the moment she walked into the room. Troy was crying as usual and Athena had begun whimpering, as well, but when she glanced over at Venus, Cheyenne went on alert and quickly lifted her daughter into her arms.

Barely able to let out the scream that was lodged in her throat, she raced from the room with the baby in her arms. She then began screaming for Quade. He and her sisters intercepted her at the end of the hall. "Cheyenne, what's wrong?" he asked, panic covering his face.

"It's Venus!" she said in a frantic voice, not even trying to remain calm. "Call 9-1-1. She's having trouble breathing."

Chapter 9

Cheyenne sat in the hospital's waiting room and closed her eyes against the rush of emotions ripping through her. Everything had happened so fast. Quade had taken Venus from her arms and had begun resuscitation procedures while Vanessa had called 9-1-1. The rescue service had arrived within minutes and now she and Quade were here, waiting for the doctor to tell them what was wrong with Venus. Vanessa and Taylor had been left behind to care for Troy and Athena.

"Our baby girl is going to be okay, Cheyenne," Quade said, taking her hand in his.

She glanced over at him and found comfort in his solid presence beside her. She loved this man, who less than an hour ago had taken their child from her arms and breathed life into her lungs. She had been in a state of panic and didn't want to think what might have happened if Quade had not been there. She tightened her hand around his and leaned over to place her head on his shoulder, finding even more comfort in doing so.

"I want to believe that, Quade. But she is so little and she looked so helpless."

"But she's a fighter, baby," he said, wrapping his free arm around her shoulder. "She can't help but be a fighter, because she has Westmoreland and Steele blood flowing through her veins."

"Yes, she's a fighter." She had needed to hear that. She needed to have hope.

"Cheyenne?"

At the sound of the feminine voice, Cheyenne glanced up to see the wives of her cousins entering the waiting room. Kylie, Jocelyn and Lena were not only her cousins-in-law, she considered them close friends, as well. And since marrying into the Steele family, they had made their husbands very happy. Quade released her to stand. Cheyenne stood, also, and gave the women hugs. Then she introduced the women to Quade.

"We came as soon as we heard. The guys are on their way, as well," Kylie was saying. "Have you spoken to the doctor yet?"

"No," Cheyenne said, shaking her head. "We've been here for almost an hour but no one has come out and told us anything. That has me worried."

No sooner had Cheyenne said the words than the man who Cheyenne recognized as one of the babies' pediatricians entered the room. She quickly raced over to him. "Dr. Miller, how is Venus?" Quade was right by her side. "This is Quade Westmoreland, my babies' father."

The man shook Quade's hand and then gave them both a reassuring smile. "We have an idea of what's wrong with Venus, but I've ordered more tests to make sure. Hyaline Membrane Disease or HMD or RDS, as it's often referred, is one common problem of babies that are born premature. Usually it's detected within the first few hours of birth, but, as in your daughter's case, sometimes later."

"What causes it?" Quade wanted to know.

"Usually from an insufficient level of surfactant in the lungs. Babies begin producing surfactant while they're still in the womb and usually before they are born they have developed an adequate amount. Evidently Venus did not."

"So what's being done to help her?" Cheyenne asked in a frantic voice.

"Venus's age is in her favor. I'm hoping her condition isn't a severe one, and there won't be any lasting effects once we begin treatment. However, in the worst case we could be looking at damage to other organs, possibly even her heart."

Cheyenne swayed against Quade and he wrapped his arms around her waist. "When can we see our daughter?" he asked in a low voice.

"Not for a while yet. She's still having difficulty breathing. I've placed her on a ventilator."

Cheyenne gasped and the arm around her tightened

as Quade continued to hold her close to him. "Thank you, Doctor," Quade said softly. "Please let us know as soon as we can see her."

After the doctor walked away Quade took Cheyenne's hand in his. "Excuse us a moment," he said to Kylie, Jocelyn and Lena, and gently pulled Cheyenne with him out of the waiting room. They walked down the hall until he suddenly turned and entered an empty room and closed the door behind him.

Still holding Cheyenne's hand, he placed her in front of him and met her gaze. The eyes staring back at him appeared grief stricken, in shock, afraid. "Get it out, Cheyenne, get it out now."

At first she just stared at him and then as if she suddenly realized what he was asking her to do, she dropped her head on his chest and began sobbing. And he held her while she cried. He closed his eyes while the weight of what the doctor had said sunk in.

He never knew, had never understood, the full extent of fatherhood until now. Fatherhood had nothing to do with a name change or wanting to create a family atmosphere for his children. It had everything to do with being there for them when they needed him, giving them what was required for them to grow and live. And, he thought further, being there for their mother, the woman who had brought them into the world, the woman who had taken his seed into her body, and kept it safe until his babies had been born.

It was about Cheyenne, the woman that he knew he

loved. Some people would actually think it was crazy considering their history, but as far as he was concerned, it made perfect sense. A part of him had known it would take a special woman to capture his heart and it wouldn't take months or years for her to do so. His parents had met and fallen in love rather quickly, so had his uncle and aunt. Then there were his brothers and cousins, some of whom had claimed they had fallen in love with their wives the moment they had set eyes on them. Now he was a living witness that such a thing was possible. Cheyenne had been a part of his life, a part of him from the moment they had made love. He had probably fallen in love with her the exact moment they had met on the beach.

Now all he wanted to do was keep her and his babies safe. He had to believe that Venus would get better and return home to them and everything with her would be all right.

He took his finger and lifted up Cheyenne's chin to look into her tear-stained eyes. Her tears were for his baby—their baby. "We have to believe she's going to be okay, sweetheart. If we both believe it, then it will happen. We bring it into existence. Do you believe me, Cheyenne?"

Cheyenne nodded. For some reason she believed him. More than anything she wanted to believe him. At the moment he was her rock, she needed his strength. And one day, she would have his love and if not, he would have hers whether he wanted it or not. Needing to be connected to him in an intimate way, she reached out and wrapped her arms around his neck and then stood on tiptoes and brought his mouth down to hers.

His kiss was gentle yet deep, passionate. He made her feel protected and cared for—even cherished and loved, although she knew she was imagining those two. But still, it didn't matter. What mattered was that he was here with her, the father of her babies, and they had to believe that everything would be all right.

She broke off the kiss and met his gaze. He took her hand in his and kissed the knuckles. "You and I are a team," he said. "Right?"

She smiled through the tears that continued to mist her eyes. "Yes, we are a team."

"And we believe everything will be fine. Right?"

She nodded. "Yes, everything is going to be fine."

And then he pulled her into his arms and kissed her again.

Cheyenne clung to those words when she and Quade were able to see their little girl hours later. It took all of her strength, as well as some of his, to look down at Venus and see all the tubes that ran from her little body and not cry out in pain.

Quade's arm tightened around her shoulder and he brought her closer to his side before leaning over to place a kiss on Cheyenne's lips. "Remember, she is a fighter."

Cheyenne nodded. She then forced a smile and said in a soft voice, "I'll never consider Troy a troublemaker again. It was his crying that brought me to the room to find Venus in respiratory distress. I don't want to think of what might have happened if for once he hadn't made a sound."

Quade didn't want to think about what would have happened, either. He was trying to hold his emotions in check and was finding it difficult to do so. At that moment he knew how it felt to love someone so much you would willingly give your life to save theirs. He felt that kind of love for his offspring. He felt that same kind of love for their mother. The woman he wanted for his wife.

"I'm sorry, but I'm going to have to ask you to leave for a moment while I make some adjustments with the machines," a nurse came up and said in a soft voice.

Instead of answering, Quade nodded and took Cheyenne's hand in his and stepped out of the room and began walking down the hall. He knew her family would be in the waiting room. They'd want an update. Quade would give them the same message he'd given them earlier. Venus's condition hadn't changed. The doctors were still waiting for some of the test results.

One thing he had discovered about the Steele family during this crisis was that they were like his family. When times got tough, they all came together. Since that morning not only had Cheyenne's four cousins been there for support, Vanessa's and Taylor's husbands, whom he had met for the first time, had stopped by, as well. Cameron Cody and Dominic Saxon seemed concerned and their sincere kindness and thoughtfulness touched Quade. He hadn't had a chance to call his family to tell them anything, which would be quite a chore since no one knew about his babies other than Chase.

They stepped into the waiting room and Quade came up short. He caught his breath, surprised, when he looked across the floor and saw several of his cousins and two of his brothers.

He shook his head, grinning when the group crossed the room to him. "How did you know?" he asked them, in a voice filled with emotion.

It was his brother Jared who spoke. "Chase had these vibes about you being deeply worried about something and when he couldn't reach you, he contacted us. He told us where you were, so we're here. You can expect Chase, Thorn and Storm later tonight. Durango and McKinnon are arriving in the morning. Ian wanted to come, but with Brooke due to deliver any day, he thought he better stay put."

Quade nodded as he glanced over at Clint, Cole, Reggie and Stone. "Thanks for coming."

A grimace appeared on Reggie Westmoreland's face. "Don't thank us yet, there's someone here that we haven't told you about yet."

Quade raised a brow. "Who?"

"Mom. She refused to be left behind, especially after hearing about the triplets." Reggie paused a moment and then said, "Get prepared. She plans to box your ears for keeping that from her. I wouldn't want to be in your shoes."

Reggie then switched his gaze to Cheyenne, slowly

looking her up and down in an appreciative glance, and said, "But then again, I do want to be in your shoes."

"You certainly have a big family," Cheyenne said to Quade hours later after she had returned to the hospital. She had gone home long enough to breast-feed the babies. While there, she had met Sarah Westmoreland, Quade's mother. Her mother and Quade's had relieved Vanessa and Taylor of babysitting duties and the two older women were getting along beautifully.

Cheyenne and Quade had met with the doctor and his update had brought smiles of relief. The tests had revealed that Venus had had a mild case of HMD, which had been treatable with the use of surfactant replacement. The ventilator had been removed a short while ago and their daughter was now breathing on her own. The doctor wanted to keep her in the hospital another day for observations and then she would be released.

Quade grinned as he settled back on the cot the nurse had brought into the room for him and Cheyenne to share for the night. They had decided they would stay at the hospital since they didn't want to leave Venus alone. "Yes, there're quite a few of us and like I told you that first day, we're very close."

"And you and Reggie are the only single ones left?"

He looked at her, smiled and said, "Yes, but I won't be single for long if you agree to marry me."

"Just to give me your name?"

Quade took her hand in his and decided now would be the perfect time to tell her how he felt. Whether she believed him or not was another matter altogether. She might feel that she didn't know him well enough considering their history. His response to that would be she knew him in a way no other woman did. While making love he'd always bared his soul to her, as well as his heart.

"Yes," he said, meeting her gaze. "To give you my name. But there's something that goes along with my name."

She lifted a brow. "What?"

"My heart."

She stared at him with disbelief written all over her face. "Are you saying that you love me?" she asked quietly.

"Yes, I am. So what do you have to say to that?" he asked. He expected her to say a lot—most of which he preferred not to hear. Especially if she was going to argue with him about how long they had known each other. That didn't matter to him. What mattered was that she was the woman he wanted to share his life.

She snuggled closer to him. "The only thing I have to say is that I love you, too."

A shocked looked covered his face. "You do?"

She smiled. "Yes, I sure do."

He leaned over and kissed her in a way that soon had her purring in his arms. When he released her, she looked into his eyes. They were ablaze with desire. "Don't even think about it, Quade."

He chuckled. "You sure?"

"Positive."

"You're right, but when I get you and Venus home, I plan to have a party to celebrate. I also plan to have my way with you."

She smiled. "You think so?"

"Baby, I know so."

She got quiet for a moment. Deciding now was the right time for them to be completely honest with each other, she said, "Quade?"

"Yes?"

"I have an idea as to why you were in Egypt."

He suddenly went still for a moment. Then he said, "I told you why I was in Egypt."

"But you didn't tell me everything. I think you left a few details out."

He met her gaze. "A few details like what?"

"You tell me."

Quade studied the look in her eyes and figured that she knew something, but how? He then remembered he had finally dozed off to sleep that night after making love to her countless times. Had she searched through his belongings? Was she a…?

"Don't even think it," Cheyenne said as if she had read his mind.

He held her gaze steadily when he asked, "Then how do you know so much about my business?"

"Because it seems a part of your business is entwined in mine."

He lifted a brow. "Meaning?"

A smile touched her lips when she said, "You got

paid to put your life on the line for the president and I did the same for the first lady."

An incredulous look appeared on Quade's face. "You worked for the PSF?"

"Yes, but only on a part-time basis when my modeling jobs just happened to be in or near a place that needed checking out. I had been a model for almost a year when I was pulled into the organization. I thought it would be daring and fun, as well as a way to serve my country."

He nodded. "And now?"

"And now I just want to raise my babies and take care of my husband."

A huge smile touched his lips. "Does that mean you will accept my marriage proposal?"

"Is it still out there?"

"You bet."

"Then, yes, I accept it, but I would love hearing you ask me again."

"No problem." He reached for her hand and took it into his. "Cheyenne Steele, will you marry me? Be my best friend, lover and the mother of all Quade's babies?"

She lifted a surprised brow. "You want more?"

"Yes, although it won't surprise me one bit if you're already pregnant, pill or no pill. And I figured Venus, Athena and Troy ought to break me in real good for any others that follow. Besides, I love being around for breast-feeding time with you."

She chuckled. "You would."

"Now let's get back to our wedding plans."

"We're making plans?"

"Might as well. My family, at least the ones that are not already here, will be showing up this weekend. Think we can plan something small by then?"

"Small?" she said laughing. "With your family? I don't know about small."

"Then I'll settle for large as long as it's this weekend. Besides, because you put Mom up in your guest room, I'm going to have to do late-night sneak-ins into your bedroom until we're legally married."

"Poor baby."

"Yeah, so see what you can pull off this weekend."

"I'll try."

He grinned and leaned up over her. "Don't sound too convincing. Maybe I should give you a little encouragement."

Cheyenne looked up at him, into the eyes of the man she loved. "Um, maybe you should."

Epilogue

"I now pronounce you man and wife. Quade and Cheyenne Westmoreland. You may now kiss your bride."

Quade didn't have to be told twice and pulled Cheyenne into his arms, taking her mouth like a starving
man. And when she practically began melting in his
arms, instead of lightening up he deepened the kiss,
going in for the kill.

"Will you at least let her breathe, Quade?"

Quade released her and shot his brother Reggie a
frown before sweeping Cheyenne into his arms and
making his way out of the church, leaving everyone
else to follow.

They had married that weekend as planned. So here
it was two weeks before Christmas and for the third
year in a row, the Westmorelands had had a Decem-

ber wedding. First it had been Chase's, then Spencer's and now his. Everyone was looking at Reggie since he was the lone single Westmoreland…at least that they knew about. Quade's father's genealogy search had located the ancestors of their great-grandfather's twin, Raphel Westmoreland. Raphel earned the reputation as the black sheep in the family after he ran off with a married woman. A huge family reunion was being planned in the spring, so the two sides could meet. Quade couldn't imagine there being more Westmorelands, but now it appeared that there were. And like everyone else, he was eager to meet all of his long, lost cousins.

He placed Cheyenne on her feet when they got outside the church. She had looked totally beautiful walking down the aisle to him, and he felt proud of the fact she was his. They had decided to put off a honeymoon for a while, at least until the babies were older. Besides, they were excited about spending their first Christmas together as a family. During the ceremony he had occasionally glanced at the triplets, who had been held in their grandmothers' arms in the front pew. Each time he saw them, he loved the mother of his babies more and more and didn't mind letting her know it.

He gazed down into Cheyenne's dark eyes. "I love you."

She smiled up at him. "And I love you, too."

And then they were showered with rice, and Quade decided now was as good a time as any to seal their vows once again with a kiss. He stepped closer, grinned down at her just seconds before pulling her into his arms. He was a man who didn't believe in wasting time.

* * * * *

TALL, DARK…WESTMORELAND!

Chapter 1

There has to be another way for a woman to have fun, Olivia Jeffries thought as she glanced around at everyone attending the Firemen's Masquerade Ball, an annual charity event held in downtown Atlanta. Already she was gearing up for a boring evening.

It wouldn't have been so bad if she hadn't arrived from Paris just yesterday, after being summoned home by her father. That meant she had to drop everything, including plans to drive through the countryside of the Seine Valley to complete the painting she had started months ago.

Returning to Atlanta had required her to take a leave of absence from her job as an art curator at the Louvre. But when Orin Jeffries called, she hadn't hesitated to drop everything. After all, he was only the greatest dad in the entire world.

He had wanted her home after making the decision to run for public office, saying it was important that she was there not only for his first fund-raiser but also for the duration of his campaign. There would be a number of functions he would need to attend, and he preferred not to go with any particular woman on a regular basis. He didn't want any of his female friends to get the wrong idea.

Olivia could only shake her head and smile. Her divorced father had taken himself off the marriage block years ago. In fact, she doubted he'd ever allowed himself to be there in the first place. He dated on occasion, but he'd never gotten serious about any woman, which was a pity. At fifty-six, Orin Jeffries was without a doubt a very good-looking man. His ex-wife, who was Olivia's mom in genes only, had left a bad taste in Orin's mouth. A taste that the past twenty-four years hadn't erased.

Her two older brothers, Duan, who was thirty-six, and Terrence, who was thirty-four, had taken after her father in their good looks. And as in the case of their father, the thought of marriage was the last thing on their minds. In a way, she followed in her dad's footsteps as well. Finding a husband was the last thing on hers.

So there you had it. They were the swinging single Jeffries, although for the moment, nothing was swinging for her, Olivia thought. There were a few people at this ball who seemed to be having fun, but most, like her, were looking at their watches and wondering when proper etiquette dictated it would be okay to leave.

Whoever had come up with the idea of everyone wearing masks had really been off their rocker. It made her feel like she was part of the Lone Ranger's posse. And because all the money raised tonight was for the new wing at the children's hospital, in addition to the mask, everyone was required to wear a name badge on which was printed the name of a nursery rhyme character, a color of a crayon or a well-known cartoon or comic-book character. How creative.

At least the food was good. The first words out of her father's mouth when he'd seen her at the airport the day before had been, "You look too thin." She figured the least she could do was mosey on over to the buffet table and get herself something to eat. Hopefully, in a little while she could split.

Reginald Westmoreland watched the woman as she crossed the room, making her way over to the buffet table. He had been watching her for over twenty minutes now, racking his brain as to who she was. Mask or no mask, he recognized most of the women at the ball tonight. He knew almost every one of them because for years he had been immersed in the science of "lip-tology." In other words, the first thing he noticed about a woman was her lips.

He could recognize a woman by her lips alone, without even looking at any other facial feature. Most people wouldn't agree, but no two pairs of lips were the same. His brothers and cousins had denounced his claim and had quickly put him to the test. He had just as quickly proven them wrong. Whether you considered it a blessing or a curse, the bottom line was that he had the gift.

And there were other things besides her lips that caught his attention, like her height. She had to be almost six feet tall. And then he was struck by the way she fit into her elegantly designed black and silver beaded dress, the way the material clung to her shapely curves. He had noticed several men approach her, but she had yet to dance with any of them. In fact, it seemed that she was brushing them off. Reginald smelled a challenge.

"So, how is the campaign going, Reggie?"

Reginald, known to all his family as Reggie, turned to look at his older brother, divorce attorney extraordinaire, Jared Westmoreland. Just last week Jared had made the national news owing to a high-profile settlement he'd won in favor of a well-known Hollywood actor.

"It officially kicks off Monday. But now that Jeffries has decided to throw his hat into the ring, things should be rather interesting," he said, referring to the older man who would be his opponent. "With Brent, I have a good campaign manager, but I still feel it might be a tight race. Jeffries is well-known and well-liked."

"Well, if you need any help, let me know, although I'm not sure how much time I can spare now that Dana's expecting and all."

Reggie rolled his eyes. Just last month Jared had found out he was going to be a father. "Dana is going to be carrying the baby, Jared, not you."

"I know, but I'm the one who's been getting sick

in the morning, and now I'm getting cravings. I never liked pickles until now."

Reggie couldn't help but smile over his wineglass. "Sounds like a personal problem to me." At the moment, his attention strayed from whatever Jared was saying. Instead, his gaze focused on the other side of the room. He noticed the woman whom he'd been watching sit down at a table. He had yet to see a man by her side, which meant she had come to the party alone.

"Umm, I wonder who she is?" he asked.

Jared followed Reggie's gaze and chuckled. "What's wrong? Don't you recognize the lips?"

Reggie shifted his gaze from the woman to his brother and frowned. "No, she's someone new. I definitely haven't met her before. Her lips don't give her away."

"Then I guess the only thing left for you to do is go over there and introduce yourself."

Reggie grinned. "I know they don't call you the sharpest attorney in Atlanta for nothing."

"Don't you know sitting alone at a party isn't good for you?"

Olivia swung her head around at the sound of the deep, throaty masculine voice to find a tall, handsome man standing beside her. Like everyone else, he was wearing a mask, but even with it covering half of his face, she knew he had to be extremely good-looking. In the dim lighting, her artist's eye was able to capture all his striking features that were exposed.

First of all, there was his skin, flawlessly smooth and

a shade of color that reminded her of rich, dark maple syrup. Then there was the angular plane of a jaw that supported a pair of sexy lips. The same ones that bestowed a slow smile on her. Apparently, he realized she was checking him out.

"In that case, I guess you need to join me," she replied, trying to remember the last time she'd been so outrageously forward with a guy and quickly deciding never. But the way the evening was going, she would have to stir up her own excitement. And now was as good a time as any to start. Maybe it was the fact that the party was so unrelentingly boring that made her long for a taste of the wild and reckless. The other men who had approached her hadn't even piqued her curiosity. She had no desire to get to know them better. But this man was different.

"I don't mind if I do," he said, easily sliding into the chair beside her while his eyes remained locked with hers. Her nose immediately picked up the scent of his cologne. Expensive. She quickly checked out his left hand. Ringless. Her gaze automatically went back to his face. Beautiful. Now he was smiling in earnest and showing beautiful white teeth.

"You're amused," she said, taking a sip of her punch but wishing she had something a little stronger.

Whoever he was, he was certainly someone worth getting to know, even if she was returning to Paris in a few months. That made it all the more plausible. It had taken her two years to get on full-time at the Louvre, and the hard work was just beginning. Once she returned, she would be working long hours, with little time to get her painting done. That was why she had brought her paints to Atlanta with her. She was determined to capture something worthwhile on canvas while she was here. The man sitting beside her would be the perfect subject.

"Flattered more than amused," he said, his voice reaching out and actually touching her, although she barely registered his words in her mind, because she was too busy watching the way his mouth moved. Sensuously slow.

She couldn't help wondering who he was. She had been gone from Atlanta a long time. After high school she had attended Pratt Institute in New York before doing her graduate work at the Art Institute of Boston. From there she had made the move to Paris, after landing a job as a tour professional, a glorified name for a tour guide.

He had to be around her brother Terrence's age, or maybe a year or so younger. She wondered if he would give her his real name, or if he would stick to the rules and play this silly little game the coordinators of the ball had come up with. His name badge said Jack Sprat. No wonder he was in such fine shape, she thought. Even in the tuxedo he was wearing, she saw broad, muscular shoulders and a nice solid chest. All muscles. Definitely no fat.

"So, Jack," she said, smiling at him the same way he was smiling at her. "What is such a nice guy like you doing at a boring party like this?"

He chuckled, and the sound sent goose bumps over her body. "Waiting to meet you so we can start having some fun." He glanced at her name badge. "Wonder Woman."

The smile that touched the corners of her mouth widened. She liked him already. "Well, trust me when I say, it's a *wonder* that I'm here at all. I really want to be someplace else, but I promised the person who paid for this ticket that I'd come in his place. And since it's all for charity, and for such a good cause, I decided to at least make an appearance."

"I'm glad you did."

And Reggie meant it. He'd thought she had a beautiful pair of lips from afar, but now he had a chance to really study them up close. They were a pair he would never forget. They were full, shapely, and had luscious-looking dips at the corners. She had them covered in light lip gloss, which was perfect; any color would detract from their modish structure.

"We've exchanged names, and I'm glad to make your acquaintance, Jack," she said, presenting her hand to him.

He grinned. "Likewise, Wonder."

The moment their hands touched, he felt it and knew that she did, too. Her fingers quivered on his, and for some reason, he could not release her hand. That realization unnerved him. No woman had ever had this kind of effect on him before, not in all his thirty-two years.

"Are you from Atlanta?"

Her voice, soft and filled with Southern charm, reclaimed his attention.

"Yes, born and raised right here," he said, reluctantly releasing her hand. "What about you?"

"Same here," she said, looking at him as if she could see through his mask. "Why haven't we met before?"

He smiled. "How do you know that we haven't?"

Her chuckle came easily. "Trust me. I would remember if we had. You're the type of man a woman couldn't easily forget."

"Hey, that's my line. You stole it," he said jokingly.

"I'll give it back to you if you take me away from here."

He didn't say anything for a minute but just sat there studying her face. And then he asked, "Are you sure you want to go off with me?"

She managed another smile. "Are you sure you want to take me?" she challenged.

Reggie couldn't help but laugh loudly, so loudly, in fact, that when he glanced across the room, his brother Jared caught his gaze and gave him a raised brow. He had five brothers in all. He and Jared were the only ones still living in Atlanta. He also had a bunch of cousins in the city. It seemed Westmorelands were everywhere, but he and Jared were the only ones who were here tonight. The rest had other engagements or were off traveling someplace.

A part of Reggie was grateful for that. He was the youngest of the Atlanta-based Westmorelands, and his brothers and cousins still liked to consider him the baby of the family, although he stood six-seven and was the tallest of the clan.

"Yes, I would take you in a heartbeat, sweetheart. I would take you anywhere you wanted to go."

And he meant it.

She nodded politely, but he knew she was thinking, trying to figure out a way she could go off with him and not take any careless risks with her safety. A woman couldn't be too trusting these days, and he understood that.

"I have an idea," he said finally, when she hadn't responded and several moments had passed.

"What?"

He reached into his jacket pocket and pulled out his cell phone. "Text someone you know and trust, and tell them to save my number. Tell them you will call them in the morning. When you call, they can erase the number."

Olivia thought about what he'd suggested and then wondered whom she could call. Any girlfriends she'd had while living here years ago were no longer around. Of course, she couldn't text her father, so she thought about her brothers. Duan was presently out of the city, since his job as a private investigator took him all over the country, and Terrence was living in the Florida Keys. She and her brothers were close, but it was Terrence who usually let her get away with things. Duan enjoyed playing the role of older brother. He would ask questions. Terrence would ask questions, too, but he was more easygoing.

Perhaps it was Duan's inquisitive mind that made him such a stickler for the rules. It had to be all those years he'd worked first as a patrolman and then as a detective for Atlanta's police department. Terrence, a former pro football player for the Miami Dolphins, knew how to have fun. He was actually the real swinging single Jeffries. He owned a nice club in the Florida Keys that really embodied the term *nightlife*.

Her safest bet would be to go with Terrence.

"Okay," she said, taking the phone. She sent Terrence a quick text message, asking that he delete the phone number from which the message was sent after hearing from her in the morning. She handed the phone back to him.

"Feel better about this?" he asked her.

She met his gaze. "Yes."

"Good. Is there any particular place you want to go?"

The safest location would be her place, Olivia thought, but she knew she couldn't do that. Her father was home, going over a campaign speech he would be giving at a luncheon on Monday. "No, but I haven't been out to Stone Mountain in a while."

He smiled. "Then Stone Mountain it is."

"And we'll need to go in separate cars," she said quickly. She had begun to feel nervous because she had never done anything like this in her life. What was she thinking? She got a quick answer when she met his gaze again. She was thinking how it would probably feel to be in this man's arms, to rub her hand across that strong, angular jaw, to taste those kissable lips and to breathe in more of his masculine scent.

"That's fine," he said in a husky voice. "You lead and I'll follow."

"And we keep on our masks and use these names," she said, pointing to her name badge.

He studied her intently for a moment before nodding his head. "All right."

She let out a silent breath. Her father was well-known in the city, and with the election just a couple of months away, she didn't want to do anything to jeopardize his chances of winning. Anything like having her name smeared in the paper in some scandal. Scandals were hard to live down, and she didn't want do anything that would be a nice addition to the *Atlanta Journal-Constitution*'s gossip column.

"Okay, let's go," she said, rising to her feet. She hoped she wasn't making a mistake, but when he accidentally brushed up against her when they headed for the exit, she had a feeling anything that happened between them tonight could only be right.

Reggie, as a rule, didn't do one-night stands. However, he would definitely make tonight and this woman an exception. The car he was following close behind was a rental, so that didn't give him any clues as to her identity. All he did know was that she was someone who wanted to enjoy tonight, and he was going to make sure she wasn't disappointed.

She'd indicated that she wanted to go someplace in Stone Mountain, and she was heading in that direction. He wondered if they would go directly to a place where they could be alone, or if they would work up to that over a few drinks in a club. If she wanted a night on the town first, there were a number of nightclubs to choose from, but that would mean removing their masks, and he had a feeling she intended for these to stay in place. Why? Was she as well-known around the city as he was? At least after Monday he would be. Brent Fairgate, his campaign manager and the main person who had talked him into running for the Senate, had arranged for campaign posters with his picture to be plastered on just about every free space in Atlanta.

Returning his attention to the car in front of him, he braked when they came to a traffic light. Just then his cell phone rang. He worked it out of his pocket. "Hello?"

"Where are you?"

He gave a short laugh. "Don't worry about me, Jared. However, I do apologize for not letting you know I was leaving."

"That woman you were with earlier isn't here, either. Is that a coincidence?"

Reggie shook his head, grinning. "I don't know. You tell me."

There was a pause on the other end. "You sure about what you're doing, Reggie?"

"Positive. And no lectures please."

"Whatever," came his brother's gruff reply. And then the call was disconnected.

The traffic began moving again, and Reggie couldn't help but think about how his life would change once the campaigning began. There would be speeches to deliver, interviews to do, television appearances to make, babies to kiss and so on and so forth. He would be the first Westmoreland to enter politics, and for him, the decision hadn't been an easy one to make. But Atlanta was growing by leaps and bounds, and he wanted to give back to the city that had given him so much.

Unlike his brothers, who had left town to attend college, he had remained here and had gone to Morehouse.

And he had never regretted doing so. He smiled, thinking that the good old days were when he got out of college and, a few years later, when he opened his own accounting firm. At the time, his best buddy had been his cousin Delaney. They were only a few months apart in age and had always been close. In fact, he was the one who had helped Delaney outsmart her five overprotective brothers right after she finished med school and needed to get some private time. He had let her use his cabin in the mountains for a little rest and relaxation, without telling Dare, Thorn, Stone, Chase or Storm where she was. Lucky for him, his cousins hadn't broken his bones, as they had threatened to do, when they discovered his involvement. The good thing was that Delaney had met her desert sheikh and fallen in love at his cabin.

Reggie's attention was pulled back to the car in front of him when Wonder Woman put on her blinker to turn into the parking lot of the luxurious Saxon Hotel. He smiled. He liked her taste, but given that they were wearing masks, he wondered how this would work. And then he got an idea and immediately pulled his cell phone out of his jacket pocket to punch in a few numbers.

"Hello?"

Reggie could hear babies crying in the background. "This is Reggie. What are you doing to my nieces and nephew?"

He heard his brother Quade's laugh. "It's bath time, and nobody wants to play in the water tonight. What's up? And I understand congratulations are in order. Mom told me you've decided to run for the Senate. Good luck."

"Thanks." And then, without missing a beat, he said, "I need a favor, Quade."

"What kind of favor?"

"I need a private room at the Saxon Hotel here in Atlanta tonight, and I know Dominic Saxon is your brother-in-law."

"So?"

"So make it happen for me tonight, as soon as possible. And I need things kept discreet and billed to me."

There was a pause on the other end. "You sure about this, Reggie?"

He shook his head. It was the same question Jared had asked him moments ago. "Yes, Quade, I'm sure. And I don't expect any lectures from you, considering when and how my nieces and nephew were conceived."

"Go to hell, Reggie."

He smiled. "Not in front of the babies, Quade. And as far as going to hell, I'll go, but only after I get a night of heaven. So make it happen for me, Quade. I'll owe you. I'll even volunteer to fly in one day and babysit."

"Damn, she must be some woman."

Reggie thought about those lips he wanted so desperately to taste. "She is."

"I'll see what I can do." And then the call was disconnected.

Smiling and feeling pretty certain that Quade would come through for him, he watched as Wonder Woman parked her car, and then eased his car into the parking spot next to hers. As soon as she turned off the engine, he got out of his car and glanced around, making sure there weren't a lot of people about. She had parked in an area that was pretty empty, and he was grateful for that.

When he got to her side of the car, she rolled down the window and looked a little flushed. "Sorry. I guess I didn't think this far ahead."

He bent down and leaned forward against her door and propped his arms on the car's window frame and smiled at her. She smelled good, and she looked good. His gaze shifted from her eyes to her lips and then back to her eyes again. He couldn't wait to taste her lips.

"Don't worry. Tonight will end the way we want," he said, with certainty in his voice and all the while thinking that if Quade didn't come through for him tonight, he was liable to kill him. At her confused expression, he said, "I've made a call, and it will only be a few moments. I'll get a call back when things get set up."

Olivia eyed the man staring at her and tried to ignore the stirring in the pit of her stomach. She couldn't help wondering just who was he and what kind of connections he had. They had to be big ones if he was able to get them a room at the Saxon from the parking lot. Would they have to do the normal check-in?

One part of her brain was screaming at her, telling her that what she was contemplating doing was downright foolish and irresponsible. No good girl, certainly not one who'd been raised to be a proper young lady, would think about having a one-night stand with a stranger.

But then the other part of her brain, the one that was daring, as well as wild and reckless, urged her on. Go ahead, Libby. Have some fun. Live a little. You haven't been seriously involved with a man for almost two years. You've been too busy. You deserve some fun. What will it hurt as long as you've taken every precaution to make sure you're safe?

And at the moment she was safe. Terrence had this man's phone number, and the hotel was definitely a respectable one. And it was one she had selected, not him. But she had to admit, she felt a little silly with the two of them still wearing their masks. At least she had taken off her name badge.

"So, Wonder Woman, what's your favorite color?"

She couldn't help but smile. He evidently felt the tension and was making an attempt to ease it. "Lavender. What's yours?"

"Flesh tone."

She grinned. "Flesh tone isn't a color."

"Depends on who's wearing it," he said softly, and then his eyes flickered to her lips. She felt the intensity of his gaze just as if it was a soft caress. Suddenly, she felt the need to moisten her lips with her tongue.

"I wish you hadn't done that," he whispered huskily, leaning his body forward to the point where more of his face was in the window, just inches from her face.

A breathless sigh escaped from her lips. "What?" she asked in a strained voice.

"Tasted your own lips. That's what I want to do. What I'm dying to do."

"What's stopping you?"

Reggie thought that was a dare if ever he'd heard one. Deciding to take her up on it, he leaned his body in closer. She was tilting her head toward his face when suddenly his cell phone rang.

Damn. He reluctantly pulled back and pulled the cell phone from his jacket.

Olivia took that time to take a deep breath, and then she listened to his phone conversation.

"Yes?" he said into the phone.

She watched a huge smile brighten his face, and at the same time, she felt intense heat gather at the junction of her thighs.

"Thanks, man. I owe you one," he said. She then watched as he clicked off the phone and put it in his pocket. He glanced over at her. "Okay, Wonder Woman. Everything is set. We're on the sixteenth floor. Room sixteen thirty-two. Ready?"

She exhaled slowly. A part of her wanted to tell him that, no, she wasn't ready. She wanted to know how he'd arranged everything from a parking lot. Another part of her needed to know how he was capable of making her feel things that no other man had ever made her feel before. How was he able to get her to take risks when she was the least impulsive person that had ever lived? At least she had been risk averse until she'd seen him at the party tonight.

She met his gaze, knowing this would be it. Once she got out of the car and walked into that hotel with him, their night together would begin. Was that what she really wanted? He was staring at her, and his gaze seemed to be asking her that same question.

She drew in a deep breath and nodded her head and said, "Yes, I'm ready."

He then opened the car door for her. "You go on ahead, and I'll follow within five minutes. The bank of elevators you should use is the one to the right of the check-in desk," he said.

"Okay."

He watched as she placed the strap of her purse on her shoulder before walking away. He smiled as she gracefully crossed the parking lot and headed toward the entrance to the hotel. He couldn't help but admire the way she looked in her dress, a silky number that swished around her legs whenever she made a movement. And she had the legs for it. Long, shapely legs that he could imagine wrapped around him, holding him inside her body during the heat of passion.

He was so into his thoughts that when she suddenly stopped walking, his heart nearly stopped beating. Had she changed her mind? Moments later he gave a deep sigh of relief when he realized she had stopped to remove her mask. He wondered if she would take the risk and turn around to let him see her face, voluntarily revealing her identity. He got his answer when she began walking again without looking back. He had a feeling that that was how the entire night would go. Identities and names would not be shared. Only passion.

He would respect her wishes, and when he joined her in the hotel room, his mask, too, would be back in place.

There was no doubt in his mind that this would be a night he would always remember.

Chapter 2

Olivia was grateful that no one seemed to pay her any attention when she walked into the huge lobby of the Saxon. It had always been her dream to spend a night in what had to be one of the most elegant hotels ever built. It was more stylish and extravagant than she had expected. There were only a few Saxons scattered about the country, in the major cities, and all had a reputation of providing top-quality service.

When she stepped onto the elevator that would carry her to the sixteenth floor, she couldn't help but again wonder about the man behind the mask and the connections he seemed to have. Reservations were hard to get because the hotel was booked far in advance, even as much as a year.

As she stepped out of the elevator and walked down

the spacious hall, she studied the decor. Everything had a touch of elegance and class. With an artist's eye, she absorbed every fine detail of not only the rich and luxurious-looking carpet on the floor but also of the beautiful framed portraits that lined the walls. She would bet a month of her salary at the Louvre that those were original Audubon prints. If they devoted this much time and attention to the hallways, she could only imagine what one of the rooms would look like.

She wondered what Jack Sprat thought of her taste, since she was the one who'd guided him here. Of course, she would pay tonight's bill, since coming here was her idea. Connections or no connections, this place was her choice and not his, so it would only be fair. The last thing she wanted to do was come off as a thoughtless, high-maintenance woman.

Moments later she stood in front of room 1632. She didn't have a key and could only assume the door was unlocked. There was only one way to find out. She turned the handle and smiled when it gave way without a problem. She slowly opened the door and stepped into the room. Quickly closing the door, she glanced around, her eyes widening. This had to be a penthouse suite. She hadn't expected this, wasn't even sure she would be able to pay for it. She had figured on a regular room, which, though costly, would have been within her budget.

She was paid well, and loved Paris, but eventually she intended to return to the United States. She planned to open an art gallery in a few years, and that took money. Every penny she earned went into her special

savings. Her father and brothers had promised to invest
in the venture, but she felt that it was her responsibility
to come up with the majority of the capital for her gallery. This little tryst was going to cost her. She would
have to dip into her savings to pay for this suite. She
wondered if just one night with a stranger could possibly be worth the sacrifice.

She crossed the room, drawn to the stately furnish-
ings. She had stayed in nice hotels before, but there was
something about a Saxon that took your breath away.
Besides the elegant luxury that surrounded you, there
was also the personalized service, culinary excellence
and other amenities, which she had often heard about,
but had yet to experience.

She walked through the sitting area to the bedroom.
Her gaze moved from the plush love seat in the room to
the bed. The bed was humongous and stately; the covering was soft to the touch. It felt as if you could actually
lose yourself under it. The bedcoverings and curtains
were done in an elegant red and a single red rose had
been placed in the middle of the bed. Very romantic.

The connecting bath was just as stunning, with a
huge Jacuzzi tub that sat in the middle of the floor,
surrounded by a wall-to-wall vanity the likes of which
she'd never seen in a hotel. Everything was his and hers,
and the bathroom was roomy, spacious.

Nervously, she walked out of the bathroom and back
into the bedroom and sat down on the edge of the bed.

When she was growing up, people had often said
she was spoiled and pampered, and in a way, she had
been. Being the only girl in the house had had its ad-

vantages. She had been only three years old when her mother left her father, ran off with a married man and destroyed not one, but two families. She would always admire her father for doing what had to be done to hold their family together. He'd worked long and hard hours as a corporate attorney and still had been there for her piano recitals and art shows and her brothers' Little League games. And one year he had even gotten elected president of the PTA. It hadn't been easy, and everyone had had to pitch in and help. And she could now admit that her brothers had made it easier for her.

Leaving home for college had been good for her. Against her father's and brothers' wishes, she had worked her way through college, refusing the money they would send her. She'd needed to encounter the real world and sink or swim on her own while doing so.

She'd learned how to swim.

She glanced at her watch. Chances were that Jack Sprat was on his way up, so now was not the time to get nervous. She had come on to him at the party, and he had come on to her. They were here because a night together was what they both wanted. So why was she thinking about hightailing it all of a sudden? Why were butterflies flying around her stomach? And what was with the darn goose bumps covering her arms?

She stood and began pacing. He would be here at any moment, so she stopped and took the time to put her mask back on. In a way she felt silly, but at the same time mysterious.

Olivia glanced at her watch again. She felt her body heating up just thinking about what would happen when he did arrive. To say she was fascinated by a complete stranger would be an understatement. If anyone had told her that within less than forty-eight hours of returning to Atlanta, she, Olivia Jeffries, would be involved in an affair to nowhere, she would not have believed them. Usually she was very conservative, but not tonight.

She caught her breath when she thought she heard footsteps coming down the hall. An anticipatory shiver ran down her spine, and she knew that in just a minute he would be there.

Reggie walked down the hallway, deep in thought. Some people engaged in casual affairs to pass the time or to feel needed. He was not one of them, and for some reason, he knew that the woman waiting on him in the hotel room wasn't, either. He would admit that there had been a few one-night stands in his history, back in the day at Morehouse, when he hadn't had a care in the world other than studying, making the grade and getting an easy lay. But now as a professional who owned a very prestigious accounting firm and as a political candidate, he picked his bed partners carefully. He hadn't been involved in any long-term affairs since right after college—and that disastrous time with Kayla Martin a few years ago, which he preferred to forget. He'd pretty much stuck to short-term affairs.

His family constantly reminded him he was the last Westmoreland bachelor living in Atlanta, but that was fine with him. Settling down and getting married were the furthest things from his mind. He was glad it wouldn't be an issue in his campaign, because his opponent, Orin Jeffries, was a long-term divorcé, and from what he'd heard, the man had no plans of ever re-marrying.

Finally, he stood in front of room 1632. Only pausing for a brief second, he reached out to open the door and then stopped when he remembered his mask. Glancing up and down the hall to make sure it was empty, he pulled the mask out of his pocket and put it on. Then, after drawing a deep breath, he opened the door.

The moment he opened the door, his eyes, that is, the portion of them that Olivia could see through his mask, met hers. They felt possessive, as if he was stamping ownership on her, when there was no way he could do that. He didn't know her true identity. He knew nothing about her other than that it seemed her need for him was just as elemental and strong as his need for her. It was a tangible thing, and she could feel it, all the way to her toes.

Yet there was something in the way he entered the room, not taking his eyes off her as he pushed the door closed behind him. And then giving the room only a cursory glance. Without a single word spoken between them, he swiftly crossed the room and drew her into his arms.

And kissed her.

There was nothing to be gained by any further talking, and they both knew it. And the moment his mouth touched hers, lightly at first, before devouring it with a hunger she felt deep in her belly, she moaned a silent acceptance of him and their night together.

This was sexual chemistry at its most potent. He was all passion, and she responded in kind. She kissed him, not with the same skill and experience he was leveling on her, but with a hunger that needed to be appeased, satisfied and explored.

The kiss intensified, and they both knew it wouldn't be enough to quench the desire waiting to be unleashed within them. Sensations were spreading through her, seeping deep into her bones and her senses. Urges that she had tried desperately to control were now threatening to consume her.

He reluctantly pulled his mouth away, and she watched as a sensuous smile touched his lips. "Tonight is worth everything," he whispered softly against her moist lips. "Not in my wildest imagination would I have thought of this happening."

Neither would I, Olivia thought. The masks were silly, but they had a profound purpose. So were the pretend names. With them, they were free to do what they pleased, without inhibitions or thought of consequences. If their paths were to cross again, after tonight, there would be no recognition, no recrimination and no need for denials. What happened in this hotel room tonight would stay in this hotel room tonight.

Reggie's gaze studied Olivia as he fought to catch his breath while doing the same for his senses. Kissing her, tasting her lips, had been like an obsession since the moment he'd laid eyes on her. The shape, texture and outline of her lips had a provocative effect on him. Some men were into the shape and size of a woman's breasts; others into her backside. He was definitely a lips man. The fullness of a pair, covered in lipstick or not, could induce a state of arousal in him. Just thinking of all the things he could do with them was enough to push him over the edge.

And then, losing control, he leaned down and kissed her again, and while his tongue dominated and played havoc with hers, he felt her loosen up, begin to relax in his arms. She wrapped her arms around his neck while her feminine curves so effortlessly pressed against him in a seamless melding of bodies. They fit together perfectly, naturally. There was nothing like having soft female limbs and a beautiful set of lips within reach, he thought.

The hand around her waist dipped, and he felt the curve of her backside through the gown she was wearing. A firm yet soft behind. He needed to get her out of her gown.

Pulling his mouth away, he swept her into his arms. At her startled gasp and with a swift glance, he met the eyes staring at him through the mask, and then his lips eased into a smile. So did hers. And with nothing left to be said, he walked to the bedroom.

Instead of placing her on the bed, he held her firmly in his arms and sat down on the love seat, adjusting her in his lap. She pulled in a deep breath and caught hold of the front of his jacket.

He smiled down at her. "Trust me. I'm not going to let you fall." She loosened her hold on him yet continued looking into his eyes, studying his features so intently that he couldn't help asking, "Like the part you can see?"

She smiled. "Yes. You have such an angular jaw. It speaks of strength and honesty. It also speaks of determination."

He raised a brow, wondering how Wonder Woman could tell those things about him from just studying his jaw. He stopped wondering when she reached out and her finger traced that same jaw that seemed to fascinate her.

"It's rigid, but not overbearing. Firm, but not domineering." She then smiled. "Yet I do see a few arrogant lines," she said, tapping the center of his jaw.

He had sat down with her in his arms, instead of placing her on the bed, so as not to rush things with her, to give her time to collect herself after their kisses. He refused to rush their lovemaking. For some reason, he wanted more, felt they deserved more. He was never one for small talk, but he figured he would take a stab at it. But now her touch was making it almost impossible not to touch. Not to undress her and give her the pleasure they both wanted. And then it came to him that the reason he was here with her had nothing to do with lust. He'd gone months without a woman warming his bed before. What was driving him more than anything was her appeal, her sexiness and his desire to mate with her in an intimate way. Only her.

He stood while cradling her tightly in his arms and moved toward the bed and gently placed her in the middle of it, handed her the rose and then he took a step back so she could be in the center of his vision. He wanted the full view of her.

Her shoulder-length hair was tousled around her face,

at least the part of her face he could see. Her dress had risen when he'd placed her on the bed. She had to know it was in disarray and showing a great deal of flesh, but she didn't make a move to pull anything down, and he had no intention of suggesting she do so. So he looked, got his fill, saw the firmness of her thighs and the shapeliness of her knees. And he couldn't help but notice how the front of the dress was cut low, showing the top portion of her full and firm breasts. He was a lips man first and a breasts man second. As far as he was concerned, he had hit the jackpot.

Olivia wondered how long he would stand there and stare. But in a way, it reassured her that he liked what he saw. No man had taken the time to analyze her this way. She might as well make it worth his while. She placed the rose to one side and reached down and unclasped her shoes before slipping them off her feet. She tossed one and then the other to him. He caught them perfectly, and instead of dropping them to the floor, he tossed them onto the love seat they had just vacated.

She was surprised. He had recognized a pair of stilettos by Zanotti. They had been another whim of hers. Shoes were her passion, and she appreciated a man who knew quality and fine workmanship in a woman's shoes when he saw it. He moved up another notch in her book.

Now it was time to take off the rest. Because she never wore panties with panty hose, that would be easy. Instead of removing her panty hose last, she decided to take them off first. He wouldn't be expecting it, and the thought of catching him off guard stirred something inside of her. With his eyes still on her, she lifted her bottom off the bed slightly to ease down her panty hose, deliberately giving him a flash to let him know that once they were gone, there would not be any covering left. After she'd removed them, she rolled the hose up in a ball and tossed them to him. As with her shoes, he made a perfect catch, and then, while she watched him, he brought the balled-up nylon to his nose and took a whiff of her scent before placing it in the pocket of his jacket.

Her gaze had followed his hands, and now it moved back to his face. She saw the flaring of his nostrils and the tightening of his fists by his sides, and she saw something else. Something she had noted earlier, when he had walked across the room to her, but that now had grown larger. His erection. There was no doubt in her mind, unclothed and properly revealed, it would put Michelangelo's *David* to shame. Her artistic eye could even make out the shape of it through his pants. It was huge, totally developed, long and thick. And at the moment, totally aroused. That was evident by the way the erection was straining against the fly of his pants.

He shifted his stance. Evidently, he'd seen where her gaze had traveled, and she watched as his fingers went to the zipper of his tuxedo pants and slowly eased it down. She could only stare when, after bending to remove his shoes and socks, he stepped out of his pants, leaving his lower body clad only in a pair of sexy black briefs. She knew they were a designer pair; their shape, fit and support said it all. The man had thighs that were firm, hard and muscular. She didn't have to see his buns to know they were probably as tight as the rest of him.

There was no need to ask if he worked out on occasion. The physical fitness of his body said it all.

And he looked sexy standing there, with a tux jacket and white shirt on top and a pair of sexy briefs covering his lower half. She figured he had decided to remove the clothes from the same part of his anatomy as she had. They were both undressing from the bottom up.

She held her breath, literally stopped breathing, when his hands then went to the waistband of his briefs. And while her gaze was glued to him, he slowly pulled the briefs down his legs.

Damn.

The man, thankfully, had no qualms about exposing himself, and for that she was grateful, because what her eyes were feasting on was definitely worth seeing. He was truly a work of art. And while her focus was contained, he went about removing the rest of his clothes. She wasn't aware of it until he stood before her, totally naked in all his glorious form.

Her gaze traveled the full length of his body once, twice, a total of three times before coming back to settle on his face. He was a naked, masked man, and she would love to have him pose for her as such. On canvas she would capture each and every detail of him. He was pure, one hundred percent male.

"It's your turn to take off the rest of your clothes, Wonder."

His words, deep and husky, floated around the already sexually charged room.

She forced her gaze from his thick shaft and moved it to his face as, on her knees, she reached behind herself and undid the hooks of her dress before pulling it over her head. It was simple, and she was naked, since she hadn't worn a bra.

Now he saw it all. And like she had earlier, his gaze moved to her lower part, zeroing in on the junction of her thighs. Suddenly she felt awkward. She wondered what he was thinking. She kept her body in great shape, and her Brazilian wax was obvious.

She met his gaze when he returned it to her face. She smiled. "I'm done."

"No, baby," he said in a tight and strained voice. "You haven't even got started."

Reggie pulled in a deep breath, meaning every word he'd just spoken. Never in his life had he been so hard and hot for a woman. Never had he wanted to eat one alive. As far as he was concerned, there would not be enough time tonight to do everything he wanted to do. So there was none to be wasted. But first...

"Is there anything you have an aversion to doing?" he felt the need to ask.

He watched how she lifted her gaze a moment, and then she said in a soft voice, "Yes. I'm not into bondage."

He chuckled. "Then it's a good thing I left my handcuffs at home." And because he saw the slight widening of her eyes, he smiled and said, "Hey, I'm just teasing. I would be crazy to tie your hands since I prefer you putting them all over me."

As far as Olivia was concerned, that was the perfect invitation. She scooted close to the edge of the bed and reached out and splayed her hands across his chest. She smiled when she heard his sharp intake of breath. And she was fascinated by the way his muscles flexed beneath her hands and by the warmth of his skin beneath her fingers.

"You're into torture?" he asked huskily, his tone sounding somewhat strained.

"Why? Do you feel like you're being tortured?" she asked innocently, shifting one of her hands lower to his stomach.

"Yes." His answer was short and precise. His breathing seemingly impaired.

"You haven't seen anything yet, Jack Sprat."

And then her hand dropped to that part of him she'd become fascinated with from the moment she'd seen it. It was large, heavy and, for tonight, it was hers. Her hand closed up, contracted and then closed up again, liking the feel of holding it, stroking it.

Breathing at full capacity, Reggie could no longer handle what his mystery woman was doing to him and pulled back and reached down for his pants to retrieve a condom packet from his wallet. Ripping the packet with his teeth, he proceeded to put the condom on.

He glanced up to see her lying back on the bed, smiling at him, fully aware of the state she'd pushed him to. He moved so quickly, it caught her off guard, and then he was there with her in the bed, pinning her beneath him on the coverlet and immediately taking her mouth captive, devouring it like he intended to devour her. And when he pulled back, he moved down to her breasts, taking the nipples in his mouth, doing all kinds of things to them with his tongue until she cried out. She pleaded with him to stop, because she couldn't take any more.

But he definitely wasn't through with her yet. Intent on proving that she wasn't the only one with hands that could torture, he used his knee to spread her legs. He then settled between them, determined to fit his erection in the place where it was supposed to be.

There was so much more he wanted to do—devour her breasts, lick her skin all over—but at that moment, the one thing he had to do before his brain exploded with need was get inside of her.

He pulled his mouth away from her breasts, and breathing hard, he stared down at her, determined to see what he could of her eyes through the mask. "This is crazy," he said, almost choking for both breath and control of the words.

"Might be," she said, just as short of breath. "But it's the best craziness I've ever experienced. Let's not stop now."

He stared at her. "You sure?"

She stared back. "Positive."

And with their gazes locked, he entered her.

He felt her small spasms before he even got into the hilt, and when her inner muscles clenched him, he pressed deeper inside of her. She was tight, but he could feel her opening wider for him, like a bloom. "That's it. Relax, let go and let me in," he said.

And as if her body was his to command, it continued to open, adjust, until it was a perfect fit and curved around him like a glove. And at that moment, while buried deep inside of her, he just had to taste her lips again. He leaned forward, took her mouth and began swallowing every deep, wrenching moan that she made.

And then he began moving back and forth inside of her, thrusting, then retreating, then repeating the process all over again, each thrust aimed with perfect accuracy at her erogenous zone. He lifted her hips, and she dug her fingertips deep into his shoulders and cried out with each stroke he took.

It was at that moment that he actually felt her body explode. Then the sensations that had rippled through her slammed through him as well. He threw his head back; and he felt the muscles in his neck pop; and he breathed in deep, pulling in her scent, which filled the air.

Shudders rammed through him, and he squeezed his eyes shut as his body exploded. His orgasm came with the force of a tidal wave, and he continued to thrust inside her as his groans mingled with her cries of pleasure. And with their bodies fully engaged, their minds unerringly connected, together they left Earth and soared into the clouds as unadulterated pleasure consumed them.

"I need to leave," she said softly.

Reggie turned his head on the pillow and looked over at Wonder. He doubted he could move. He could barely breathe. It was close to morning. They'd made love all night long. As soon as they had ended one session, they'd been quick and eager to start another.

He knew she had to leave. So did he. But he didn't want their one and only night together to end. "You do know there is no reason why we can't—"

She quickly turned toward him and placed a finger on his lips. "Yes, there is. I can't tell you my true identity. It could hurt someone."

He frowned. She wasn't wearing a ring, so quite naturally, he had assumed she wasn't married. What if she...

As if reading his mind, she said, "I don't have a husband. I don't even have a boyfriend."

"Then who?" he asked quickly, trying to understand why they couldn't bring their masquerade to an end. He probably had more to lose than she, because his campaign for the Senate officially began Monday.

"I can't say. This has to be goodbye—"

Before the words were completely out of her mouth, he reached out and pulled her into his arms, knowing this would be the last time he would kiss the lips he had grown so attached to.

Moments later he released her mouth, refusing to say goodbye. She wiggled out of his arms and began re-dressing. He watched her do so, getting turned on all over again.

"I'm getting money out of the ATM to pay for the room," she informed him.

He frowned at her words. "No, you're not."

"I must. It was my idea for us to come here," she said.

"Doesn't matter. Everything has been taken care of, so they won't take any money from you at the front desk. Last night is on me, and I don't regret one minute of spending it with you."

Olivia slipped back into her shoes and gazed across the room at him. He was lying in bed, on top of the

covers. Naked. So immensely male. "And I don't regret anything, either," she said, meaning every word.
She was tempted to do as he wanted—cross the room,
remove his mask and remove hers as well—but she
couldn't. She couldn't even trust herself to kiss him
goodbye. It had to be a clean break for both of them.
"And you sure you don't want me to pay for the room?"
she asked.

"Yes, I'm sure."

"At least let me give you something toward it and—"

"No," he said, declining her offer.

She didn't know how much time passed while they
just stared at each other. But she knew she had to leave.
"I have to go now," she said, as if convincing herself
of that.

He shifted on the bed to take the rose, and offered it
to her. She closed the short distance between them to retrieve it. "At least let me walk you to the door," he said.

She shook her head. "No. I'll see myself out."

And then she quickly walked out of the bedroom.

Reggie pulled himself up in the bed when he heard
the sound of the hotel door closing. He sat on the edge
of the bed, suddenly feeling a sense of loss that touched
his very soul and not understanding how such a thing
was possible.

He stood up to put on his clothes, and it was then
that he snatched off the mask. It had served its purpose.
He reached for his shirt and tie and noticed something
glittering on the carpet. He reached down and picked
it up. It was one of the diamond earrings that she had
been wearing.

He folded the earring in the palm of his hand. He knew at that very moment that if he had to turn Atlanta upside down, he would find his Wonder Woman.

He would find her, and he would keep her.

Chapter 3

"So, Libby, how was the party?"

Olivia, who had been so entrenched in the memories of the night before, hadn't noticed her father standing at the bottom of the stairs. She glanced down at him and smiled. "It was simply wonderful." He didn't need to know that she was speaking not of the party per se but of the intimate party she'd gone to at the Saxon Hotel, with her mystery man.

It had been just before six in the morning when she slipped into her father's home, and knowing he was an early riser, she had dashed up the stairs and showered. She had also put in a call to Terrence, leaving a message on his cell phone that it was okay to delete the text message she had sent to him the night before. And then she had climbed into bed. By the time her head had hit the pillow in her own bed, she had heard her father moving around.

She had enjoyed the best sleep in years. She had awakened to a hungry stomach, and the last person she had expected to meet when she took the stairs to go pillaging in the kitchen was her father. Typically, after early morning church services on Sunday, he hit the country club with his buddies for a game of golf. So why was he still here?

Orin met his daughter on the bottom stair and gave her a hug. "I'm glad you enjoyed yourself. I felt kind of bad that I couldn't attend the ball with you, but I did have to work on that speech."

She looked up at him and, not for the first time, thought that he was definitely a good-looking man, and she was glad he took care of himself by eating right and staying active. "No problem, Dad."

Not wanting him to ask for details about the party, she quickly asked a question of her own. "So why are you home and not out on the golf course?"

He smiled as he tucked her arm in his and escorted her to the kitchen. "Cathy threatened me with dire consequences today if I left before she got the chance to come over and go over my speech."

Olivia smiled but didn't say anything for a moment. Cathy Bristol had been her father's private secretary for almost fifteen years, and Olivia couldn't help but wonder when her father would wake up and realize the woman was in love with him. Olivia had figured it out when she was in her teens, and when she'd gotten older had asked her brothers about it. Like her dad, they'd been clueless. But at least Duan and Terrence had opened their eyes even if her father hadn't. Cathy was a forty-eight-year-old widow who had lost her husband over eighteen years ago, when he died in a car accident, leaving her with two sons to raise.

"So when is Cathy coming? I'd love to see her."

Her father smiled. "Around noon. I'm treating her to lunch here first before I put her to work."

"To review your speech?"

"Yes," he said when they reached the kitchen and he sat down at the table. "She's good at editing things and giving her opinion. As this is my first speech, I want to impress those who hear it. It will be one of those forums in which all the candidates speak."

Olivia nodded as she grabbed an apple out of the fruit bowl on the table and sat down across from him.

Orin frowned. "Surely that's not all you're having for breakfast."

"Afraid so," she said before biting into her apple.

"You're so thin," he pointed out. "You should eat more."

Olivia could only smile. There was no way she could tell her father that she had eaten quite a lot last night. After making love several times, they had ordered room service, eaten until their stomachs were full and then gone back to bed to make love some more.

Deciding to get her father off the subject of her weight, she said, "So, tell me something about this guy who has the audacity to run against my father."

Orin leaned back in his chair. "He's one of those Westmorelands. Prominent family here in Atlanta. He's young, in his early thirties, and owns an accounting firm."

Olivia nodded. She recalled the name, and if she wasn't mistaken, Duan and Terrence had gone to school with some of them. They were a huge family. "So what's his platform? How do the two of you differ?"

"On a number of issues, we're in agreement. The main thing we differ on is whether or not Georgia can support another state-financed university. He thinks we can, and I don't. We have a number of fine colleges and universities in this area. Why on earth would we need another one? Besides, he's inexperienced."

Olivia couldn't help but smile at that, because her father didn't have any political experience, either. In fact, she and her brothers had been shocked when he'd announced he was running for a political office. The only thing they could come up with as to the reason was that his good friend and golfing buddy Senator Albert Reed was retiring and wanted someone to replace him whom he knew and could possibly influence. Not that her father was easily influenced, but he was known to give in under a good argument, without fully standing his ground.

"And young Westmoreland will run on his name recognition since he has a couple of celebrities in the family. One of his cousins is a motorcycle racer, and another is an author."

And your son just happens to be a very well-known former NFL player, she wanted to say. Who you have called upon to appear at a couple of rallies. So you are just as bad.

Olivia said nothing but listened as she took another bite of her apple. At least she tried to listen. More than once her mind took a sharp turn, and she found her thoughts drifting to breath-stopping memories of the tall, dark and handsome man she had met and spent a wonderful night with. She could vividly recall his kisses and the way he had been methodically slow and extremely thorough each time he'd taken her mouth in his, eating away at her lips, unrestrained, unhurried and not distracted.

And there were the times his mouth had touched her everywhere, blazing a trail from her nape to her spine, then all over her chest, tasting her nipples and making her intensely aware of all her hidden passion—passion he'd been able to wrench from her.

The only bad thing about last night was the fact that she had lost one of the diamond earrings she had purchased a year ago in Paris. The earrings had been a gift to herself when she landed her dream job. She would love to get it back, but knew that wouldn't be happening. But she would be the first to admit that the night spent in her one-time lover's arms had been worth the loss.

The ringing of the doorbell claimed her attention and brought her back to the present.

"That must be Cathy," Orin said. He quickly rose from the table and headed to the front door.

Olivia studied her father and couldn't do anything but shake her head. He seemed awfully excited about Cathy's arrival. Olivia couldn't help wondering if perhaps her father had finally awakened and smelled the coffee and just wasn't aware he'd been sniffing the aroma. She had been around her brothers long enough to know that when it came to matters of the heart, men had a tendency to be slow.

She turned in her seat when she heard a feminine voice, Cathy's voice. Olivia smiled when she saw the one woman she felt would be good for her father and again wondered why her father hadn't asked Cathy to be his escort for some of these functions. Cathy was very pretty, and Olivia thought, as she glanced at the two of them walking into the kitchen, that they complemented each other well.

Brent Fairgate waved his hand back and forth in front of Reggie's face. "Hey, man, are you with us, or are you somewhere in la-la land?"

Reggie blinked, and then his gaze focused on the man standing in front of him, before shifting to the woman standing beside him, Pam Wells. Brent had hired Pam as a strategist on a consulting basis.

"Sorry," he said, since there was no use denying they hadn't had his attention. "My mind drifted elsewhere for a moment." There was no way he was going to tell Brent that he was reliving the memories of the prior night. Brent was the most focused man that Reggie knew. Reggie was well aware that Brent wanted him to be just as focused.

"Okay. Then let's go back over the layout for tomorrow," Brent said, handing him a folder filled with papers. "The luncheon is at the Civic Center, and both you and Jeffries will be speaking. The order will be determined by a flip of a coin. You got the speech down pat.

Just make sure you turn on your charm. Jeffries will be doing likewise. Without coming right out and saying it, you will have to make everyone see you as the voice of change. You will have to portray Jeffries as more of the same, someone who represents the status quo."

"Okay. Give me some personal info on Jeffries, other than he's the Holy Terror's father," Reggie said.

Early in his professional football career, Terrence Jeffries had been nicknamed the "Holy Terror" by sportscasters. Reggie understood that Terrence was now a very successful businessman living in the Florida Keys.

"He also has another son, who's a couple years older than the Holy Terror," Pam replied. "He used to be on the Atlanta police force, but now he owns a private investigation company. He's low-key and definitely not in the public eye like Terrence."

Reggie nodded. "That's it? Two sons?"

Pam shook her head. "There's also a daughter, the youngest. She's twenty-seven. An artist who lives in Paris. I understand she's returned home for the campaign."

Reggie lifted a brow. "Why?"

Pam smiled. "To act as her father's escort for all the fund-raisers he'll be expected to attend. From what I understand, he hasn't dated a lot since his wife up and left him."

Reggie frowned. "And when was that?"

"Over twenty-something years ago. He raised his kids as a single father," said Pam.

Reggie nodded, immediately admiring the man for taking on such a task. He was blessed to have both of his parents still living and still married to each other. He couldn't imagine otherwise. He had heard his siblings and cousins talk about the hard work that went into parenting, so he admired any person who did it solo.

"As you know, Orin Jeffries is a corporate attorney at Nettleton Industries. He's worked for them for over thirty years. And he's almost twenty-five years older than you. He'll likely flaunt the age difference and his greater experience," Brent added.

Reggie smiled. "I'm sure that he will."

"Do you need me to look over your speech for tomorrow?" Brent asked.

Reggie met his friend's gaze. "I haven't written it yet." Concern touched Brent's features, and not for the first time, Reggie thought his best friend worried too much.

"But I thought you were going to do it last night, right after you came home from the Firemen's Masquerade Ball," Brent said.

Reggie sighed. There was no way he was going to mention that he hadn't made it home from the ball until this morning, because he had made a pit stop at the Saxon Hotel. Actually, it had been more than a pit stop. The word *quickie* in no way described what he and Wonder Woman had done practically all through the night. They had refused to be rushed.

Before Brent could chew him out, Reggie said, "I'll do it as soon as the two of you leave. If you want to drop by later and look it over, then feel free to do so."

A stern look appeared on Brent's face. "And don't think that I won't."

Reggie rolled his eyes. "Just don't return before six this evening."

Brent raised a brow. "Why?"

"Because I need to take a nap."

Brent chuckled. "You never take naps."

Determined not to explain anything, Reggie said, "I know, but today I definitely need one."

As soon as Pam and Brent left, Reggie called and checked in with his parents. Usually on Sunday he would drop by for dinner, and he didn't want his mother to worry when he didn't make an appearance.

After convincing Sarah Westmoreland that he was not coming down with a flu bug and that he just needed to rest, he was ready to end the call, but she kept him on the phone longer than he'd planned to give him a soup recipe…like he would actually take the time to make it. Not that she figured he would. She was just hoping he had a lady friend available to do his bidding.

He couldn't help but smile as he climbed the stairs to his bedroom. His mother's one wish in life was to live to see her six sons all married and herself and his father surrounded by grandchildren. A bout with breast cancer a few years ago had made her even more determined to see each one of her sons happily married.

Her dream had come true—almost. Jared's recent announcement that he and his wife, Dana, would become parents in the fall meant that all of James and Sarah Westmoreland's sons—with the exception of him— were married and either had kids or were expecting them. Quade had blown everyone away with his triplets. But then multiple births ran in the Westmoreland family.

When he reached his bedroom, he began stripping off his clothes, remembering when he had stripped for an audience of one the night before. He had been aware that Wonder Woman's eyes had been directed on him while he'd taken off each piece...the same way his eyes had been on her.

As he slid between the covers, he promised himself that once he woke up, he would have slept off the memories and would be focused on the present again. That morning he'd thought about trying to find his mystery woman, and he still intended to do that, but he owed it to Brent and his campaign staff to stay focused and put all his time and energy into winning this election.

But still...

He thought about the lone earring he had in his dresser drawer. On the way into the office, he would stop by Jared's favorite jewelry store, Garbella Jewelers, to see if they could possibly tell him anything about the earring, like who had made it and, possibly, from which store it had been purchased. Checking on something like that shouldn't take too long and wouldn't make him lose focus.

As he felt himself drifting off to sleep, his mind was flooded with more memories. He wondered how long this fascination, this mind-reeling, gut-wrenching obsession with his mystery woman, would last.

He wasn't sure, but he intended to enjoy it while it did.

* * *

Olivia sat in the chair across the room, and her observant eye zeroed in on her father and Cathy. She tried not to chuckle when she noticed how they would look at each other when the other one wasn't watching. Boy, they had it bad, but in a way, she was glad. Sooner or later, her father would realize that Cathy was the best thing to ever happen to him. Even now, after working as his secretary for over fifteen years, their relationship was still professional. She knew in time that would change, and she would do her part to help it along.

"Dad?"

Orin looked up from his seat behind his desk and glanced over at her. Cathy was standing next to his chair. They'd had their heads together while Cathy critiqued his speech. "Yes, sweetheart?"

"Why did you send for me to be your escort for all these fund-raising events when you had Cathy right here?"

As if on cue, Cathy blushed, and her father's jaw dropped as if he was surprised she would ask something like that. Before he could pick up his jaw to respond, Cathy spoke, stammering through her explanation.

"T-there's no way Orin can do something like that. I'm his secretary."

Olivia smiled. "Oh." What she was tempted to say was that secretary or no secretary, Cathy was also the woman her father couldn't keep his eyes off. She couldn't wait until she talked to Duan and Terrence.

And then, as if by luck or fate, since it also seemed to be on cue, her cell phone rang, and when she stood and pulled it out of her back jeans pocket, she saw the call was from Terrence.

Knowing it was best to take the call privately, she said, "Excuse me a moment while I take this." She quickly walked out of the room and closed the office door behind her.

"Yes, Terrence?"

"What the hell is going on with you, Libby? Why did you text me from an unknown number and then call this morning and ask that the text be deleted?"

Olivia nervously licked her lips. One thing about Terrence was that he would ask questions, but if she gave him a reason that sounded remotely plausible, he would let it go, whereas Duan would continue to ask questions.

"Last night I went to this charity party in Dad's place and met a guy. He asked me to follow him to a nightclub in Stone Mountain, and I did, but I felt I should take precautions."

"That was a good idea. Smart girl. So how was the club?"

"Umm, nice, but it didn't compare to Club Hurricane," she said, knowing he would like to hear that she thought the nightclub he owned in the Keys was at the top of the list.

"You're even smarter than I thought. So how's Dad? He hasn't dropped out of this Senate race yet?"

Olivia smiled. Terrence and Duan were taking bets that sooner or later, when Orin Jeffries got a taste of what real politics were like, he would call it quits. At first she had agreed with them, but now she wasn't so sure. "I don't know, Terrence. I think he's going all the way with this one."

"Umm, that's interesting. I still think Reed pushed Dad into running for his own benefit. I'm going to give Duan a call. We might need to talk to Dad about this."

"You might be too late. The first forum is tomorrow, and he's giving a speech. He's been working on it for two days. The only good thing coming out of all this is that he and Cathy are working together," she said.

"Libby, they always work closely together. She's his secretary."

"Yes, but they are working closely together in a different way, on issues other than Nettleton Industries business. In fact, she's over here now."

She could hear her brother chuckle. "Still determined to play Cupid, are you?"

"I might as well while I'm here, since I have nothing else to do." She thought of Jack Sprat. She had been tempted earlier to pull out her art pad and do some sketches to pass the time. She had thought about drawing her mystery man with the mask and then playing around to see if she could draw sketches of how she imagined he might look without the mask. She had eventually talked herself out of it.

"Well, I'll be coming home in a couple of weeks, so stay out of trouble until then, sport."

She laughed. "I can't make you any promises, but I'll try."

Chapter 4

Brent had given his speech a thumbs-up, so Reggie felt confident it would go over well. He walked around the luncheon reception, greeting all those who had arrived to attend the forum. This would be the first of several gatherings designed to give voters a chance to learn each candidate's agenda. He had met Orin Jeffries when he'd first arrived and thought the older man was a likable guy.

A number of his family members were present and a number of his friends as well. These were people who believed in him, supported him and were counting on him to make changes to some of the present policies.

A career in politics had been the last thing on his mind and had never been his heart's desire, until recently. He'd become outraged at the present senators' refusal to recognize the state's need for an additional college. More and more young people were making the decision to acquire higher learning, and the lower tuition costs of state universities compared to private universities were a key factor in the process. It was hard enough for students to get the funds they needed to go to college, but when they were refused entrance into schools because of campus overcrowding, that was unacceptable. Anyone who wanted a college education should be able to get one. Georgia needed another state-run college, and he was willing to fight for it.

The University of Georgia was the oldest public university in the state and had been established by an act of the Georgia General Assembly over two centuries ago. Just as there had been a need for greater educational opportunities then, there was a need now. In fact, land had been donated for that very purpose ten years ago. Now some lawmakers were trying to use a loophole in the land grant to appropriate the land to build a recreation area—a park that would be largely composed of a golf course.

Reggie was aware that getting elected would only be the first hurdle. Once he got in the Senate, he would then have the job of convincing his fellow lawmakers of the need for an additional state university as well.

He glanced at his watch. In less than ten minutes, lunch would be served, and then halfway through lunch, each person seeking office would get an opportunity to speak. There were about eight candidates in attendance.

Deciding he needed to switch his focus for a moment, he thought about his visit to Garbella Jewelers that morning. Mr. Garbella's assessment of the earring was that it was a fine piece of craftsmanship. The diamonds were real and of good quality. He doubted the piece had been purchased in this country. He thought the way the diamonds were set was indicative of European jewelry making. Mr. Garbella had gone on to say that the pair had cost a lot of money. After visiting with the jeweler, Reggie was more determined than ever to find his Wonder Woman and return the missing earring to her.

Quade and his cousin Cole, who'd both recently retired—Quade from a top security job with the government and Cole from the Texas Rangers—had joined forces to start a network of security companies, some of which would include private investigation. He wondered if they would be interested in taking him on as their first client.

He looked at his watch again before glancing across the room and meeting Brent's eye. He had less than ten minutes to mingle, and then everyone would be seated for lunch. He hated admitting it, but he felt in his element. Maybe a political career was his calling, after all.

Olivia waited until just moments before the luncheon was to begin to make an entrance and join her father. According to his campaign manager, Marc Norris, her entrance was part of a coordinated strategy. He wanted her to ease into the room and work one side of it while her father worked the other. Subtle yet thorough.

When he had mentioned his strategy that morning while joining Olivia and her father for breakfast, she had gotten annoyed that the man assumed she didn't have any common sense. Evidently, Norris doubted she could hold her own during any discussion. But not to cause any problems, she had decided to keep her opinions to herself.

She saw noticeable interest in her from the moment she stepped into the room. Most people knew that Orin Jeffries had a daughter, but a number of them had forgotten or shoved the fact to the back of their mind in the wake of his two well-known sons. Practically everybody in the country knew of the Holy Terror, whether they were football enthusiasts or not. Since retiring from football, Terrence had been known for his work in a number of high-profile charities. He also commentated on a popular radio talk show, *Sports Talk,* in South Florida, which might go into syndication the next year. Duan had made the national headlines a few years before, when his undercover work as a detective had resulted in the exposure of a couple of unsavory individuals who'd been intent on bringing organized crime to Georgia.

But it didn't bother her in the least that her brothers' good deeds had somehow made people forget about her. Besides, she hadn't lived in this country in four years, returning only on occasion to visit, mainly around the holidays.

She began mingling, introducing herself as Orin Jeffries's daughter, and actually got a kick out of seeing first surprise and then acknowledgment on many faces. One such incident was taking place now.

"Why, Olivia, how good it is to see you again. It's

been a while since you've been back home. But I do remember you now. You must be extremely proud of your father and brothers."

"Yes, I am, Mrs. Hancock, and how is Beau? I understand he's doing extremely well. You must be proud of him."

She watched the older woman's eyes light up as she went into a spiel about her son. She was a proud mother. Olivia knew Beau from school. Unless he had changed over the years, Beau Hancock was an irrefutable jerk. He'd thought he was the gift to every girl at Collinshill High School.

She glanced down at her watch. She had ten minutes left before everyone would take their seats for lunch. She had called the Saxon Hotel on the off chance that someone from housekeeping had come across her diamond earring and turned it in. That hadn't been the case. A part of her was disappointed that it had not been.

There was still one section of the room she needed to cover. Mrs. Hancock, in singing Beau's praises, had taken up quite a bit of her time. Now she was again making her way through the crowds, speaking to everyone, as Norris had suggested.

"You're doing a marvelous job working the room," Senator Reed whispered. The older man had suddenly appeared by her side.

She forced a smile. For some reason, she'd never cared for him. "Thanks."

She had already met several of the candidates since entering the room, but she had yet to meet the man who would be her father's real competition, Reggie West-moreland.

As she continued mingling and heading to the area where Reggie Westmoreland was supposedly rubbing elbows with the crowd, her curiosity about the man who opposed her father couldn't help but be piqued. She started to ask Senator Reed about him but changed her mind. The senator's opinion wouldn't be the most valuable.

"You look nice, Olivia."

She glanced up at the senator, who seemed deter-mined to remain by her side. He was a few years older than her father, and for some reason, he had always made her feel uncomfortable.

"Thanks, Senator." She refrained from saying that he also looked nice, which he did. Like her father, he was a good-looking man for his age, but Senator Reed always had an air of snobbery about him, like he was born with too low expectations of others.

"It was my suggestion that your father send for you." When she stopped walking and glanced at him, with a raised brow, he added, "He was in a dilemma, and I thought bringing you home to be his escort was the perfect answer."

She bit back a retort, that bringing her home had not been the perfect answer. Being in that dilemma might have prompted her dad to ask Cathy to attend some of those functions with him. No telling how things would have taken off from there if the senator hadn't butted in.

She was about to open her mouth, to tell Senator Reed that her father was old enough to think for himself, when, all of a sudden, for no reason at all, she pulled in a quick breath. She glanced up ahead, and no more than four feet in front of her, there stood a man with his back to her.

The first thing she noticed about him was his height. He was taller then the men he was talking to. And there was something about his particular height, and the way his head tilted at an angle as he listened to what one of the men was saying, that held her spellbound.

He was dressed in a suit, and she could only admire how it fit him. The broadness of his shoulders and the tapering of his waist sent a feeling of familiarity through her. She stopped walking momentarily and composed herself, not understanding what was happening to her.

"Is anything wrong, Olivia?"

She glanced up at Senator Reed and saw concern in his eyes. She knew she couldn't tell him what she was thinking. There was no way she could voice her suspicions to anyone.

She needed to go somewhere to pull herself together, to consider the strong possibility that the man standing not far away was her Jack Sprat. Or could it be that she was so wrapped up in the memories of that night that she was quick to assume that any man of a tall stature who possessed broad shoulders had to be her mystery man?

"Olivia?"

Instead of saying anything, she shifted her gaze from the senator to look again at the man, whose back was still to her. It was at that precise moment that he slowly turned around, and his gaze settled on her. In a quick second, she pulled in a sharp breath as she scanned his face, and her gaze settled on a firm jaw that had an angular plane. Her artist's eye also picked up other things, and they were things others would probably not notice—the stark symmetry of his face, which was clear with or without a mask, the shape of his head and the alignment of his ears from his cheeks. These were things she recognized.

Things she remembered.

And she knew, without a doubt, that she was staring into the face of the man whom she had spent the night with on Saturday. The man whose body had given her hours upon hours of immeasurable pleasure. And impossible as it seemed—because they'd kept their masks in place the entire time—she had a feeling from the way he was staring back at her just as intently as she was staring at him that he had recognized her, too.

"Olivia?"

She broke eye contact with the stranger to gaze up at the senator. The man was becoming annoying, but at the moment, he was the one person who could tell her exactly what she needed to know. "Senator Reed, that guy up there, the one who turned around to look at me. Who is he?"

The senator followed her gaze and frowned deeply. "The two of you had to meet eventually. That man, young lady, is the enemy."

She swallowed deeply before saying, "The enemy?"

"Yes, the enemy. He's the man that's opposing your father in his bid for the Senate."

Olivia's head began spinning before the senator could speak his next words.

"That, my dear," the senator went on to say, "is Reggie Westmoreland."

It was her.

Reggie knew it with every breath he took. Her lips were giving her away. And he wasn't sure what part of him was recognizable to her, but he knew just as sure as they were standing there, staring at each other, that they were as intimately familiar to each other as any two people could be.

It was strange. He'd been standing here with Brent, his brother Jared, his cousins Dare and Thorn, and Thorn's wife, Tara. They'd all been listening to Thorn, a nationally known motorcycle builder and racer, who was telling them about an order he'd received to build a bike for actor Matt Damon. Then, all of a sudden, he'd felt a strange sensation, followed by a stirring in the lower part of his gut.

He had turned around, and he'd looked straight into her face. His Wonder Woman.

He couldn't lay claim to recognizing any of her other facial features, but her lips were a dead giveaway. Blatantly sensual, he had kissed them, tongued them, licked them and tasted them to his heart's content. He knew the shape of them in his sleep, knew their texture, knew what part of them was so sensitive that when he'd touched her there, she had moaned.

She looked totally stunning in the stylish skirt and blouse she was wearing. The outfit complemented her figure. Even if he hadn't met her before, he would be trying his best to do so now. Out of his peripheral vision, he noted a number of men looking at her, and he understood why. She was gorgeous.

He lost control, and his feet began moving toward her.

"Reggie, where are you going?" Brent asked.

He didn't respond, because he truly didn't know what he could say. He continued walking until he came to a stop directly in front of the senator and the woman. The senator, he noted, was frowning. The woman's gaze hadn't left his. She seemed as entranced as he was.

He found his voice to say, "Good afternoon, Senator Reed. It's good seeing you again."

It was a lie, and he realized the senator knew it, but he didn't care. Approaching him would force the man to make introductions, and if it took a lie, then so be it.

"Westmoreland, I see you've decided to go through with it," replied the senator.

Reggie gave the man a smile that didn't quite reach his eyes. "Of course." He then shifted his gaze back to the woman. The senator would be outright rude not to make an introduction, and one thing Reggie did know about the senator was that he believed in following proper decorum.

"And let me introduce you to Olivia Jeffries. Olivia, this is Reggie Westmoreland," the senator said.

At the mention of her name, Reggie's mind went into a tailspin. "Jeffries?" he replied.

"Yes," the senator said as a huge, smug smile touched his lips. "Jeffries. She's Orin Jeffries's daughter, who is visiting from Paris and will remain here during the duration of the campaign."

Reggie nodded as his eyes once again settled on Olivia. He then reached out his hand. "Olivia, it's nice meeting you. I'm sure your father is excited about having you home."

"Thank you," replied Olivia.

They both felt it the moment their hands touched, and they both knew it. It was those same feelings that had driven them to leave the party on Saturday night and to go somewhere to be alone, with the sole purpose of getting intimately connected. Reggie opened his mouth to say something, and then a voice from the microphone stopped him.

"Everyone is asked to take a seat so lunch can be served. Your table number is located on your ticket."

"It was nice meeting you, Mr. Westmoreland," Olivia said, not sure what else to say at the moment.

She honestly had thought she would not see him again, not this soon, not ever. And now that he knew their predicament—that she was the daughter of the man who was his opponent in this political race—she hoped that he would accept the inevitable. Nothing had changed. Even with their identities exposed, there could never be anything between them beyond what had happened Saturday night.

"It was nice meeting you as well, Ms. Jeffries," said Reggie. And then he did something that was common among Frenchmen but rare with Americans. Bending slightly, he lifted her hand to his lips and kissed it before turning and walking away.

Chapter 5

Olivia found that every time she lifted her fork to her mouth, her gaze would automatically drift to the next table, the one where Reggie Westmoreland was sitting. And each time, unerringly, their gazes would meet.

After their introduction, she had excused herself to the senator, smiling and saying she needed to go to the ladies' room. Once there she had taken a deep breath. It was a wonder she hadn't passed out. With his mask in place, Reggie Westmoreland had been handsome. Without his mask, he took her breath away. While standing in front of him, she'd had to tamp down her emotions and the sensations flowing through her.

His eyes were very dark, almost chocolate, and their shape, which she had been denied seeing on Saturday night, was almond, beneath thick brows. It had taken everything in her power to force her muscles to relax. And when he had taken her hand and kissed the back of it before walking off, she'd thought she would swoon right then and there.

"Libby, are you okay? You've barely touched your meal," her father said, interrupting her thoughts.

She glanced over to him and smiled. "Yes, Daddy, I'm fine."

"Westmoreland is the cause of it," said Senator Reed, jumping in. "She met him right before we took our seats. He probably gave her an upset stomach."

Her father frowned. "Was he rude to you, sweetheart?" he asked, with deep concern tinged with anger.

She was opening her mouth to assure her father that Reggie hadn't been rude when Senator Reed said, "He was quite taken with her, Orin."

She ignored the senator's comment, thinking that he didn't know the half of it. Instead, she answered her father. "No, he wasn't rude, Dad. In fact, although we spoke only briefly, I thought he was rather nice." She smiled. "Quite the charmer."

"The enemy is never nice or charming, Olivia. Remember that," the senator said, speaking to her like she was a child. "I strongly suggest that during this campaign, you stay away from him."

She was opening her mouth to tell the senator that she truly didn't give a royal damn about what he would strongly suggest when her father spoke.

"You don't have to worry about Libby, Al. She's a smart girl. She would never get mixed up with the likes of Westmoreland."

The likes of Westmoreland? Was there something about Reggie that her father and the senator knew but that she didn't? she wondered. Granted, that might be true, since she had arrived in the country on Friday. But still, she heard intense dislike in her father's voice and pondered the reason for it. Did it have to do only with the campaign, or was there more? Marc Norris was the only other person at their table, and he wasn't saying anything. But then Norris didn't look like the type to gossip. She didn't know him well. In fact, she had just met him on Friday evening.

"Well, if I didn't know better, I'd think Olivia and Westmoreland had met before," replied Senator Reed.

The senator's words almost made her drop her fork. She had to tighten her grip on it. She thought about Reggie. Had their reaction to each other been that obvious?

There was a lag in the conversation at the table, and she knew from the brief moment of silence that the men were waiting for her to respond one way or the other. So she did. "Then it's a good thing that you know better, Senator, isn't it?"

She said the words so sweetly, there was no way that he or anyone else could tell if she was being sincere or smart-alecky. Before any further conversation could take place, one of the sponsors of the event got up and went to the podium to announce that the speeches were about to begin.

"Okay, Reggie. What's going on with you and that woman at the other table? The one you can't seem to keep your eyes off," Brent said in a whisper as he leaned close to Reggie.

Reggie lifted a brow. "What makes you think something is going on?"

Brent chuckled. "I have eyes. I can see. You do know she's Jeffries's daughter."

Reggie leaned back in his chair. He couldn't eat another mouthful, although he hadn't eaten much. He was still trying to recover from the fact that he and his mystery woman had officially met. "Yes, the senator introduced us. And grudgingly, I might add. He didn't seem too happy to do so," Reggie said.

"Figures. He probably wants her for himself." At Reggie's surprised look, Brent went on to explain. "Reed is into young women big-time. I once dated someone who worked at his office. He tried coming on to her several times, and she ended up quitting when the old man wouldn't give up no matter how many times she tried turning him off. The man takes sexual harassment to a whole new level."

Reggie's jaw tightened. The thought that the senator could be interested in Olivia, even remotely, made his blood boil. "But he's friends with her father."

"And that's supposed to mean something?" Brent countered, trying to keep his voice low. "I guess it would mean something to honorable men, but Reed is not honorable. We don't have a term-limit law here, so it makes you wonder why he isn't seeking another term. Rumor has it that he was given a choice to either step down or have his business—namely, his affairs with women half his age—spread across the front pages of

the newspapers. I guess since he's still married and his
wife is wealthier than he is, although she's bedridden,
he didn't want that."

Reggie shook his head. "Well, he shouldn't concern
himself with Olivia Jeffries."

"And why is that?"

Reggie didn't say anything for fear of saying too
much. In the end, he didn't have to respond, because it
was his turn to speak.

"You gave a nice speech, Dad. You did a wonderful job," Olivia said once she and her father got home.

"Yes, but so did Westmoreland," Orin said, heading
for the kitchen. "He tried to make me look like someone who doesn't support higher education."

"But only because you are against any legislation
to build another state university," she reminded him.

"We have enough colleges, Libby."

She decided to back away from the conversation because she didn't agree with her father on this issue.
The last thing she wanted was to get into an argument
with him about Reggie Westmoreland and his speech.
If nothing else, she had reached the conclusion at dinner that neither her father nor the senator wanted her to
get involved in any way with the competition.

She glanced at her watch. "I think I'm going to
change and then go to the park and paint for a while."

"Yes, you should do that while you still have good
sunlight left. And feel free to take my car, since I won't
need it anymore today. That rental car of yours is too

small," Orin said, already pulling off his tie as he headed up the stairs.

She could tell he was somewhat upset about how the luncheon had gone. Evidently, he had assumed, or had been led to believe, that winning the Senate seat would be a piece of cake. It probably would have been if Reggie Westmoreland hadn't decided to throw his hat into the ring at the eleventh hour.

And she had to admit that although her father's speech had been good, Reggie's speech had been better. Instead of making generalities, he had hammered down specifics, and he had delivered the speech eloquently. And it had seemed that as his gaze moved around the room while he was speaking, his eyes would seek her out. Each time they'd done so and she'd gazed into them, she'd felt she could actually see barely concealed desire in their dark depths. She had sat there with the hardened nipples of her breasts pressed tightly against her blouse the entire time.

And all she'd had to do was to study his lips to recall how those same lips had left marks all over her body, how they, along with his tongue, had moved over these same breasts, licking, sucking and nibbling on them.

After the luncheon was over, instead of dallying about, she had rushed her father out, needing to leave to avoid any attempts Reggie might have made to approach her again. She would not have been able to handle it if he had done so, and it would only have raised Senator Reed's suspicions. For some reason, the older man was making her every move his business.

Olivia had changed clothes and was gathering her

art bag to sling over her shoulders when her cell phone rang. Not recognizing the local number, she answered the call.

"Hello?"

"Meet me someplace."

She got weak in the knees at the sound of the deep, husky voice. She really didn't have to ask, but she did so anyway. "Who is this?"

"This is Reggie Westmoreland, Wonder Woman."

Olivia pulled into the parking lot of Chase's Place, wondering for the umpteenth time how she had let Reggie Westmoreland talk her into meeting him there. The restaurant, he'd said, was closed on Mondays, but since he knew the owner, there would not be a problem with them meeting there for privacy.

When she'd indicated she did not want to be seen meeting with him, he'd told her to park in the rear of the building. She hated the idea of everything being so secretive, but she knew it was for the best.

Of all the never-in-a-million-years coincidences, why did she have to have an affair—one night or otherwise—with the one man her father could not stand at the moment?

Doing as Reggie had advised, she drove around to the rear and parked beside a very nice silver-gray Mercedes, the same one she'd seen Reggie driving Saturday night. After getting out and checking her watch for the time, she walked up to the back door of the restaurant and knocked. It opened immediately. A man who was almost as tall as Reggie and just as handsome opened the door and smiled at her before stepping aside to let her in.

"Olivia?" he asked, continuing to smile, as he closed the door behind her.

She was so busy studying his face, noting the similarities between him and Reggie, that she almost jumped when he uttered her name. Like Reggie, he was extremely handsome, but she didn't miss the gold band on his finger. "Yes?" she said finally.

"I'm Chase Westmoreland," he said, extending his hand. "Reggie is already here and is in one of the smaller offices, waiting for you. I'll take you to him."

"Thanks." And then, because curiosity got the best of her, she asked, "Are you one of Reggie's brothers?"

The man's chuckle floated through the air as he led her down a hallway. "No, Reggie has five brothers, but I'm not one of them. I'm his cousin."

"Oh. The two of you favor one another," she pointed out.

"Yes, all we Westmorelands look alike."

After walking down a long hallway, they stopped in front of a closed door. "Reggie is in here," Chase said, grinning. "It was nice meeting you."

Olivia smiled. "And it was nice meeting you as well, Chase." And then he was gone. She turned toward the closed door and took a deep breath before turning the handle.

Reggie stood the moment he heard voices on the other side of the door. This was the only place he could think of where he and Olivia could meet without fear of a reporter of some sort invading their privacy. The political campaign had begun officially today, and already all the sides were trying to dig up something on the others.

He'd told Brent that he wanted a campaign that focused strictly on the issues. He wasn't into dirty political games. He felt the voters should get to know the candidates, learn their stance on the issues and then decide which offered more of what they were looking for. If they wanted something different, then he was their man, and if they were used to the do-nothing agenda that Reed had implemented over the past four years, then they needed to go with Jeffries, since it was a sure bet that he was Reed's clone.

As soon as the door opened, his heart began hammering wildly in his chest, and the moment Olivia walked into the room and their gazes met, it took everything he possessed not to cross the floor and pull her into his arms and taste those lips he'd enjoyed so much a couple of nights ago.

Instead of coming farther into the room, she closed the door behind her and then leaned back on it, watching him. Waiting. His hands balled into fists at his sides. He smiled and said, "Wonder Woman." It wasn't a question; it was a statement. He knew who she was.

The butterflies in Olivia's stomach intensified as they flew off in every direction. As she looked across the room at the extremely handsome man, she couldn't help but pose the one question that had been on her mind since they'd met earlier, at the luncheon. "How did you recognize me?" she asked in a soft-spoken voice.

He smiled, and she actually felt her heart stop. She felt her body begin to get hot all over. "Your lips gave you away. I recognized them. I would know your lips anywhere," he said. His voice was deep and throaty.

Olivia frowned, finding that strange. But it must have made some sense, at least to him, because he *had* been able to recognize her.

"What about you? You recognized me also. How?" he asked.

"I'm an artist, at least I am in my spare time. I study faces. I analyze every symmetrical detail. Although you were wearing a mask, and I couldn't see the upper part of your face, I zeroed in on the parts I could see." She decided not to tell him that there was more to it than his face. It had been his height that had first drawn her attention, and the way he'd tilted his head and his broad shoulders. If she could find the words to describe him, they would be, in addition to handsome—tall, dark... Westmoreland.

"I guess both of us can see things others might miss," he said.

"Yes, I guess we can," she agreed.

The room got silent, and she could feel it. That same sexual chemistry that had overtaken them that night, that had destroyed their senses to the point where they hadn't wanted to do anything else but go somewhere and be alone together, was still potent.

"Please come join me. I promise not to bite."

His words broke into her thoughts, and she couldn't help but smile. It was on the tip of her tongue to say, yes, he did bite and that she'd had numerous passion marks on her body to prove it. However, she had a feeling from the glint in his eyes that he'd realized the slipup the moment she had. His eyes darkened, and she felt heat settling everywhere his gaze touched.

She breathed in a deep breath before moving away from the door. She glanced around. The room was apparently a little game room. It had a love seat, a card table, a refrigerator and a television.

"This is where my cousins and brothers get together to play cards on occasion," said Reggie, breaking into her thoughts. "They used to rotate at each other's homes, but after they married and started having kids, they couldn't express themselves like they wanted whenever they were losing. So we decided to find someplace to go where we could be as loud and as colorful as we wanted to be."

She nodded and remembered how things were when her brothers used to have their friends over for poker. Some of their choice words would burn her ears. She then crossed the room to sit on the love seat.

He remained standing and was staring at her, making her feel uncomfortable. She cleared her throat. "You wanted to meet with me," she said, reminding him of why they were there.

He smiled. "Yes, and do you know why?"

"Yes," she said, holding his gaze. "It wouldn't take much to figure out that now that you know my father is one of the men you'll be running against in a few months, you want to establish an understanding between us. You want us to pretend that Saturday night never happened and that we've never met."

He continued to stare at her intently. "Is that what you think?"

She blinked. "Yes, of course. Under these circumstances, there's no way we can be seen together or even let anyone in on the fact that we know each other."

"I don't see why not. I'm running against your father, not you, so it shouldn't matter," he said.

Olivia felt her heart pounding hard in her chest. "But it does matter. Orin Jeffries is my father, and he and his campaign staff consider you the enemy," she said truthfully, although she hadn't meant to do so.

Reggie shook his head. "It's unfortunate they feel that way. I'm not his enemy. I'm his opponent in a Senate race. It's nothing personal, and I was hoping no one would make it such."

Olivia didn't know what to say. She knew Senator Reed, who seemed to be calling the shots as to how her father ran his campaign, could be ruthless at times. She had overheard the whispered conversations that took place at her table during lunch. She knew that the man had no intentions of letting this be a clean campaign, and that bothered her because it was so unlike her father to get involved in something so manipulative and underhanded.

"I'm sorry, but it will be personal. I don't agree, but politics is politics," she heard herself saying, knowing it wasn't an acceptable excuse. "If I became involved with you in any way, it would be equal to treason in my father's eyes. Things are too complicated."

"Only if we let them be. I still say us meeting and

going out on occasion don't involve your father, just me and you."

She shook her head as she stood. It was time to go. She really should not have come. "I need to go."

"But you just got here," he said softly in that sexy voice that did things to her nervous system.

"I know, but coming here was a mistake," she said.

"Then why did you?" he asked softly.

She met his gaze and knew she would tell him the truth. "I felt that I should. Saturday night was a first of its kind for me. I've never left a party with someone I truly didn't know, and I've never had a one-night stand. But I did with you because I felt the chemistry. One of the reasons I came today was that I needed to see if the chemistry between us was real or a figment of my imagination."

"And what's your verdict?" he asked, holding her gaze.

She didn't hesitate in responding. "It's real."

"Does that frighten you?"

"It does not so much frighten me as confuse me. Like I said, I've never responded to a man this way before."

"And what was the other reason you came tonight?"

"We never took our masks off, and I needed to know how you were able to recognize me today. I got the answers to both of my questions, so I should leave now."

"But what about me? Aren't you interested in knowing why I wanted to see you again? Why I asked for us to meet?" He was staring intently at her, and his gaze seemed to touch her all over.

"Why did you want to see me?" she asked.

He slowly moved across the room to stand in front of her, and her pulse began beating rapidly, and heat began to settle between her thighs from his closeness. "Your lips were one reason."

"My lips?" she asked, raising a brow. He seemed to be searching her face, but she could tell his main focus was her lips.

"I claimed them as mine that night," he said in a husky whisper. "I just needed to know if they still are."

And before she could catch her next breath, he pulled her into his arms and captured her mouth with his.

They were still his.

This was what he needed to know. This was the very reason he had kept breathing since Saturday, Reggie thought as he hungrily mated with Olivia's mouth. The memories that had consumed him over the past forty-eight hours had nothing on the real thing. And she was responding to his kiss, feasting on his mouth as greedily as he was feasting on hers. Their masks were gone but not their passion.

He hadn't expected the fires to ignite so quickly, but already they were practically burning out of control. Her body was pressed fully against his, and he could feel every heated inch of her, just like he was certain she could feel every inch of him. Hard. Aroused. He knew he needed to pull back from her mouth to take a much-needed breath, but he couldn't. He had thought of kissing her, dreamed of kissing her, every since the morning they'd parted. His tongue was tangling with hers, and it seemed he couldn't get enough.

Instantly, he knew the moment she began withdrawing, and he pulled back, but not before tracing the outline of her lips with the tip of his tongue while tamping down on the stimulating effect the kiss had had on him.

"I really do need to leave." Her words lacked conviction, and he couldn't help but notice that she had wrapped her arms around his neck and hadn't yet released him. He also took note that her mouth was mere inches from his, and she hadn't pulled back.

Making a quick decision for both of them, he said, "Please stay and let's talk. Will you stay a while longer if I promise not to kiss you again? There's so much I want to know about you. I won't ask you anything about your father and his campaign, just about you."

"What good would it do, Reggie?" she asked, saying his name for the first time. The sound of it off her lips produced flutters in the pit of his stomach.

"I think it will appease our curiosity and maybe help us make some sense as to why we became attracted to each other so quickly and so deeply," he responded. "Why the chemistry between us is so strong."

Olivia pulled her arms from around his neck, thinking that what he was suggesting wasn't a good idea, but neither was kissing. But then she really didn't want to leave, and she had to admit that she'd wondered why they had hit it off so quickly and easily. But it didn't take a rocket scientist to figure out some of the reasons. He was an extremely handsome man, something she had recognized even with the mask. And his approach that night had not been egotistical or arrogant. She had somehow known he was someone she could have fun with and whose company she could enjoy.

And those things had been verified in the most intimate way.

"And we'll just talk?" she asked, making sure they understood each other.

"Yes, and about no one but us. That way you can't feel disloyal to your father."

She inhaled deeply. "But I still do," she admitted openly.

He didn't say anything for a moment. "Let me ask you something." At her nod, he asked, "If we would have met at any other time and if I was not your father's political opponent, would he have a problem with you dating me?"

She knew the answer to that, since her father had never been the kind of dad who cross-examined his children's dates. He had always accepted her judgment in that area. Now, her brothers had been another matter, especially Duan. "No, I think he wouldn't have a problem with it," she said truthfully.

"That's good to know, and that's why we should move forward on the premise that the campaign should not affect our relationship." His voice and smile conveyed that he truly believed what he was saying.

"But how can it not?" she asked, wishing things were that simple.

"Because we won't let it," he responded. "First of all, we need to acknowledge that we are in a relationship, Olivia."

She shook her head. "I can't do that, because we really don't have a relationship. We just slept together that night."

"No, it was more than that. It might have been a one-night stand, but I never intended *not* to find you after you left the Saxon on Sunday morning. In fact, I took this to a jewelry store this morning to see if I could trace where it was originally purchased," he said, pulling her diamond earring from his pocket. "It might have taken me a while, but eventually, I would have found you, even if I had to tear this town up doing so," he said, handing the earring to her.

She took it and studied it, remembering just when she had purchased the pair. It had been when she'd gotten her first position at the Louvre Museum. These diamonds had cost more than the amount of her first paycheck. But it had been a way for her to celebrate.

"Thank you for returning it." She slipped the earring into her pants pocket and then looked back at him. "So, what do you want to talk about?"

"I want to know everything about you. Over dinner. In here. Just the two of us."

She licked her lips and noticed immediately how his gaze had been drawn to the gesture. "And you promise no kissing, right?"

He chuckled. "Not unless you initiate it. If you do, then I won't turn you down."

She couldn't help but smile at that. "You mentioned dinner, but the restaurant isn't open today."

"No, it isn't, but Chase will make an exception for us. Will you join me here for dinner so we can talk and get to know each other?"

She was very much aware that if her father knew she was here, spending time with Reggie, he would think she was being disloyal, but she knew she truly wasn't. If at any time Reggie shifted the conversation to her father, as if pumping her for information about him, she would leave. But for now, she owed it to herself to do something that made her happy for a change, as long as she was not hurting anyone. If Duan or Terrence had been caught up in a similar situation, there was no way her father would have asked them to stop seeing that person. She should not be made the exception.

Olivia knew Reggie was waiting for her answer. "And our time here together will be kept confidential?"

He smiled. "Yes. Like I said, this is about you and me, and not the campaign. As far as I'm concerned, one has nothing to do with the other."

"Then, yes, I'll join you here for dinner," she said after taking a long, deep breath.

Chapter 6

"I know your favorite color is lavender, but tell me something else about Olivia Jeffries, and before you ask, I want to know everything," Reggie said as he sat in the chair at the table while Olivia sat across from him, on the love seat, with her feet curled beneath her. They were both sipping wine and trying to rekindle that comfort zone between them.

Chase had been kind enough to take their food order and had indicated that he would be serving dinner to them shortly. He had given them a bottle of wine, two wineglasses, a tablecloth and eating utensils. Together, the two of them had set the table.

Reggie wondered if being here with him reminded her of how intimate things had been between them on Saturday night. They had shared dinner then, but only after spending hours making love, to the point where they were famished.

"I'm the baby in the family," she said, smiling. "I have two older brothers."

"And I know the Holy Terror is one of them," Reggie said, grinning. "He went to school with a couple of my cousins and two of my brothers. In fact, my brother Quade was on his football team in high school. I understand the Holy Terror has mellowed over the years."

Olivia chuckled. "It depends on what you mean by 'mellowed.' Both of my brothers tend to be overprotective at times, but Duan is worse than Terrence, since he's the oldest. Duan is thirty-six, and Terrence is thirty-four."

"And you are?" he asked, knowing a lot of women didn't like sharing their age.

"I'm twenty-seven. What about you?"

"Thirty-two."

Reggie took a sip of his wine and then asked, "Is Duan the one you sent the text message to on Saturday night?"

"Are you kidding?" she said, chuckling. "Duan would have been on the first flight back home, and he would not have erased your number. He would have had you thoroughly checked out. He has a lot of friends in law enforcement. He used to be a police detective. Now he owns a private investigation company. I sent the text message to Terrence. I can handle him a lot easier than I can Duan."

Reggie nodded. "So why is a beautiful girl like you living so far away from home, in Paris?"

She smiled. "Working. I've always wanted to work at the Louvre Museum in Paris, and I was hired right out of grad school as a tour guide. I had to start at the bottom, but I didn't mind if that's what it would take to work my way up the ladder to be an art curator. It took me almost four years, but I finally made it. I've been a curator for almost a year."

"Congratulations," he said and meant it.

"Thanks."

"So do you plan to make Paris your permanent home?" he asked, watching her sip her wine. He liked the way her lips curved around her glass. He had noticed this detail about her on Saturday night, and it had been a total turn-on...just like it was now.

"I love living over there. I miss being home sometimes, but I've managed to return for the holidays. My brothers and I make it a point to be home for Christmas. But my dream is to return home in a few years, when I've saved up enough money to establish an art gallery." She smiled wistfully.

He nodded. "So over the years, you've come home only during the holidays?"

"Yes."

He wondered if that had anything to do with the fact that her mother had walked out on them a couple of days before Christmas, according to Brent. Reggie could only imagine how disruptive that particular Christmas had to have been for them. "And how long do you plan to stay this time?"

She didn't say anything at first, just stared into her

wineglass for a while. Finally, she said, "Until the election is over."

She glanced up and met his gaze, and he breathed in deeply and said, "We won't let that matter now, remember?" he reminded her gently.

"Yes," she said softly. "I remember." She shifted positions in her seat. "So, now, tell me about Reggie Westmoreland."

He took another sip of his wine and then leaned forward in his chair, resting his arms on his thighs. "I'm the youngest son of my parents. Multiple births run in my family. My father is a fraternal twin. My uncle John and my aunt Evelyn have five sons and one daughter."

"Chase is one of their sons?" she interrupted.

He smiled. "Yes, and Chase is a twin. His twin, Storm, is a fireman. So in their birth order, my cousins are Dare, who is the sheriff of College Park, Thorn, who races and builds motorcycles, Stone, who is a writer and writes adventure novels as Rock Mason, the twins Chase and Storm, and Delaney, the only girl. Delaney and I are the same age and are very close."

"I've heard about Thorn, and, of course, I've read a few Rock Mason novels. And I remember reading years ago about your cousin Delaney and how she married a sheikh. That's awesome."

"Yeah, we all think it is, although I have to say, her brothers weren't too happy about it at first, especially with her leaving the country to live in the Middle East. But her husband, Jamal, is a real nice guy, and everyone looks forward to her trips home. All my cousins are married with children."

"What about your siblings? I understand there are quite a few. Are there twins on your side, too?" she asked.

"Yes. My oldest brother is Jared, and he is a divorce attorney here in the city. Spencer lives in California and is the financial adviser in the family. Durango lives in Montana and is a park ranger. He's thinking about retiring to play a bigger role in his horse-breeding business. And then there are the twins—Ian and Quade. Ian owns a resort on Lake Tahoe, and Quade used to work for the government, but now he owns a number of security firms around the country. Quade and his wife are the parents of triplets, and they live in Carolina, although they have another home in Jamaica."

"Wow! You weren't kidding when you said multiple births run in your family. Are your brothers married?"

"Yes, and happily so. I'm the only single Westmoreland living in Atlanta. My father has a brother, Uncle Corey, who lives in Montana. He also has triplets, Casey, Clint and Cole, and they are all married."

At that moment, there was a knock on the door, and seconds later Chase entered with their food. "Everything smells delicious," Olivia said, getting to her feet to help place the plates on the table.

Chase smiled. "I hope the two of you enjoy it," he said, then left them alone again.

Once they were seated at the table, Reggie glanced over at her and smiled. "I'm glad you decided to stay."

Olivia returned his smile.

During dinner Olivia was so tuned in to Reggie that she could only stare at him and listen to everything he was saying. He told her about the other family of Westmorelands, the ones living in Colorado, whom his father had discovered when he decided to research the family history a year ago. A family reunion was being held later this month in Texas, where both the Atlanta-based Westmorelands and the Denver-based Westmorelands would be getting together and officially meeting for the first time. It sounded exciting, especially to someone whose family was limited to two brothers and a father. Both of her sets of grandparents were deceased, and both of her parents had been only children.

"Would you like some more dessert?" he asked.

Reggie's question reclaimed her thoughts, and she smiled over at him. He had kept his word, and although the attraction they shared was there, flowing blatantly between them, they had been able to harness it while sharing information about each other. A part of Olivia wasn't sure why they had decided to spend time together when nothing would ever come of it, but they had. Once again, the desire to be together, if only to breathe the same air and share conversation, had driven them to defy what others around them felt they should do.

"No, thanks. I do have to leave. I told my father I was going to the park to paint."

"I'm glad you agreed to meet with me and I'm sorry if I placed you in an awkward position."

"You didn't," she said. "I mentioned to Dad that I was going to the park before you called. I just didn't tell him of my change of plans, because he was resting."

"Would you have done otherwise?" he asked her.

She knew she would be honest and said, "No, he

would have forbidden it. And that's the reason why, as much as I enjoyed sharing dinner and conversation with you, Reggie, we can't do it again. I hope you understand."

He met her eyes. "No, I don't understand, because like I said earlier, Olivia, the campaign doesn't concern our relationship."

"The press won't see it that way, and they would have a field day with the story of you and I being involved. I refuse to sneak around to see you." She stood. "I need to go."

Reggie stood as well. He knew he couldn't detain her any longer, but he was more determined than ever to see her again and spend time with her. And he didn't want them to sneak around, either. There had to be a way, and he was determined to find it. "I enjoyed our time together, Olivia."

She held out her hand to him. "So did I. Thank you."

Reggie took the hand she offered, felt the heat the moment he touched it and knew she felt the heat as well. His fingers tightened on hers, and they both were aware of the sensations flowing between them. This wasn't the first time such a thing had happened. It always did when they came in contact with each other.

It was she who tugged her hand away first. "And thanks again for returning my earring."

"You're welcome."

And then Olivia turned and moved toward the door. Before she opened it, she glanced back over her shoulder, saw his unwavering stare, deciphered the intense desire in his eyes. She still felt the heat of his touch on her hand.

She wanted to go back to him, wrap her arms around his neck, but she knew she could not. She would not regret the time she'd spent with him on Saturday night or today. But she was realistic enough to know that as long as Reggie Westmoreland was her father's opponent in the Senate race, her father would never accept her dating a Westmoreland. So from this day forward, she would have fond memories of their times together, but they would have to sustain her throughout the campaign and later, when she returned to Paris.

"Olivia?"

She had already opened the door to leave when she heard him call her name. Swallowing deeply, she stopped and turned around. "Yes?"

"No matter what, you will forever be my Wonder Woman."

She felt the tightness in her throat and fought the tears that had begun clouding her eyes. *And you, Reggie Westmoreland, will forever be the man that I wished I'd had the opportunity to get to know better,* she thought.

Their gazes held for the longest time, and then she turned and walked out the door and closed it behind her.

Olivia was surprised to find her father had already gone to bed by the time she returned home. At some point, he had come downstairs and fixed a pot of vegetable soup, which he'd left warming on the stove for her. A part of her felt awful about her deceit. She'd been served a delicious full-course meal at Chase's Place, while her father had been home, eating alone.

She quickly realized that he'd not eaten alone when she noticed two of everything in the sink and the lipstick on the rim of one of the coffee cups. She smiled. The lipstick was the shade Cathy usually wore, which meant there was a good possibility that her father's secretary had joined him for dinner.

She went upstairs and was about to undress for her shower when her cell phone rang. "Hello."

"Hey, Libby, I heard you were home."

"Duan! Where are you? How have you been?"

She heard her brother's deep laugh. "Still asking a thousand questions, are you? I've been fine. How are things there?"

"Umm, so-so. Dad gave his first speech today, and I thought it was great, but he feels his opponent did better."

"Well, did his opponent do better, Libby?"

His question threw her. Why would Duan ask her something like that? "Let's just say that they both did well, but Westmoreland made a direct hit on all the issues, whereas Dad just skated across the surface, like Senator Reed used to do."

"Politics as usual," Duan said. "I told Dad that I don't know squat about politics, but I'd think the people would want some fresh and innovative ideas. With Senator Reed tagging along, there's no way Dad can represent change."

Olivia nodded. She was glad she wasn't the only person in the family who thought that.

Duan went on. "And it's a shame that he's running against Reggie Westmoreland. I heard he's a nice guy. His cousin Dare is the sheriff of College Park. I've worked with Dare before, and I like him. Most of the Westmorelands that I know are good people."

"Dad thinks he's the enemy," Olivia said.

"I'm sorry that Dad feels that way. I was hoping this would be a clean campaign. I bet it's Senator Reed who's trying to make it dirty."

She could hear the dislike in her brother's voice. "So you will make it home for the barbecue next Saturday?" she asked him. In two weeks there would be a massive outdoor cookout in Atlanta-Fulton County Stadium for people to come out and meet all the candidates. Their father had asked her and her brothers to be there for the event so that the Jeffries family could show a united front.

"Yes, I'm in Detroit, but I hope to have everything wrapped up by then."

"Good." She looked forward to seeing both of her brothers. "Be safe, Duan."

"I will."

After leaving Chase's Place, Reggie decided to stop by and visit with his parents. He'd always admired his parents and the strength of their marriage. Everyone in the family knew the story of how James and Sarah Westmoreland had met and how it had been love at first sight. He couldn't help but chuckle when he thought about it now.

His mother and his aunt Evelyn had been the best

of friends since childhood and had both been born and raised in Birmingham, Alabama. After graduating from high school, Evelyn had come to Atlanta to visit her aunt for the summer. During her first week in the city, she'd gone on a church picnic and met John Westmoreland. It had been love at first sight, and deciding not to waste any time, John and Evelyn had eloped the following week.

Evelyn had called Sarah to tell her the news, and being the levelheaded person that his mother was, Sarah could not believe or accept that someone could meet and fall in love at first glance. So Sarah had gone to Atlanta to talk some sense into Evelyn, only to meet John's twin brother, James, and fall in love with him at first sight as well. Two weeks later Sarah and James had married.

That had been nearly forty years ago, and his parents' marriage was still going strong. There had been his mom's cancer scare a few years back, when she'd been diagnosed with breast cancer. But thankfully, she was now doing fine, although she made sure never to miss her annual checkups. His mother was a strong and determined woman who had the love and admiration of her family.

Although Reggie knew it was his mother's desire to see her last son happily wedded, he was in no hurry. He had a good career as an accountant, with a very prestigious client list, and in a couple of months, he would know if his future would include politics.

His thoughts then shifted to Olivia Jeffries. He had enjoyed the time they had spent together tonight. In bed or out, she was someone he liked being with, and it bothered him that she had refused to see him again because of her father. The last thing they needed was to let anyone or anything get in the way of what could be a promising relationship. He understood that she would be leaving the country to return to Paris once the election was over, but Saturday night and today had proven that they were good together. He had actually enjoyed sitting in the coziness of that room at Chase's Place with her while they did little more than engage in conversation with each other.

He had enjoyed studying her while she talked, watching her lips move with each and every word she enunciated. And she had been wearing the same perfume she'd had on Saturday night. It had been hard sitting there across from her, knowing that he had tasted every inch of her skin, had been inside her body and had brought her pleasure.

By the time he pulled into his parents' driveway, he knew there was no way he could willingly walk away from Olivia Jeffries. He didn't like the thought of the two of them sneaking around to see each other so her father wouldn't find out, but at the moment he didn't care. The bottom line was that he wanted to see her again and would do anything and everything in his power—even blackmail—to make it happen.

If Olivia thought she had seen or heard the last of him, she was sorely mistaken.

Chapter 7

"I see you had a guest for dinner last night, Dad."

Olivia watched her father actually blush across the breakfast table and thought it was kind of cute that he seemed a little embarrassed.

"Ahh, yes, Cathy stopped by, and I invited her to stay for dinner."

"Oh, and why did she come by? Are the two of you working on another speech?"

"No, no," her father was quick to say. "She thought I wasn't in a good mood after yesterday's luncheon and wanted to cheer me up. She stopped by the bakery and brought me my favorite Danish. I thought that was kind of her."

"I think so, too, but then Cathy is a kind person. I like her."

Her father lifted a brow. "Do you really?"

Olivia looked over at him. She could tell her response was important to him. "Yes, and I always have. Over the years I thought she was not only a good secretary to you but a nice person, too. When I was younger and was dealing with a lot of girl stuff, I would often call Cathy."

Her father looked surprised. "You did?"

"Yes. Come on, Dad. You have to have known it was hard for me being the only girl in the house, and I couldn't talk to you, Duan and Terrence about *everything*."

"No, I guess not. I'm glad she was there for you then," her father said.

"Yes, and I'm glad she's here for you now, Dad."

Olivia watched as Orin's blush deepened. "Everything between me and Cathy is strictly business."

She was forced to hide her smile behind the rim of the coffee cup she'd brought to her lips. "Of course, Dad. I wasn't insinuating anything."

Half an hour later, after her father had left for work, Olivia decided to get dressed and go to the park and paint like she had planned to do the day before. She was about to head downstairs when her cell phone rang. For some reason, she knew who the caller was without looking. Her heart skipped several beats before she clicked the phone on. "Hello."

"Please meet with me again, Olivia."

She closed her eyes and breathed in deeply as the sensuous sound of his voice floated through her. "Reggie, I thought we decided that we wouldn't see each other again."

"I thought so, too, but I couldn't sleep last night. Thoughts of you kept invading my mind. I want to see you, Olivia. I want to be with you. Meet me today at noon. The Saxon Hotel. The same room number."

Her mind was suddenly flooded with memories of everything that had taken place in that room. And he wasn't the only one who'd been unable to sleep last night. Her body had been restless. Hot. She had dreamed of him several times, and at one point she had sat on the edge of the bed for what seemed like hours, recovering from the pleasurable memories that had swept through her, interrupting her night and filling her with a need she had never felt...until meeting Reggie.

"Will you come, Olivia? Please."

His voice was deep, quiet, yet persuasive. The sound of it poured over her skin like warm cream, and she couldn't fight it, because deep inside she wanted to be with him as much as he wanted to be with her.

She needed to see him again, to know, to understand and to explore the pull between them. Was it just sexual, or was it something else? Despite her decision not to become involved with him, she knew that she had to be with him at least one more time. These memories she was collecting would have to be enough to sustain her for the rest of her life.

"Yes," she said finally. "I'll meet you at noon."

Reggie paced the hotel room, glancing at his watch every so often. It was a few minutes before noon. He had had a news conference at nine but hadn't counted on a slew of reporters bombarding him after the news conference was over. Nor had he counted on the rumor that had quickly spread that his accounting firm, which employed over a hundred people, was facing possible bankruptcy and definite layoffs.

It was a lie that could easily be proven false, but not before mass pandemonium erupted at his business, and he'd spent part of the morning calming his employees' fears. He didn't have to think twice about where the lie had been generated, which made him angrier than hell. He'd never suspected that Orin Jeffries would allow his campaign staff to stoop so low.

For a moment he'd thought he would have to cancel this meeting with Olivia, but a part of him had refused to do it. She had consented to meet with him, and he would have moved heaven and hell to be here. Now he couldn't help wondering if she would show up. What if she had changed her mind? What if—

At that moment the door opened and Olivia walked in and his entire body went completely still. It seemed as if his heart picked that exact moment to stop beating. He was very much aware of how good she looked dressed in a pair of black tailored slacks and a light blue linen blouse.

She closed the door behind her and leaned against it, saying nothing but holding his gaze as intently as he was holding hers. He could now admit that although he had been drawn to her lips, the total package was what had captured his interest. She had the kind of presence that demanded attention, and just like at the Firemen's Masquerade Ball and yesterday, she was getting his again today. In droves.

In addition to checking her out, he was trying to get a read on her but couldn't. The sexual chemistry had hit the airwaves the moment she had walked through the door. With them, it couldn't be helped. But what about her attitude? he wondered. She had said yesterday that she didn't want them to become involved. Yet when he had defied her wishes and had called and asked her to meet with him here, she had accepted.

What was she expecting from him? What was he expecting from her?

He definitely knew what he wanted, but wanting and expecting were two different things. For the moment he was just glad to have her here, in this hotel room, alone with him. Had she come to spend time with him or to chew him out for having the audacity to call and ask her to meet with him? He was certain he was about to find out.

"Hello, Olivia."

"Reggie." And then, with her gaze still locked firmly with his, she moved away from the door and walked toward him.

His heart somehow began beating again, and it was only when she came to a stop directly in front of him that he allowed his gaze to shift and took note of the cut of her blouse. The low, square cut showed the nice swell of her breasts. They were breasts he had tasted before and was dying to taste again. Not surprisingly, something primal stirred inside him. His heart rate increased, and he breathed in deeply as a way to slow it down.

He cleared his throat. "I ordered lunch," he heard himself say and watched as she glanced behind him to see the table that had been set for two. "I'll call them to deliver the food when we're ready to eat," he said and drew a somewhat shaky breath.

She reached out and smoothed her hand along the back of his neck. "Are you hungry now, Reggie?" she asked, her voice an octave lower than he remembered.

He swallowed thickly. The feel of her fingers on his skin was pure torture. "It's up to you, since you're my guest."

A smile touched her lips at the corners. "In that case, we can wait. I'd rather do this now." And then she leaned up on tiptoe and connected her mouth to his.

At that moment whatever control he had been holding on to broke, and he instantly swept her into his arms without disconnecting their mouths. He wanted to head directly for the bedroom, but at that moment the only thing he could do was stand there with her in his arms and savor her this way, not sure when or if he would be granted the opportunity to do so again. He intended to make this their day, just like Saturday had been their night.

On the way to the hotel, Brent had tried to pin him down as to where he was going. He had told his friend that he was to be disturbed only if there was an emergency. He could tell Brent had wanted more information, but none had been forthcoming. What he did on his personal time was his business, and this lunch was on his personal time. And he was feasting on what he enjoyed most. Olivia's mouth.

He wasn't sure what had changed her mind since yesterday, when she had been adamant about not getting involved with him, but he was just glad she had. There was only so much a man could take.

He finally pulled back from her mouth. It was then that she nuzzled against his ear. The tip of her tongue trailed a path beneath it, and then she whispered. "I want to make love with you again—"

Before she could finish her words, he headed in the direction of the bedroom, sidestepping the table set for two. She laughed when he gently tossed her on the bed, then captured her laughter with his mouth when he quickly joined her there. And then it was back on. The heat was blazing. They didn't have a moment to waste, and they both knew it. As they lay fully clothed in bed, with their mouths joined in the most intimate way, their tongues dueled, tangled and mated. She refused to stay still. She was moving all over the place, and he eventually placed a thigh over hers. She had become wild, so bold and wanton. And he loved it.

She pulled her mouth back and met his gaze, their hearts pounding loudly in the room. "Make love to me, Reggie. Now," she said.

She didn't have to say the words twice. He moved off the bed and quickly undressed, trying not to rip the buttons off his shirt in his haste. And then, when he was completely naked, except for the condom he had taken the time to put on, he went for her, pulled her toward him to remove her blouse and bra before tackling her shoes, slacks and panties.

When he had pulled the latter two down her hips to reveal the lushness of her feminine mound, he knew he had to taste her right then. He tossed the items of clothing aside and held down her hips at the same time that his mouth lowered to her, kissing her intimately, with a hunger and greed that made her tremble and moan incoherently. But he didn't let up. His tongue was desperate to reacquaint itself with the taste it had relished on Saturday, and he intended to get his fill. And her body responded, generating the sweetness he wanted, and he mercilessly savored her.

He felt her hands lock around his head as if to hold his mouth in place, but that wasn't needed. He wasn't going anyplace until he got enough, and that wouldn't be anytime soon. He proved his point by plunging his tongue deeper inside of her, absorbing the wetness of her sensuality, which was being produced in abundance just for him.

Reggie finally pulled back and licked his lips, while his eyes traveled down her entire body, taking in every inch and every curve, the texture of her skin and the fullness of her breasts, which seemed to be begging for his mouth.

Leaning upward, he brushed his lips against a taut nipple, liking the sound of the quick breath that got caught in her throat. He proceeded to sample her nipples, finding both tantalizingly hot.

"Come inside me, please."

Olivia's tortured moan had Reggie moving his body over hers. When his heated shaft was at the opening of her feminine mound, he met her gaze, and then, with a hungry growl, he pushed deep inside of her.

Olivia closed her eyes as pleasure washed through her. What was there about being joined to Reggie that made her feel such joy, such mind-blowing pleasure and such spellbinding ecstasy? She felt him lift her legs, and she wrapped them around his waist while he thrust inside of her with whipcord speed and precision. Everything about him was affecting her in an elemental way, and she could barely stifle her moans as she was consumed by a tide of red-hot passion. It was only with him that she could feel not only taken but possessed. Only with him could she be not only driven but also contained. And he was making love to her without any restraint and with a voracious need, which was fueling her own. And every time the hard muscles of his stomach pressed against hers, pinning her beneath him, she trembled from the inside out.

And then an orgasm rammed through her. Never before had she felt anything so profound. She cried out his name. And he used his tongue, lips and mouth to absorb her cries of pleasure, her moans of passion. Instead of letting up, he pressed on and thrust deeper.

The flames ignited, flared and then burned in the very center of her, and when an explosion ripped through her a second time, he was there, and she felt his shaft expand before exploding in his release. And as passion tumbled her over into the depths of turbulent, sensual waters, she cried his name once more before she felt herself drowning in a sea of ecstasy.

Propped up on his elbow, Reggie stared down at Olivia. In the middle of the day, she had actually drifted off to sleep. He smiled, understanding why. He had shown her no mercy in taking them both through waves and waves of pure pleasure. Somewhere in the back of his mind, he heard the sound of his cell, but at that moment he chose to ignore it. His main focus, his total concentration, was on the most beautiful creature he had ever laid eyes on.

He glanced over at the clock on the nightstand. They had been in the room for two hours already—two hours of nonstop lovemaking in which he would get hard again before even coming out of her. They would start another bout of lovemaking right on the tail end of the previous one. Nothing like this had ever happened to him before. He felt totally obsessed with this woman.

He could vividly recall the first moment he had seen her at the Firemen's Masquerade Ball. He had known then, just like he knew now, that she was the one that he would make his. At the time he just hadn't known the depth to which he would do so. Now he did.

And he also understood why his brothers and cousins seemed so happy these days, so blissfully content. They had been able to find that one person who they knew was their soul mate. The question of the hour was, how was he going to convince Olivia that she was his? Especially considering the fact that they were sneaking around just to be together.

He wanted to introduce her to his family. He especially wanted her to get to know his mother and his brothers' and cousins' wives. He wanted to take her to the Westmoreland family reunion, which would be held in Texas at the end of the month. He wanted to take her to one of Thorn's motorcycle races later this year. There were so many things he wanted to share with her. But the most important thing of all was his life.

There was no need to tell her that he loved her, because she wouldn't understand that one thing about being a Westmoreland was recognizing your mate when you saw her or him. Although, he thought, with a smile, he would have to admit some of his cousins and brothers had refused to accept their fate at first. But in the end it hadn't done any good. Love had zapped their senses just the same. And it had done the same thing to him. It had hit him like a ton of bricks on Saturday night, and like his parents, he had fallen in love at first sight.

She had her defenses down now, but he wouldn't be surprised if they were back up before she left the hotel today. It didn't matter. He was not going to let her deny them what was rightfully theirs to have. She didn't know it yet, but in time she would. No matter what the situation was between him and her father regarding the campaign, it had no bearing on the two of them.

He noticed her eyes fluttering before they fully opened, and then she was staring up at him. She had to be hungry now. He would feed her, and then he would make love to her again.

Or so he thought. Suddenly she lifted her body and pushed him back onto the covers to straddle him, placing her knees on the sides of his hips to seemingly hold him immobile. She tilted her head back and looked down at him. And smiled. He felt the effects of that smile like a punch to his gut, and his shaft suddenly got hard, totally erect.

"I thought you would be hungry," he said, reaching out and placing the palm of his hand at the back of her neck.

"I am," she whispered, holding his eyes with her own. "For you."

He drew her head down to brush his lips against hers. "And I for you."

When he released her mouth, she glanced at him with a confused look in her eyes. "What are you doing to me, Reggie Westmoreland? How do you have the ability to make me feel wild and reckless? Make me want to yield to temptation?"

A hot rush of desire sent shivers through his body. "I should be asking you the same thing, Olivia Jeffries."

And then she lowered herself on him, and he knew it was a good thing he'd already donned a new condom, because there was no way he could have said stop when she embedded him inside of herself to the hilt. The look on her face told him that she was proud of her accomplishment. She had wanted, so she had taken.

And then she began moving, slowly at first and then with a desperation that sent fire surging through his loins and made it feel as if the head of his shaft was about to explode. But she kept moving, dangling her twin globes in front of his face with every downward motion.

He reached out and grabbed hold of one, brought it to his mouth, and she threw her head back as she continued to ride him in a way he had never been ridden before. The woman had power in her thighs, in her hips and in her inner muscles, and she was using them to make shivers race all through him.

In retaliation, he covered her breasts with his kisses, using his lips and tongue to push her over the same edge that he was close to falling from. And when an explosion hit, he bucked until they were almost off the bed, but then her thighs nearly held him immobile. His body was locked so tightly with hers, he wondered if they would be able to separate when the time came. And at that moment he really didn't care if they couldn't. He would love to stay inside of her forever, in the place where he would one day plant his seed for their child.

That thought triggered another explosion inside of him, and he groped hard for sanity when Olivia came apart on top of him. Her inner muscles clamped him tightly, and she drew every single thing she could out of him. His lungs felt like they were about to collapse in his throat when he tried to keep from hollering out. Burying his face in her chest, he found a safe haven right between her breasts. He knew from this day forward that whatever it took, one day he would make her totally, completely and irrevocably his.

"We never ate lunch, did we?" Olivia asked as she slid back into her slacks.

"No, and I owe you an apology for that," Reggie said, pulling up his pants. He stopped what he was doing and stared at her, watched how she was struggling with the buttons on her blouse.

"Come here, Olivia."

She glanced over at him and smiled before crossing the room to him. "I don't know why I wore this thing when it has so many buttons. It's not like I didn't know that you would be taking it off me."

He didn't say anything as he took over buttoning her blouse. She was right. It did have a lot of buttons. That wouldn't have been so bad if his attention hadn't been drawn to her flesh-toned bra. "Your bra is my favorite color," he said, smiling down at her.

"I figured as much when I put it on," she said, grinning. "You were right. Flesh tone is a color."

"If you're hungry, we can still—"

"No. I noticed your cell phone went off a few times. You need to get back to work."

He chuckled. "Have you noticed the time, Olivia? The day is practically over. We've been here for five hours. It's past five o'clock." And he really wasn't bothered by it. "There. All done," he said, dropping his hands to his sides before he was tempted to do something, like pull her into his arms and kiss her.

"Thanks. Now I definitely need to know something," she said, looking up at him.

"What?"

"Do you have stock in this place?"

Another smile touched his lips. "Wish I did, but no."

"Then what kind of connections do you have?" she asked, with an expression on her face that said she was determined to know.

"My connection is my brother Quade. Dominic Saxon is his brother-in-law. Both recently became fathers. Quade has triplets—a son and two daughters and Dominic's wife, Taylor, gave birth to a son a few months ago."

"Oh. Proud fathers, I gather."

Reggie smiled. "Yes, they are."

He slipped into his shirt while he watched her stand before the dresser's mirror to redo her makeup. Although he knew he would probably get some resistance, he decided to go ahead and have his say. "I got the room again for this Saturday night, Olivia."

Olivia met his gaze in the mirror before slowly turning around to stare at him. He had just issued an open invitation, and it was one he wanted her to accept. She continued to stare into his dark eyes, and then she shifted her gaze to study his face. There was something, something she couldn't decipher, in his eyes and on his face.

"Coming here today was risky, Reggie," she finally said softly.

"I know," was his response. "But I had to see you."

"And I had to be with you," she said honestly.

Too late she wondered why she would admit such a thing to him, but deep down she knew the reason. She wanted him to know that she had wanted to be here and that she thought their time together was special.

Reggie crossed the room to her, and without giving him the chance to make the first move, she reached up and drew his mouth down to hers. And he kissed her with a gentleness that he had to fight to maintain.

When she released his mouth, he gazed down at her. "Sure you had enough?"

She licked her lips. "For now." She then smiled. "I'll get the rest on Saturday."

He lifted a hopeful brow. "You will come?"

She smiled. "Yes, I will come."

Although he knew they needed to finish getting dressed and be on their way, he reached out, caught her around the waist and pulled her gently into his arms, immediately reveling in the way her body seemed to cling to his, perfectly and in sync. And then he lowered his mouth to hers for a kiss that would keep him going strong until Saturday night, when they would come together once again.

Chapter 8

"Cathy will be calling you later today, Libby."

Olivia lifted her gaze from her cereal bowl to glance over at her father, with a questioning look on her face. "For what reason?"

"To schedule all those fund-raisers that you and I will need to attend over the next couple of weeks, beginning this Saturday."

Panic shot through Olivia. "Not this Saturday night, I hope."

Her father quirked a thick brow. "No, it's Saturday midday at the home of Darwin Walker and his wife."

She nodded. Darwin and Terrence used to play together for the Miami Dolphins. Last year Darwin, who, like Terrence, had retired from the NFL, moved to Atlanta after accepting a coaching position with the Falcons.

"And why are you concerned about Saturday night? Do you have plans or something?" Orin asked.

Olivia swallowed. She hated lying to her father, but there was no way she could tell him the truth. Running for political office had made him somewhat unreasonable, especially when it came to Reggie. She was convinced that the only reason he didn't like Reggie was that he was the main person standing in the way of him becoming a senator. However, she intended to do as Reggie had suggested and believe that the election had no bearing on what was developing between them.

She met her father's gaze. "Yes, I have plans. I ran into a friend at the party Saturday night, and we're getting together again this weekend." At least what she'd said wasn't a total lie.

Her father's features softened. "That's good. I've been feeling badly about asking you to put your life in Paris on hold to come here and be my escort for all these campaign events. I'm glad you've managed to squeeze in some fun time."

If only you knew just how much fun I've had thanks to Reggie, she thought.

Both she and her father resumed eating, and the kitchen became quiet. There was something she needed to ask him, something she truly needed to know. The issue had been bothering her since she'd heard about it yesterday.

She glanced across the table at her father. He had resumed reading the paper and was flipping through the pages. She hated interrupting, but she had to. "Dad, can I ask you something?"

"Sure, sweetheart," Orin said, looking up to meet her gaze and placing the newspaper aside. "What is it?"

"Reggie Westmoreland," she said and watched her father's jaw flex.

"What about him, Libby?"

"Did you authorize any of your staff members to put out that false statement about his company facing bankruptcy and layoffs?"

Her father frowned. "Of course not. Why would I or my staff do something like that?"

"To discredit him."

His features tightened. "And you believe I would do something like that or give my staff permission to do so?"

"I don't want to believe that, but I'm not naive. I know how dirty politics can be, Dad."

Orin leaned back in his chair. "Are you taking up for Reggie Westmoreland?" he asked, studying her features.

She sighed deeply. "No, Dad, I'm not taking up for anyone. Such tactics can backfire, so my concern is actually for you."

What she didn't say was that she was sure Reggie was aware of the rumor, which had circulated yesterday, but he hadn't mentioned it to her. Although he had to have been upset about it, Reggie had given her his full concentration and had kept his word not to mix his competition with her father and his relationship with her.

Now it was her turn to study her father's features, and she could see that what she'd said had him thinking. Was he so disjointed from his campaign staff that he truly didn't know what was going on? Did he not know what they were capable of?

"I'm having a meeting with my campaign staff this morning, and if I discover that someone on my staff is connected to yesterday's story in any way, they will be dismissed."

She came close to asking if that included Senator Reed. She had a feeling he was behind the rumor. "Thanks, Dad. I think it will be in your best interest in the long run."

"Where were you yesterday, Reggie? I tried reaching you all afternoon," Brent said, looking across the breakfast table at his friend. They were sitting in Chase's Place, where they had met for breakfast.

Reggie shrugged. "I was busy. Did anything come up that you couldn't handle?"

"Of course not." Brent set his coffee cup down, and his blue eyes studied Reggie intently. "But it would have been nice if I'd been able to contact you. Someone from *Newsweek* called to do an article on you. We're not talking about a local magazine, Reg. We're talking about *Newsweek*. You know how long I've been trying to get you national coverage."

Yes, Reggie did know, and he felt badly about it. But at the time all he could think about was that he wanted to spend uninterrupted time with Olivia. "I'm sorry about that, Brent."

"You're seeing her, aren't you?"

Reggie lifted a brow and met Brent's stare. "It depends on who you're referring to."

"Orin Jeffries's daughter."

Reggie leaned back in his chair. He and Brent had been friends for a long time, since grade school, actually. After attending college at Yale, Brent had worked for a number of years in Boston before moving back to Atlanta a few years ago to care for his elderly parents. A couple of months ago, Reggie had been the best man at Brent's wedding.

As far as Reggie was concerned, other than his brothers and cousins, there wasn't a man he trusted more. He met his best friend's eyes. "Yes, I'm seeing her."

Brent let out a deep sigh. "Do you think that's smart?"

Reggie chuckled. "Considering the fact that I plan to marry her sometime after the election, yes; I would have to say it's smart."

Brent's jaw dropped. "Marry!" And then he quickly glanced around, hoping no one had heard his outburst. After turning back around, he nervously brushed back a strand of blond hair that had fallen onto his face. "Reggie, you just met the woman on Monday at that luncheon."

"No," Reggie said, smiling, as he absently swirled the coffee around in his cup. "Actually, we met before then."

Brent lifted a brow. "When?"

"Saturday night, at the Firemen's Masquerade Ball."

"Saturday night?"

"Yes," replied Reggie.

"That wasn't even a week ago. Are you telling me

you decided once you saw her at a party that you were going to marry her?"

"Something like that. And at the time I didn't know who she was. I found out her true identity on Monday, at that luncheon, the same time she found out mine." Reggie could only smile. Brent was staring at him like he had totally lost his mind. "Trust me, my friend, I haven't lost my mind. Just my heart."

Brent took a sip of his orange juice. His expression implied that he wished the juice was laced with vodka. "Do the two of you understand the implications of what you're doing? Hello," he said, putting emphasis on that single word. "Her father is your opponent in a Senate race."

"We're aware of that. However, we've decided that has nothing to do with what's going on between us," Reggie said.

"And you love her?" Brent asked incredulously.

"With all my heart and then some," Reggie answered truthfully.

He had thought about it a lot last night. To be honest, he hadn't been able to think about anything else. As crazy as it might seem to some people, yes, he had fallen in love with her. He had never been totally against marriage, especially since his family over the past seven years—starting with Delaney—seemed to be falling like flies into matrimony. He just knew he wouldn't ever settle down until the right woman came along. Because of his career and his decision to get into politics, he hadn't expected that to happen anytime soon. He thought he would at least be in his late thirties when he tied the knot, although he knew his mother wished otherwise.

"And she feels the same way?"

Brent's question invaded Reggie's thoughts. "Not sure. I've never asked her. In fact, I haven't even shared my feelings with her yet. It will be best to wait until after the campaign."

Brent took another gulp of his orange juice. "I swear, Reggie, you're going to give me heart failure."

Reggie smiled. "Don't mean to. I'm sure you remember when you met Melody. What did you tell me? You claimed you had fallen in love with her instantly."

"I did. But her father wasn't my political opponent," Brent countered.

"Shouldn't matter, and we intend not to let it affect our relationship, either. So wish us luck."

Brent couldn't help but smile. "Hey, man, what you need are prayers, and I'll be the first to send one up for you."

Olivia stepped off the elevator and glanced around. Over the years, not much in her father's office had changed. The placement of the furniture was still the same. She remembered coming here as a child after school and sitting on the sofa and watching television— but only after she had completed her homework. Duan and Terrence had been into after-school sports, so instead of letting her go home to an empty house, her father had hired a private car to pick her up from school and bring her here.

"Libby, it's good to see you. You didn't need to come in to meet with me."

Olivia couldn't help but return Cathy's warm smile. "I didn't mind. I wanted to get out of the house, anyway."

That much was true. She had tried to paint, but the only subject that had readily come to mind was Reggie, and she couldn't risk her father finding sketches of him all over the place. She slid into the chair next to Cathy's desk.

"If you wanted to see your dad you're too late. He stepped out. I think he went over to his campaign headquarters," Cathy was saying, with a concerned expression on her face. "He was on the phone earlier with his campaign staff, and he wasn't a happy camper. He suspects someone released that false information on Westmoreland yesterday. Now it says in this morning's paper that your father's campaign is turning to dirty politics."

Olivia sighed. She'd been afraid that would happen. "Well, I'm glad Dad is addressing it. Otherwise, it could backfire even more if whoever is responsible keeps it up."

"I agree."

Olivia liked Cathy. She was attractive, responsible, and Olivia knew the woman had her father's interests at heart. At least her father was beginning to notice Cathy as a woman, although he was moving way too slowly to suit Olivia. "Well, as you can see, I brought my planner," she said to Cathy. "Dad wants me to pencil in all those important dates of those campaign events.

I still don't understand why he just didn't ask you to go with him."

Cathy blushed. "Your father would never do that. I'm his secretary."

Olivia rolled her eyes. "You're not just his secretary, Cathy. You're his right hand in more ways than one, and I'm sure he knows it. Frankly, I'm concerned about him and the election. Sometimes I think he wants to become a senator, and other times I'm not sure. What's your take on it?"

Cathy hesitated in responding, and Olivia knew it was because she thought that to say anything negative about Orin or the campaign might be construed as disloyalty. "I think that if it had been left up to your father, he would not have run," Cathy said hesitantly.

"Then why did he?"

"Because Senator Reed talked him into it."

Olivia shook her head, still not understanding. "My father is a grown man who can make decisions on his own. Why would he let Senator Reed talk him into doing anything? That doesn't make sense. It's not like they have a history or have been friends for a terribly long time. It's my understanding that they met playing golf just a few years ago."

Cathy shook her head. "No, their relationship goes back further than that."

Olivia blinked, surprised. She had a feeling Cathy knew a lot more than she was telling. Definitely a lot more than Olivia or her brothers knew. "So, what's the relationship?"

Cathy, Olivia noted, was nervously biting her lips. "I'm not sure it's my place to say, Libby," she said.

Olivia knew that if she didn't get the information from Cathy, then she would never get it. Deciding to go for broke, she said in a low and soft voice, "I know you love Dad, Cathy." At the woman's surprised look, Olivia lowered her voice even more. "And I'm hoping Dad realizes, and very soon, what a jewel he has in you, not only as an employee, but, more importantly, as a woman who, I know, has his back. But I'm honestly worried that something is going on that my brothers and I wouldn't agree with, and if that's the case, then we need to know what it is."

Cathy stared at her for a long moment. "Your father feels indebted to the senator."

Olivia raised a brow. "And why would he feel that way?"

Cathy didn't say anything for a long while. "Because of your mother," the older woman said.

Olivia's head began spinning. "How does my mother have anything to do with this? My brothers and I haven't heard from her in over twenty-something years. Are you saying that my father has? That he and my mother are in contact with each other?"

"No, that's not what I'm saying."

With a desperate look in her eyes, Olivia took hold of the woman's hand. "Tell me, Cathy. You need to tell me what's going on and what my mother has to do with it."

"Years ago, your mother ran off with another man, a married man," Cathy said.

Olivia nodded. She knew all that. Although she had

been only three then, years later she had overheard one of her grandparents talking about her mother in whispers. "And?"

"The man's wife had a child."

"Yes, I know that as well," Olivia said. "I also know the woman was so torn up about what happened that eventually she and her child moved away."

"Yes, but what you probably don't know is that eventually, a couple of years later, that woman committed suicide. She could never get over losing her husband."

Olivia gasped. Cathy was right. She hadn't known that. "How awful."

Cathy nodded sadly in agreement. "Yes, it was. And what's even worse, when she decided to stall her car on the train tracks and just sit there waiting for the train to come, she had her child in the car with her. They were both killed."

Tears she couldn't hold back sprang into Olivia's eyes. It was bad enough that her mother's actions had broken up a family, but they had also caused a woman to end her own life and that of her child.

"I didn't want to tell you," Cathy said softly, handing Olivia a tissue.

Olivia dabbed at her eyes. "I'm glad you did. But what does all that have to do with Senator Reed?"

Now it was Cathy who reached out to hold Olivia's hand. "The woman who committed suicide was his sister, Libby, and your father feels responsible for what eventually happened to her and her little girl because of what your mother did."

* * *

The first thing Olivia did when she got home was to pull out her sketch pad and water colors, determined to go to the park. Painting always soothed her mind, and she needed it today more than ever.

She had come home soon after her conversation with Cathy; otherwise, she would have gone looking for her father just to cry in his arms. It just wasn't fair that he felt responsible for the choices his wife had made over twenty years before, choices that had ultimately led to a sad tragedy. And if Senator Reed was intentionally playing with her father's conscience, he would have to stop.

Once at the park, she found several scenes she could concentrate on and tried her hand at doing a few sketches, but her concentration wavered. A part of her wanted to call her brothers and tell them what she'd found out, but she resisted doing so. They would be in town next weekend, and she would tell them then. They would know how to handle the situation. She loved her father and if he really wanted to enter politics and become a senator, then he had her support. But if he was being railroaded into doing something out of misplaced guilt, then she definitely had a problem with that.

For the first time in years, she thought about the woman who had given birth to her. The woman had walked out of her, her father's and her brothers' lives without looking back. When Duan had gotten old enough, he had tried contacting her, to satisfy his need to know why Susan Jeffries's maternal instincts had never driven her to stay in contact with the three kids she had left behind. Instead of finding a woman who regretted what she had done, he had found a selfish individual who had been married four times and had never given birth to another child. Instead, she had been living life in the fast lane and was the mistress of a race-car driver, apparently working on hubby number five. That had been six years ago. There was no telling what number she was on now.

The more Olivia thought about her mother, the more depressed she became, and she found that even painting couldn't soothe her troubled mind. It was strange that the happiest of her days were those she'd spent with Reggie. Not just sharing a bed with him, but sharing a bit of herself like she'd never shared with a man before. They would talk in between their lovemaking. Pillow talk. She felt so good around him.

A child's laughter caught her attention, and she glanced across the pond to see a mother interacting with a child that appeared to be about three, the same age she'd been when her mother left. The woman seemed to be having fun, and the exuberance on the face of the little girl left no doubt that she, too, was having the time of her life. That's what real mothers did. They put smiles on their children's faces, not sad frowns that lasted a lifetime.

Aware that she had begun thinking of her poor excuse for a mother again, she shifted her thoughts back to Reggie. She would love to see him now, be held by him and kissed by him. It was hard to believe that they had met less than a week ago, but since then they had shared so much.

Half an hour later she was still sitting on the park

bench, thinking about Reggie. They had spent most of yesterday together. Would he want to see her today? Would he meet her somewhere if she were to call, just to hold her in his arms and do nothing more?

Olivia swallowed. There was only one way to find out. She took her cell phone out of her bag and dialed his number.

"Hello. This is Reggie Westmoreland."

The sound of his sexy voice oozed all over her. "Hi. This is Olivia. I didn't want to call you, but I didn't have anyone else to call."

"Olivia, what's wrong?"

She swiped at a tear. "Nothing really. I just need to be held."

"Where are you?"

"At a park. I came here to paint and—"

"What's the name of the park?"

"Cypress Park."

"I know where it's located. I'm on my way."

"No, it's out in the open. Is there a place near here where we can meet?" she asked.

There was a pause, and then he said, "Yes, in fact, there is. My cousin Delaney and her husband, Jamal, own a town house a few blocks away. It's on Commonwealth Boulevard. Delaney's Square."

"A town house just for her?" Olivia asked.

"Jamal was the first tenant and decided to buy out the others so he, Delaney and the kids could have their privacy whenever they came to town. I have a key to check on things when they're not here. Go there now, sweetheart. I'll be waiting."

* * *

Olivia recognized Reggie's car parked in front of a massive group of elegant buildings, all townhomes, around ten of them, on a beautiful landscaped property.

She strolled up the walkway to the center building; her pulse rate increased with every step she took. When she reached the front door, she glanced around. She lifted her hand to knock on the door, but before her knuckles could make contact, the door opened and Reggie was there. He captured her hand in his and gently pulled her inside and closed the door behind her.

Olivia looked up at him, and he gently pulled her into his arms. He wrapped his arms around her waist and pressed her face to his chest.

She inhaled deeply. He smelled of man, a nice, robust scent that sent shivers down her spine. This was what she needed. To be held in his arms. Riding over here, she kept thinking about how it would feel to be in his arms again. Her life was in turmoil, and right now he was a solid force in her mixed-up world.

Suddenly, she felt herself being lifted in his arms, and she linked her arms around his neck. "Where are you taking me?" she asked when he began walking.

"Over here, to the sofa, so I can hold you the way I want to, and so you can tell me what's bothering you."

Olivia pressed her lips together, not sure she could do that without implicating her father, and that wouldn't be good. He didn't need to know that her father had felt compelled to enter the Senate race because Senator Reed, a man he felt indebted to, had encouraged him to do so, and that her father's heart might not be in it.

Reggie adjusted her in his arms when he sat down on the sofa and angled her body so that she could look up at him. "What happened, Olivia? What happened to make you call me?"

She hesitated and then decided to tell him some of what was bothering her, but not all of it. "I was at the park and saw this mother and child. The little girl was about the age I was when my mother walked out on my dad, my brothers and me. Seeing them made me realize how easy it was for my mother to walk away without looking back."

"And she's never tried contacting you?" Reggie asked, softly stroking the side of her face with the pad of his thumb.

Oliver shook her head. "No, she never has."

Reggie tightened his hold on Olivia, and she clung to his warmth. She wasn't sure how much time passed before she lifted her head to look at him. He looked at her, studied her face. "Are you okay?" he asked softly.

She nodded. "I am now. But I have to go. Dad will worry because it's getting late."

He stood with her in his arms and let her slide down his body until her feet touched the floor. For a long moment, she stood there and stared at him, realizing that he hadn't kissed her yet. He must have read her mind, because he lowered his mouth to her. She craned her neck to meet him halfway and let out a deep sigh when their lips met.

His tongue was in her mouth in a flash, moving around in a circular motion before winding around hers, taking it in total possession. She wrapped her arms around his neck and groaned out loud when he deepened the kiss. Sensations throbbed within her, and she felt a shiver pass through her body.

Moments later, she pulled back from the kiss, gasping for breath. Nobody could kiss like Reggie Westmoreland. She was totally convinced of that. They had to stand there a moment to catch their breaths. In a way, it did her heart good to know he had been just as affected by the kiss.

"Do you want me to show you around before you go?" Reggie asked her in a ragged voice, taking her hand in his.

Olivia glanced around. The place was absolutely beautiful, with its sprawling living room that was lavishly decorated in peach and cream, its bigger-than-life dining room and kitchen and its spiral staircase. Fit for a king. And from what she'd read, Sheikh Jamal Ari Yasir would one day inherit that title.

"Yes, I'd love to see the rest of it."

Reggie showed her around, and she was in total awe of the lavishly decorated bedrooms and baths, and when they toured one of the beautifully decorated guest rooms, with a huge four-poster bed, he didn't try to get her in it. Instead, he looked at her. "Saturday night will be ours. Today you just needed me to hold you," he whispered.

His words went a long way to calm her, soothed her troubled mind and actually made her feel special, mainly because she had called and he had come. "Thank you for coming, Reggie."

He looked down at her and pulled her closer to him. "I will always come when you call, Olivia."

She met his gaze, thinking that was a strange thing to say. They didn't have a future together. At the end of two months, she would be returning to Paris.

"Come on. Let me walk you to your car," Reggie said huskily as he placed his arms around her shoulders.

Olivia regretted that her time with Reggie was about to end and appreciated that he had been there for her when she had needed him. That meant a lot.

Chapter 9

The following week Olivia kept busy by attending several functions with her father. She had decided not to discuss her conversation with Cathy with him. Instead, she would meet with her brothers and get their take on the matter when they came to town later that week.

She had to catch her breath whenever she thought of the times she and Reggie had spent together, especially on Saturday night. On Wednesday he had called and asked her to have a midday snack with him at Chase's Place. It was then that she had met Chase's wife, Jessica, who was expecting the couple's first child. Jessica, who liked to bake, had treated her to a batch of brownies, which had been delicious. Olivia wondered what Reggie had told Chase and Jessica about their relationship, and if they knew that she was the daughter of his opponent in the Senate race.

Olivia couldn't help but note over the past few days that her father seemed excited about this weekend. He would have his three children home to attend the huge barbecue that was being planned for all the candidates on Saturday evening.

Tonight she would attend yet another political function with her father. All the candidates would be there. She and Reggie would have to pretend they barely knew each other. They had talked about it on Wednesday, and she knew he wasn't overjoyed at the thought of that, but he had promised to abide by her wishes. She wasn't crazy about them sneaking around to see each other, either, but under the circumstances, it was something they had to do.

She smiled as she continued to get dressed, thinking that sneaking around did have its benefits. It made them appreciate the time they were together, and they always found ways to put it to good use. It would be hard tonight to see him and not go over to him and claim him as hers. And a part of her felt that he was hers. Whenever they were together, he would use his mouth to stamp his brand all over her, and she would do likewise with him.

She tried not to think about the day when the campaign would finally be over and she would have to return to Paris. She was even thinking about calling the Louvre to see if she could extend her leave for a couple more weeks. She wanted to be able to be with him in the open after the election. She didn't want to think about how he and her father would feel about each other then, depending on which one of them was victorious.

She glanced at her watch. She needed to hurry, because the last thing she wanted was to make her father late to a campaign event. Besides, although she had just seen Reggie yesterday, she was eager to see him again.

Reggie clung to his patience when he glanced at the entrance to the ballroom. He had thought about Olivia most of the day and couldn't wait to see her. Last night he had begun missing her and wished he could have called her to ask her to meet him somewhere. This sneaking around was unpleasant, and his patience was wearing thin. He wasn't sure he would be able to hold out for another month. Because her brothers would be arriving in town this weekend, she'd said it wouldn't be wise for her to try to get away for a tryst at the Saxon on Saturday night, after the barbecue. The fact that Duan and Terrence Jeffries would be in town until next Wednesday meant his and Olivia's time together would basically be nonexistent.

"And how are you doing this evening, Westmoreland?"

Reggie turned to look at Senator Reed. The one man he really didn't care to see. "I'm fine, Senator. And yourself?" he asked, more out of politeness than a sense a caring.

"I'm doing great. I think, for you and Jeffries, it will be a close election."

Reggie wanted to say that this view was not reflected in the most recent poll, which indicated that he had a substantial lead, but he refrained from doing so. "You think so?" he said.

"Yes, but what it all will eventually boil down to is experience."

Reggie smiled.

"And the candidate I endorse," the senator added.

What the senator didn't add, Reggie quickly noted, was that he was not endorsing him. That was no surprise. The man had already endorsed Orin Jeffries and was working with Jeffries's campaign. "Sorry you think that, Senator, since I'm equally sure that I don't need or want your endorsement."

"And I'm equally sorry you feel that way, because I intend to prove you wrong. I will take great pleasure when you lose." The older man then walked away.

"What was that about?" Brent asked when he walked up moments later.

"The good senator tried convincing me of the importance of his endorsement."

Brent snorted. "Did you tell him just where he could put his endorsement?"

Reggie chuckled. "Not in so many words, but I think he got the picture."

Brent glanced to where the senator was now standing and talking to a wealthy industrialist. "There's something about that man that really irks me."

"I feel the same way," Reggie said. He was about to tilt his glass to his lips when he glanced at the ballroom entrance at the exact moment that Olivia and her father walked in. He immediately caught her gaze, and the rush of desire that sped through his body made him want to say the hell with discretion, cross the room and pull her into his arms. But he knew he couldn't do that.

Brent, who was standing beside Reggie, followed his gaze. "Do I need to caution you about being careful? You never know who might be watching you two. I don't trust Reed. Although he's backing Jeffries, I wouldn't put anything past him."

Reggie's gaze remained on Olivia's face for a minute longer, until she looked away.

Senator Albert Reed frowned as he watched the interaction between Olivia and Reggie. He had a strong feeling that something was going on between them, but he didn't have any proof. And that didn't sit well with him. He had suggested to Orin that he send for his daughter under the pretense that she could be an asset. But the truth was that he really wanted Olivia for himself.

He had discovered that women her age enjoyed the company of older men, especially if those men were willing to spend money on them. With his wife bedridden, he had needs that only a younger woman could fulfill.

When he had seen all those pictures of Olivia that Orin had on the wall in his study, he had made the decision that he wanted her as his next mistress. Getting her into his bed would be the perfect ending to his quest for revenge against the Jeffries family for what Orin's slut of a wife had done. Orin felt guilty, and as far as Senator Reed was concerned, his guilt was warranted. He should have been able to control his unfaithful wife.

He took a sip of his drink as he continued to watch

Olivia and Reggie looking at each other. Umm, interesting. It was time to take action. Immediately.

"I'm sure England is just beautiful this time of the year."

Olivia nodded as Marie Patterson rattled on and on to the group of four women about her dream to one day spend a month in England. Then Olivia took a sip of her drink and glanced around the room, her gaze searching for one man in particular. When she found him, their gazes met and held.

She knew that look. If they had been alone, she would have crossed the room to him and wrapped her arms around his neck while he wrapped his around her waist. He would have brought her close to him and pressed his hard, muscular body against hers to the point where she would cradle his big, hard erection at the junction of her thighs.

"So, what about Paris, Ms. Jeffries? I understand you've been living there for a while. Is the weather there nice?"

Olivia swung her attention back to Mrs. Patterson when the woman said her name. She took a quick sip of her wine to cool off her hot insides before answering. "Yes, the weather in Paris is nice."

When the conversation shifted from her to the latest in women's fashion, Olivia's gaze went back to Reggie. He was talking to a group of men. Because the men had that distinguished Westmoreland look, she could only assume that they were relatives of his—brothers or cousins.

She was about to turn her attention back to the group

of women around her when Senator Reed, who was standing across the room, caught her eye. He was staring at her. For some reason, the way he was looking at her made her feel uncomfortable, and she quickly broke eye contact with him.

Reggie had endured the party as long as he could and was glad when Brent indicated he could leave. He headed for the door, but not before finding Olivia. He smiled at her and nodded. He knew she would interpret the message.

He had been in his car for about five minutes when she called. "Where are you, sweetheart?" he immediately asked her.

"The ladies' room. I'm alone, but someone might walk in at any minute. You wanted me to call you?"

"Yes," he said hoarsely. "I want you."

The depths of his words almost made Olivia groan. She turned to make sure she was still alone in the ladies' room. "And I want you, too," she whispered into her cell phone.

There was a pause. And then he said, "Meet me. Tonight. Our place."

Olivia inhaled deeply. Meeting him later wouldn't be a problem, because her father was a sound sleeper. She knew it would be their last time together for a while. Her brothers would be arriving sometime tomorrow. She could pull something over on her dad, but fooling her brothers was a totally different matter. "Okay, I'll be there. Later."

She then clicked off her cell phone.

* * *

"Did you enjoy yourself tonight, Libby?"

Olivia glanced over at her father as they walked up the stairs together. "Yes, I had a good time, and the food was excellent."

Orin couldn't help but chuckle. "Yes, it was good, and I was glad to see you eat for a change, instead of nibbling."

When they reached the landing, he placed a kiss on her forehead. "Good night, sweetheart. I'm feeling tired, so I'm going on to bed. What about you?"

"Umm, I may stay up a while and paint. Good night, Dad. Sleep tight."

He chuckled. "I will."

As soon as Olivia walked into her room and closed the door behind her, she began stripping out of her clothes, eager to get to the Saxon Hotel and meet Reggie. Going to her closet, she selected a dress. She felt like going braless tonight. Within minutes she was slipping her feet into a pair of sandals and grabbing her purse. Opening the door, she eased out of her room, and within seconds she was down the stairs and out of the house.

She couldn't wait until she was with Reggie.

Reggie stood when the door to the hotel room opened and Olivia walked in. Without saying anything, she tossed her purse on the sofa and then crossed the room to him. The moment she was within reach, he pulled her into his arms and swept her off her feet.

On other nights he had stamped his ownership all

over her body, but tonight he wanted to claim her mouth, lips and tongue and locked all three to his. At the party she had been so close, yet so far, and he had wanted her with a force that had him quaking.

He pulled his mouth back. He was moving toward the bedroom when she began wiggling in his arms. "No. Here. Let's make love in here."

The moment he placed her on her feet, she went for his clothes, pushing the shirt off his shoulders and greedily kissing his chest. He was tempted to tell her to slow down, to assure her that they had all night, but he knew that they didn't. She would need to leave before daybreak.

Her hands went to the buckle of his pants, and he watched as she slid down the zipper before easing her hand inside to cup him. He threw his head back and released a guttural moan as sensations spiraled through him, almost bringing him to his knees. And when she began stroking him, he sucked in a deep breath.

"I want this, Reggie," she said as she firmly held his shaft.

"And I want to give it to you," he managed to say, slowly backing her up to the wall.

When they couldn't go any farther, he reached out and pulled down the straps of her dress and smiled when he saw she wasn't wearing a bra. Her breasts were bared before his eyes. He licked his lips. "Are you wearing anything at all under this dress?" he asked when his mouth went straight to her breasts.

"No."

"Good."

He lifted up the hem of her dress and planted his hand firmly on her feminine mound. "And I want this."

Taking a step back, he tugged her dress the rest of the way down, and the garment drifted to the floor. His gaze raked up and down her naked body. "Nice."

He then removed his clothes, and, taking a condom out of his wallet, he put it on. Then he reached out and lifted her by the waist. "Wrap your legs around me, Olivia. I'm about to lock us together tightly, to give you what you want and to get what I need."

As soon as her legs were settled around his waist and his shaft was pointing straight for the intended target, he tilted her hips at an angle to bury himself deep inside of her and then drove into her. She arched her back off the wall, and his body went still. Locked in. A perfect fit. Silence surrounded them, and they both refused to move.

Flames roared to life within him, and he felt himself burning out of control, but he refused to move. Instead, he held her gaze, wanting her to see what was there in his eyes. It was something he couldn't hold in any longer, but first he wanted to see if she could read it in his gaze.

Olivia stared back at Reggie. She saw desire, heat and longing. She felt him planted deep inside of her. But it was his gaze that held her immobile. In a trance. And she knew at that moment why she kept coming back, kept wanting to be with him when she knew that she shouldn't.

She loved him.

The result of that admission was felt instantly: her

body shivered. In response, Reggie, she noted, never wavered in his relentless stare, and then he spoke in a deep, husky voice. "I love you."

She immediately stifled a deep sigh before reaching up and placing her arms around his neck and saying, "And I love you."

Reggie's lips curved into a smile before he leaned down and sank his mouth onto hers as his body began moving, slowly, then fast, in and out of her with power- ful thrusts, stirring passion, fanning the fire and then whirling them through an abyss of breathless ecstasy. Over and over again, he made love to the woman he loved and captured her moans of pleasure in his mouth. And when she shattered in his arms and he followed her over the edge, he knew he wasn't through with her yet.

They had just begun.

He tightened his hold on her, and on weak legs, he moved toward the bedroom. For them, time was lim- ited tonight. Their passion was raging out of control. But moments ago they had let go and claimed love, and when they tumbled onto the bed together, he knew that tonight was just the beginning for them.

"Wake up, sweetheart. It's time to go."

Olivia lifted her eyes and gazed up at Reggie. He was standing beside the bed, fully dressed. "What time is it?" she asked sleepily, forcing herself to sit up.

"Almost four in the morning, and I got to get you home," he said.

She nodded. Although they had driven separate cars, it was the norm for him to follow behind her and see her safely inside her house. Excusing herself, she quickly went to the bathroom, and when she returned moments later, he was sitting on the edge of the bed.

He reached out his hand to her. "Come here, baby."

And she did. She went to him, and he pulled her down onto his lap and kissed her so deeply and thoroughly, she could only curl up in his warmth and enjoy. When he finally lifted his mouth from hers, he gazed down at her lips.

"You have beautiful lips," he whispered softly.

"Thank you."

His gaze then moved to her eyes. "And I meant what I said earlier tonight, Olivia. I love you."

She nodded. "And I meant what I said earlier, too. I love you." She didn't say anything else for a minute, and then she added, "Crazy, isn't it?"

"Not really. My dad met my mom, and they were married within two weeks. Same thing with my aunt and uncle. Westmorelands believe in love at first sight." He paused for a second. "This changes everything."

She lifted a brow. "What do you mean?"

"No sneaking around."

She wondered why he thought that. "No, Reggie. It changes nothing." She eased out of his arms and began getting dressed.

"Olivia?"

She turned to him. "My father is still running against you, and the election is not until the end of next month and—"

"You would want us to sneak around until then?" he asked incredulously. When she didn't answer, he said,

"I want you to meet my family. I want you to attend my family reunion with me in Texas in a few weeks. I want you by my side and—"

"I have to think about my father. He would not want us to be together," she said.

"And I told you in the beginning, this doesn't involve your father. You are a consenting adult. You shouldn't need your father's permission to see me."

"It's not about his permission. It's about me being there for him, Reggie. I owe my father a lot, and I refuse to flaunt our affair in front of him," she persisted.

"And I refuse to sneak around to see you any longer. That's asking a lot of me, Olivia. I love you, and I want us to be together."

"But we are together, Reggie."

He was silent for a moment, and then he said, "Yes, behind closed doors. But I want more than that. I want to take you out to dinner. I want to be seen with you. I want to do all those things that a couple does together when they are in love."

Olivia sighed. "Then you will have to wait until after the election."

They stared at each other for the longest time. Then Reggie said quietly, "When you're ready to let nothing get in the way of our relationship, our love, let me know, Olivia."

Then he turned and walked out of the hotel room. As soon as the door closed behind him, Olivia threw herself on the bed and gave in to her tears.

Olivia slowly walked out of the Saxon Hotel, with a heavy heart. She'd told a man that she loved him, and then she'd lost him in the same day. She had stayed in the hotel room and cried her eyes out, and now she felt worse than ever.

Crossing the parking lot, she stopped walking when she glanced ahead and saw Reggie leaning against her car. She stared at him, studied his features, not wanting to get her hopes up. Inhaling deeply, she moved one foot in front of the other and came to a stop in front of him.

They stood, staring at each other for a long moment, and then he reached out and pulled her into his arms and kissed her.

Moments later he pulled back slightly and placed his forehead against hers. "I love you, and I want you with me, out in the open, not sneaking around, Olivia. But if that's the only way I can have you right now, then that's what I'll take."

Olivia felt a huge weight being lifted off her shoulders, but she knew it was at Reggie's expense. He deserved to have a woman by his side, one that he could take to dinner, take home to meet Mom and invite to his home.

Leaning closer, she snuggled into his arms, close to his warmth and his heart. She knew that this was the man that would have her heart forever.

Chapter 10

"You've been rather quiet, Libby. Aren't you glad to see us?"

Olivia glanced over at Duan and forced a smile. "Yes. I missed you guys."

"And we missed you," Terrence said, coming to join them at the breakfast table. "So why haven't you been your usual chipper self the past couple of days?"

She sighed, thinking there was no way she could tell her brothers what was really bothering her. But she could tell them what Cathy had shared with her. "I'm fine. I'm just in a funky mood right now. It will pass soon," she said.

Her brothers had flown in yesterday for the barbecue to be held that afternoon. It was an event she wasn't looking forward to, because she knew that Reggie would be there. It would be hard to see him and not want to be with him.

"There is something I need to talk to you two about while Dad is at campaign headquarters. It's something that Cathy told me, and it might explain why Dad decided to run for the Senate."

Duan raised a brow. "What?"

She then told her brothers everything that Cathy had shared with her. She saw Duan's jaw flex several times.

"I knew there was a reason I didn't like Senator Reed," Duan said.

"Same here," Terrence said. His eyes had taken on a dark look, and she now understood why the sportscasters had dubbed him the Holy Terror when he played professional football.

"I think we should talk to Dad to make sure he's entered politics for the right reason," Duan said. "If he did then he has our blessings. If he didn't, then I think he should reconsider everything before going any further."

Olivia nodded. "I agree."

"And what do the three of you agree on?"

Olivia, Duan and Terrence glanced up. Their father had walked into the kitchen, and he had Senator Reed with him. Olivia looked at her brothers. "It's nothing that we can't talk about later, Dad," she said quickly. She then glanced at Senator Reed, who was looking at her oddly. "Good morning, Senator."

The man had a smug look on his face when he responded. "Good morning, Olivia." He then slid his gaze to her brothers. "Duan. Terrence."

They merely nodded their greeting.

Her father studied her and her brothers and then reached into his pocket and pulled out an envelope. "Can you explain this, Olivia?" he asked, tossing several photographs on the table.

Olivia picked them up and studied them. They were photographs taken of her in Reggie's arms two nights ago in the parking lot of the Saxon Hotel. Several were of them kissing. "Who took these?" she asked, glancing at her father.

It was Senator Reed who spoke. "We have reason to believe Westmoreland himself is responsible. It seems you put more stock in the affair than he did. I was able to get these before the newspapers printed them."

Olivia glanced back at the photographs, and when Duan held out his hand for them, she handed them over to him. The room got quiet while Duan looked at the pictures before passing them on to Terrence.

"Were you having an affair with Westmoreland, Libby? Knowing he is my opponent in the Senate race?" Orin asked his daughter, as if he was insulted by such a possibility.

Refusing to lie, Olivia lifted her chin. "Yes. Reggie and I met at the Firemen's Ball two weeks ago. It was a masquerade party, so we didn't know each other's identity."

"But what happened once you found out?" her father asked quietly.

She sighed deeply. "Once we found out, it didn't matter. Our involvement had no bearing on your campaign," she said.

Senator Reed chuckled. "And I'm sure he convinced

you of that. It's obvious he wanted to make a spectacle of you and your father. It's a good thing I stepped in when I did."

Olivia glared at the man. "You would like my father and brothers to believe the worst of Reggie, wouldn't you?" she said in a biting tone. "Well, it truly doesn't matter, because it's what I don't believe that does."

"And what don't you believe, Libby?" Duan asked, standing next to her.

She glanced up at her oldest brother. "What I don't believe, Duan, is that Reggie had anything to do with this." She turned back to her father. "And knowing that only makes me wonder who does."

At that moment the doorbell rang. "I'll get it," Terrence said, walking away, but not before gently squeezing his sister's elbow, giving her a sign that she had his support.

"So if you don't believe Westmoreland sent out these photos, Libby, then who did?" Orin asked his daughter.

"That's what I'd like to know," said a male voice behind them.

Olivia swung around. Terrence had escorted Reggie into the kitchen.

Orin frowned. "Westmoreland, what are you doing here?"

Reggie looked at Orin. "Someone thought it was important that a courier deliver these to me before eight in the morning," he said, throwing copies of the same pictures Olivia had just seen on the kitchen table. "I figured someone was trying to play me and Olivia against each other, and I wasn't having it."

Reggie then turned to Olivia. "I had nothing to do with those photos, Olivia."

"I know you didn't," she said softly.

"Well, the rest of us aren't so gullible," Senator Reed snapped.

Duan stepped forward. "Excuse me, Senator, but why are you here? What goes on in this family really doesn't concern you."

The man seemed taken aback by Duan's words. "If it wasn't for me, those pictures would have been on the front page of today's paper. I saved your father the embarrassment of this entire town knowing that his daughter is having an affair."

Terrence's smile didn't quite reach his eyes as he came to stand beside Duan. "You do mean his *grown* daughter, don't you?"

"She is having an affair with *him,*" Senator Reed said, almost at the top of his voice, pointing at Reggie.

"And what business is it of yours?" Olivia snapped.

"It is my business because I had your father bring you home for *me,*" Senator Reed snapped back. The entire room got quiet, and the senator realized what he'd said. Five pairs of eyes were staring at him. "What I meant was that I—"

"We know exactly what you meant, Al," Orin said in a disgusted voice, seeing things clearly now. "And just to set the record straight, I didn't ask my daughter to come home for you. The only reason I summoned Olivia home was to be here with me for the campaign."

Seeing he had lost his footing with Orin, Senator Reed said, "Aw, come on, Orin. You know how I spout off at the mouth sometimes. Besides, why are you getting mad at me? She is the one who is sneaking around with your opponent behind your back. She reminds you of your ex-wife, don't you think?"

Before anyone could blink, Orin struck the senator and practically knocked him to his knees. "Get up and get out, and don't ever come back. You're no longer welcome in my home, Al," Orin said, barely holding back his rage.

The senator staggered to his feet. "Fine, and you can forget my endorsement," he said heatedly, limping toward the door.

"I don't need it," Orin shot back. "I plan to pull out of the race."

When the door slammed shut, Olivia quickly moved over to her father. "Dad, are you going to pull out because of what I did?" she asked softly.

Orin pushed a strand of hair out of her face. "No, sweetheart. Your old man realizes that he's not cut out to be a politician. Al had convinced me that running for office was what I needed to do, but it was not truly what I wanted to do. I never really had my heart in it."

He glanced down at the pictures on his kitchen table and then over at Reggie. "I hope for your sake that you care for my daughter, Westmoreland."

Reggie smiled as he came to stand beside Olivia. "I do. I'm in love with her, sir," he said.

Orin's features eased into a satisfied smile. "And the way she defended you a few moments ago, I can only assume that she's in love with you, too."

"I *am* in love with him," Olivia affirmed.

"Good." Orin then looked at his two sons. "It seems our family will be increasing soon. What do you think?"

Duan chuckled. "He loves her. She loves him. It's all good to me."

Terrence smiled. "As long as they don't decide to marry before today's barbecue. I was looking forward to checking out the single ladies there today."

Orin rolled his eyes and shook his head. He then offered Reggie his hand. "Welcome to the family, son," he said.

The barbecue was truly special. Orin made the announcement that he was pulling out of the Senate race, and he gave his endorsement to Reggie. In the next breath, Orin announced that there would be a Jeffries-Westmoreland wedding in the very near future.

With Olivia by his side, Reggie introduced her to all the many Westmorelands in attendance.

"Just how many cousins do you have?" she asked him a short time later.

He smiled. "Quite a number. Just wait until you meet the Denver Westmorelands at the family reunion in a few weeks."

"Have you met them all?" she asked curiously.

"No, but I'm looking forward to doing so."

Olivia nodded. So was she. She and Reggie had discussed her move back to the States, and a wedding was planned for next month after the election. She was truly happy.

Reggie held her hand as they walked around the grounds, greeting everyone. She smiled, thinking she was beginning to like the idea of becoming a politician's wife.

"You know what I think?" Reggie whispered to her when they claimed a few moments to be alone.

She glanced up at him. "No, what do you think?"

He smiled. "I think we should go to the Saxon Hotel tonight and celebrate. What do you think?"

She chuckled. "I think, Reggie Westmoreland, that you are a true romantic."

He pulled her into his arms. "If I am, it's because I've got a good teacher." And then he sealed his words with a kiss.

Epilogue

The following month, in a church full of family and friends, newly elected senator Reginald Westmoreland and Olivia Marie Jeffries exchanged vows to become man and wife. Reggie thought Olivia was the most beautiful bride he had ever seen. His mother was crying. The last Atlanta-based Westmoreland was now married.

At the reception, when they made their rounds to speak with everyone, Reggie got to spend time again with his new cousins, the Westmorelands of Denver. Everyone had met and gotten acquainted at the family reunion. Talk about a good time. And it was great knowing there were more Westmorelands out there. Everyone on both sides was looking forward to spending time together, getting to know each other and having family reunions each year.

"I can't believe how the men in the Westmoreland family favor each other," Olivia said, glancing across the room at five of Reggie's cousins from Denver—Jason, Zane, Dillon and the twins, Adrian and Aidan. They were just five of the tons of cousins from Colorado, and she had liked all of them immediately, including the women her age.

Olivia had enjoyed the family reunion and getting to know Reggie's family. And they had accepted her with open arms. She felt blessed to be a part of the Westmoreland clan.

Later that night Reggie presented his wife with her wedding gift. They had flown to the Caribbean right after the wedding reception to spend a week at the Saxon Hotel that had recently been built in St. Thomas.

"This, sweetheart, is for you," Reggie said, handing her a sealed envelope. They had just enjoyed dinner in the privacy of their room.

"Thank you," Olivia said, opening up the envelope. It contained a key. And then she glanced at the card. She suddenly caught her breath and then stared over at Reggie as tears sprang into her eyes. "I don't believe it."

"Believe it, darling. You once told me what you wanted, and as your husband, I want to make it happen for you. Years ago I bought the building and when my first partner and I dissolved our business partnership, I kept the building. I think it would be perfect for your art gallery. It's in a good location."

She got out of her seat and went around the table to thank Reggie properly. He pulled her into his lap and kissed her with the passion she had gotten used to receiving from him.

"Thank you," she said through her tears. "I love you."

"And I love you, my Wonder Woman."

Reggie gathered her into his arms, and when she leaned up and caught his mouth with hers, he shivered as a profound need rushed through him. This was their wedding night. They were in a Saxon Hotel. And they were in each other's arms.

Life was wonderful.

* * * * *

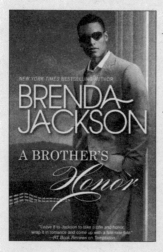

REQUEST YOUR FREE BOOKS!

2 FREE NOVELS PLUS 2 FREE GIFTS!

KIMANI™ ROMANCE

Love's ultimate destination!

A Brand-New Madaris Family Novel!

NEW YORK TIMES BESTSELLING AUTHOR

BRENDA JACKSON

COURTING JUSTICE

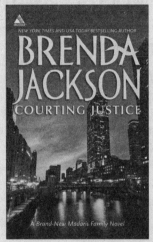

Winning a high-profile case may have helped New York attorney DeAngelo DiMeglio's career, but it hasn't helped him win the woman he loves. Peyton Mahoney doesn't want anything more than a fling with DeAngelo. Until another high-profile case brings them to opposing sides of the courtroom…and then their sizzling attraction can no longer be denied.

"Brenda Jackson is the queen of newly discovered love, especially in her Madaris Family series."
—*BookPage* on *Inseparable*

Available now wherever books are sold.